Bob Berzins can usually be found on the Peak District moors near his home in Sheffield, rock climbing or fell running. Although many of these areas are within the National Park and have protected conservation status, the ravages of our biodiversity crisis and climate crisis are all too apparent, and Bob spends much of his time campaigning for wildlife and the environment. He's written numerous blogs and a self-published novel, *Snared.*

Bob Berzins

THE LAST CROW

AUSTIN MACAULEY PUBLISHERS™

LONDON * CAMBRIDGE * NEW YORK * SHARJAH

A CIP catalogue record for this title is available from the British Library.

ISBN 9781035859894 (Paperback)
ISBN 9781035859900 (ePub e-book)

www.austinmacauley.com

First Published 2024
Austin Macauley Publishers Ltd®
1 Canada Square
Canary Wharf
London
E14 5AA

Chapter 1

The wind pushed into his face, squeezing sleep from his eyes and rattling the hawthorn above him. Darkness shielded all movement until he pulled his eye down to the gun sight. Now the slope was alive in shades of grey and white, with larger shapes moving, digging amongst the trees.

His long wait was surely over, but the badgers continued their search for earthworms and there was no clear shot. The easterly carried away his scent, leaving them unaware.

He was lying on the edge of a holloway, an ancient route connecting woodland, fields and villages, marking the boundary of land ownership before barbed wire. Beyond him, the badger setts were just as old with their own history of family and community. That was lost on Logan Porter because badgers were vermin full of disease and he didn't have to hide his disgust any more. There was a bounty. He had full protection from the law and police to back it up.

He heard the scuffle of large, solid animals rolling in leaf litter and two shapes breaking free of the trees. The larger one stopped as the other ran down the slope. The dominant male was chasing a juvenile, who followed a well-worn path. Just as far as the peanuts Logan had piled on the run. Night or day, a badger's world was smell and here was a feast. The animal glowed white through the night scope, leaving plenty of time to pull the trigger. The crack of the gun sent the clan into panic, but Logan's only thought was the victim on the ground and as he approached, his torch revealed the badger was still twitching. Logan glanced towards the sett, but the animals had retreated to the safety of their refuge. Hunger would drive them out tomorrow and they'd try a different entrance. So he'd block those that he knew about and if the wind was in favour, lure them towards the holloway once more.

Although a juvenile, the badger weighed about 15kg, so it took some effort to swing it into a clear plastic sack, rear end first. Logan had clear instructions for this one and he reached into his pocket for the calling card before fastening the sack. Warming to his task after hours of lying still, he carried the badger back to his quad bike and swung the sack into the box on the front. Back home, it was strange to leave his pick-up in the yard, it would stick out like a sore thumb where he was going. *Make sure you don't get spotted.* So, the badger went into the boot of his wife's hatchback, a car that blended into urban streets. It was a short journey on empty roads, one that he'd recced a few days before. The rows of terraced houses were linked by cut-throughs and alleys so it was easy enough to park on the street behind and nip through to the back door with his parcel, just as he'd been told.

It was a shame that badger hadn't been added to the pile of culled animals in the outhouse, waiting to be counted and collected. He would have been paid £50 for the carcass and those clear plastic sacks, one on top of the other gained him respect from every dairy farmer in the area. They knew who he was, an essential worker. Bit by bit he was making himself irreplaceable until he could draw the real money. It was that respect that made him push out his chest and helped him cope with just a few hours of snatched sleep. Even though this one had to be kept secret, £300 for a special delivery made him smile.

Back home, the tea was sweet and a few biscuits set him up for his day job. There wasn't time to check the two entrances to the fox earth were still blocked, but he'd dragged concrete slabs over those and they weren't going anywhere. His terriers had cleared the foxes out and Upper Denling Wood was such good cover he knew the adults would still be hiding nearby. And there'd be cubs, but at this time of year, he probably needed to call them juveniles. He pulled the terriers out of their kennel and threw them into the box on the quad bike, where he'd stored the badger a few hours before. It was time to meet the rest of the hunt.

Chapter 2

Raven tried to stop the chatter in his brain. A deep breath in followed by a long slow breath out and then for a moment, he was calmer but exhausted. Half an hour had disappeared since he'd been dragged out of a few hours of dead man's sleep. It was becoming familiar but there was no comfort in that.

Instead, in his nightmare darkness wrapped itself around his head, squeezing, stopping his breath. His arm had flown to the side in a reflex grasping at nothing. And then the choking began; a wet towel across his face, bringing him awake.

He'd been lying diagonally across the bed, one arm suspended in space, feeling the panic of lungs without air. Slowly his eyes had adjusted to the glow of street lamps and he tried to find the familiar shapes of the bedroom, his refuge. But the surroundings jabbed back at him, a bony finger pressing on a nerve, the one that hurt him most. He was reduced to this: arms heavy and useless, lungs blocked.

Trying a shallow breath, then deeper and after a few moments, strength returning, he moved his arm, rolled over and reached out but the bed was cold and empty.

Of course, it was, what did he expect?

There would be no more sleep, so he'd lifted his legs onto the floor and pulled on some clothes. First, a soft fleece hoody and leggings, then thick socks to soothe his feet. He hung onto the banister and walked downstairs.

This wasn't the first time and there was a groove in the sofa where he pulled his legs up. He listened to the sound of his breath and felt his lungs soothing the tension. But the thoughts kept trying to muscle through his mindfulness.

Through the corner of his eye, there was movement on the pavement outside. He turned to look, but they'd gone. Someone out to do him harm, he was sure. Then he stopped himself. He couldn't live like this. It was just a neighbour walking home after a night out, nothing more. After a moment, there were footsteps at the back of the house. That was real. He unfolded his legs and ran through to the kitchen, fumbling for the key.

He yanked the door open, there was something on the ground, but he jumped over it and ran around the back of the other houses and onto the street. Nobody. They must have been quick to get completely out of sight or they were hiding. The next block of four terraced houses had a locked gate to prevent access to the back. So, Raven walked a bit further before he realised he couldn't poke around the back of every house on the street.

It wasn't the time of year for birds to sing but that didn't deter the robin. And yes, the sky had changed from black to grey. On the short walk back to his kitchen, Raven tried to calm down his imagination. He'd barely glanced at the package on the floor and now it was building up in his mind.

"Just take a proper look in a minute," he muttered, feeling his wet socks flapping on the paving slabs.

Outside his door, in the first light of the day was a thick, clear plastic sack, sealed at the top. Wrapped tightly inside was a badger and as Raven forced himself to look closer, there was a wire snare pulled tight at its neck. The message couldn't have been any clearer: *we know who you are and where you live.*

The scar on his side flared in pain.

Chapter 3

Hunting had never gone away, despite the legislation. And it was a twelve months of the year activity. Chloe had been a regular with the saboteurs when she was a student, but some bad experiences and a full-time job pulled her away. Right now after all the upheaval in her life she longed for something that completely absorbed her and friends who looked out for her with a simple shared purpose. A few phone calls had put her back on the contact list as if she'd never been away. This morning's 5.00 a.m. collection saw half a dozen of them congregated around a copse of trees in farmland just outside town. It felt like the remnants of a larger wood, now surrounded by open fields. In the centre of the trees was a fox earth with all entrances likely to have been blocked. And this was the dilemma for the sabs: if they went into the trees to unblock the earth that would just send the foxes running into the open. Leaving the earth blocked left them nowhere safe. There would be at least one vixen and her cubs hiding in the undergrowth. As shapes became clearer in the dawn, the yapping of hounds grew louder.

Chloe followed everyone else pulling up their face coverings. Bodycams and handheld video cameras were turned on. And a few moments later, the first voices.

"Fucking sabs are here!"

Two riders pulled their horses to a stop, yanking on the bridles. The whipper-in, on horseback, halted the dogs and cracked the bone-handled whip to stop the hounds straying from the pack. His companion shouted at the sabs:

"You're trespassing."

Someone leant over to Chloe's ear and whispered, "That's Jeremy Cockerill. He's a local magistrate."

Huntsman Cockerill had clearly been up early that morning. Flushed, clean-shaven cheeks, black jacket, white jodhpurs and polished black boots.

And with each word clearly enunciated: "Get off my land. I'm phoning the chief constable."

"Bollocks," was the reply. "I'm phoning her myself. You're in breach of the Hunting Act 2004."

The stand-off was broken by the shriek of hounds, whipped for moving restlessly and the chug of a quad bike carrying a thickset man wearing his own face covering. The quad circled around the back of them and Chloe twisted her neck anxiously. Again the whisper in her ear: "Logan Porter, their terrier man."

There was a large metal box on the front of the quad, where the terriers were kept until they were put underground into an earth. Chloe couldn't see into the box on the back but there would be spades and shotguns in there.

Then suddenly another rider, a woman, dug her heels into her horse's flanks and galloped towards the sabs. Chloe froze until an arm reached around her waist and yanked her out of the way. She looked around in panic, but horse and rider were making a wide loop around the field, to the side of the copse. That was the signal to unleash the hounds.

Two blasts on the horn and the dogs were running towards the trees. Cockerill looked on approvingly. The hounds had been trained and this was a test. Then he raised the horn to his lips, repeating the short urgent sound.

The sabs spread out, trying to stop the dogs from entering the trees shouting "Leave it," as loud as they could, to pull the hounds back. But despite her shouts Chloe had to stand helplessly as the hounds ran straight past her into the *covert*.

Everyone ran as fast as they could to the far side of the trees where they could see the hounds chasing more than one fox through the undergrowth. There weren't enough riders to encircle the copse which would have kept the foxes inside so after less than a minute a vixen burst out of the trees, then three juveniles followed all running in different directions. Seconds later, the hounds appeared. In a crescendo of high-pitched barking and yelps, they followed the vixen.

It made Chloe shudder. Thirty-two hounds in full cry chasing four small wild animals. And the vixen was sacrificing herself for the sake of her offspring.

Then suddenly, the engine of the quad bike roared and mud was flying from the tyres as it raced across the field cutting between the vixen and the hounds. The calls from the whipper-in and blasts from the huntsman changed tempo to slow mournful sounds.

The pack was a mix of older experienced hounds and younger dogs. The sabs were watching the results of several months of training. Like most hunt packs, older hounds here were discarded after five years and up to a third of the pack was replaced each year. The dogs would chase and kill when that was the command. And equally, they would stop when told.

Chloe couldn't believe the pack with the scent of blood would actually stop, but that's what happened. All except for one, who continued to chase the vixen beyond the quad bike until the calls of *'back to 'im'* were heard.

"That one's dead meat for sure," Chloe heard from one of her colleagues.

Sure enough, when the hound returned, they heard the whipper-in roar, "Gunner!"

The dog approached for a crack in the ribs from the long solid handle of the whip.

"Bastards," said Chloe. Not just the old dogs were discarded.

Hounds, horses and the quad bike made their way slowly out of the field.

Chloe turned to the other sabs, "What the hell went on there?"

There was some discussion and they agreed the *cubbing* season was coming to an end. Today was a small victory: the hunt likely changed its behaviour because of the sabs. If they hadn't been around, the vixen at least would have been chased and killed, or maybe the vixen was spared because there weren't enough paying members of the hunt to enjoy it. The hounds were trained, they would chase to command and new litters of foxes were being dispersed. Full-blown hunting was just around the corner.

Chloe felt flat and depressed and lagged behind the others walking back to the minibus. Then she felt the same arm that had saved her from the horse, a tender strength across her back and squeezing her shoulder.

"Are you alright?" she heard.

She was better now, for sure, but needed more friendly faces. A debrief in the Dragon would help.

Chapter 4

Another corpse and the life pulled from a living creature. Raven pushed the disgust, anger and despair to one side and photographed the badger. This would be another crime report, fat lot of good that would do. He stored the badger in the outhouse and went back inside. Then started to search for the police website but realised that could wait. There was time to get out on a shooting moor before work. His bag was already packed, so he pulled on some outdoor clothes, had a drink of water and went out to his van.

It was an effort to concentrate on the road and the speed limit, so he imagined a driving instructor was in the passenger seat. It didn't feel like that long ago since he was taking his test. The car park didn't have any white lines or even a tarmac surface, so he was spared any manoeuvres and stuck the van close to the side of a bush. Some of the stones on the path had the familiarity of lifelong friends and moorland air cleared his lungs and his mind. It was a well-travelled route.

Fronds of bracken were showing golden tips and this dense vegetation had attracted small birds: wrens and stonechats liked the cover and the insects. And as he climbed higher his eyes scanned from side to side, looking for signs of quad bikes and six-wheel all-terrain vehicles. Gamekeepers left large footprints in their obsession for a sky full of red grouse and it wasn't long before he saw the bright red comb or eye patch of a male.

The bird spotted him and flew out of the heather with barely a sound, hugging the carpet of purple flowers, a tactic that had contributed to its survival. Raven stepped off the path, his legs kicking up clouds of pollen. Finally, he stopped on top of a bluff and surveyed the landscape. Close by some of the heather had turned a rusty red colour as the flowers faded. The curlews and other waders were back at their estuaries, breeding completed, but it felt like the imprint of their calls remained, hanging over the moor. A few naive years ago, he might have expected buzzards being mobbed by crows and peregrine falcons swooping on their prey. But this was the High Ridge Estate, a grouse shooting moor. Waders, meadow pipits and songbirds were tolerated and really not much else.

The shooting season had started in a fanfare of publicity but soon he'd heard the coded language: poor weather at breeding and a difficult harvest. So, he wasn't seeing twenty or more grouse lifting into the air as they were disturbed.

In the distance, some of the trees were starting to turn and a few had lost their leaves already. He scanned down to these areas, expecting to see some sign of gamekeepers checking traps. And as he concentrated, there, the grey outline of a pick-up truck. Raven turned to his video camera on a short tripod.

He didn't have long to wait before a faint honking sound announced the arrival of Canada geese, a mix of adult birds with clear markings and the pale brown wash of juvenile feathers. He imagined the birds were leaving the moors for a winter in the lowlands. Every time he saw a scene like this, there was an ache in the pit of his stomach. This was the knot of anxiety that gnawed away at his sleep. Two birds fell to the ground before he heard the shot. Then another two fell at the second blast of pellets. The calls were frantic now, wing beats rapid. One of the juveniles was struggling to fly and dropped to the ground a hundred yards from the others.

Swinging the camera back around, Raven saw the gamekeeper emerge from the trees. Dressed in sniper camouflage, including a face covering, he jogged over to where the juvenile had fallen, shotgun in hand. The goose was writhing on the ground, unable to fly any more. A boot crashed down on its head and another on its body, releasing a last cry that escaped into the morning stillness.

Then another familiar scene, the gamekeeper, hand clasped around a long, graceful neck, dragging the bird along the ground back to the others. The geese were dumped in the trees; their rotting flesh would attract foxes, badgers, buzzards or crows, lured into a trap or the sights of the gamekeeper's gun.

Finally, the pick-up disappeared and Raven packed up his camera. It would make a good video for social media but in the eyes of the law, the gamekeeper had dispatched some vermin for the benefit of conservation. The gamekeeper was supposed to have tried all possible non-lethal methods to discourage these birds but a gun remained the first and only choice.

Just short of the car park the gate was open and parked on the side of the path was another pick-up. The rear of the vehicle was covered over in a hard top with a blacked-out window. On top of the cabin was a tell-tale spotlight, used to dazzle animals before they were shot.

As he drew level, Raven glanced across to see a mobile phone obscuring the driver's face. He was being filmed. Back at his van, he waited a few moments until the pick-up nosed into the car park. Raven took his own photograph and then a deep breath. They were trying to provoke him into losing his temper, so he calmly and slowly set off back to town. He had to go home to get his tools and he didn't want the gamekeeper to know his address. But given this morning's delivery, it was already too late for that. The pick-up following him sucked the light out of the morning.

Chapter 5

Finn Sutherland was settling into his new job. These southern estates were closer to the money. He'd arrived after the breeding season at High Ridge and there were far too few grouse for his liking. But the clients had been grateful and pressed the fifties into his hands.

Early mornings with a gun in his hand made him feel in touch with nature. Anything you do in daylight they'll be watching you, that was his brief. So it was pretty simple, all the real work had to be done at night. This morning had just been a bit of target practice. A pump action shotgun and he would have taken down all the geese.

The owner was expanding his interests and it was Finn's job to ensure there was plenty of sport. Fairview Mill was a new business opportunity. When the land adjoining High Ridge came up for sale, Nathan Parbolde had snapped it up. This was lowland scrub and woodland with the heather and grouse of High Ridge a long way up the hill. The mill buildings now provided lunch facilities with basic fare downstairs for regular clients and opulence upstairs for the VIPs. Mill Lane was a public road littered with the corpses of pheasants and Finn's pick-up squashed the bodies even flatter. Twenty thousand young birds or poults had been delivered six weeks before with the partridges going into closed pens on rough grassland. The pheasants went into large open-top pens in woodland and it was these birds that had started to fly out and wander into the traffic. Archie and Jayden had been taken on for the seasonal work of feeding the horde of fowl.

Finn took pride in keeping losses to a minimum. He couldn't do anything about the road traffic victims and those would only increase as the pheasants matured. But he could stop the tide of predators drawn to carrion on the roads and the open pens. He pulled into the car park and glanced at his phone.

"Done," was the message from Ryan, his assistant. Finn scrolled down his contacts and stopped at Superintendent Farlow. As he tapped the handset symbol on the screen, Finn stared across the car park where two pheasants were pecking at the ground. They still had the muted plumage of juveniles and it would only be a few weeks before the punters were blasting them from the sky.

Farlow picked up and there was no need for any preamble. "More trap damage I'm afraid, sir. And theft. Ryan managed to get the VRM and I'll send you a couple of photos and the location."

Finn had the measure of the newly promoted officer. An obsequious 'sir' would boost Farlow's self-importance and 'VRM' showed Finn had been paying attention to police jargon when he'd been briefed.

"I'll pass it on to the crime bureau when I get those. Leave it with me."

There was no need to mention any names; they both knew exactly who they were targeting. The pheasants trotted into the undergrowth. There were enough signals to email the photos and a couple of grid references. Then it was time for Finn to do his rounds.

He saw Jayden in one of the large pens, a large bucket in either hand one full of grain and the other full of dead birds. It was an outdoor battery farm, with more than a thousand birds crammed together. The weak didn't survive. Not all birds were the same age, due mainly to when the poults had been delivered. That worked well for Finn ensuring a steady flow of pheasants reaching maturity and flying out of the pens. But it did leave the problem of predators still taking some birds no bigger than chicks.

Finn had to shout above the noise of the birds.

"Any sign of visitors?"

Jayden shook his head. "Don't think so, but can't really tell. I think it's the other pheasants that have had a go at these," he said shaking the bucket full of carcasses.

They were reared on grain but when the pheasants moved out of the pens, they would eat insects or even small reptiles if they could be caught. Finn glanced up at the wooden post that provided a handy perch near the pen and he could see the trap was unused. He'd like to leave it there all the time. A pheasant or partridge wouldn't perch on anything so small but it was ideal for tawny owls. *There were more vermin killing the smaller birds in his pen.*

Finn swivelled the safety catch on the spring trap, leaving it flat and easy to slip into his pocket. It was a debate in his mind if he should clip these traps to their posts. A tawny owl wasn't big enough to fly off with an unsecured trap but crows or sparrowhawks were. And then they might be found somewhere nearby and people would start making all sorts of accusations. A bird landed on the plate of the trap and a bar on a powerful spring crushed their legs. A short chain kept the trap and bird attached to the post. Nice and simple. But the trouble was these traps had been illegal for more than fifty years. It was the same story all around now with conservationists meddling in things they didn't understand. So, the trap went into his pocket. Maybe the pheasants were now too big for the owls to take but the traps would be put out again until Finn was sure.

Then it was time to check the partridges up the hill. Each release pen had an area of around 20 square metres and contained around 200 birds. The pens had wire mesh sides and lighter plastic netting formed a roof. The losses here were down to disease not predation and as Finn approached the first pen, the birds panicked and clambered over the corpses with barely enough room to flap their wings before they were tangled in another bird. The remaining ground in the pen had a layer of grain, husks and droppings. The purpose here was to harden up the birds before release but keeping them enclosed any longer would just kill more.

He'd have a word with Jayden and Archie and they'd release some of the partridges this afternoon. The birds would go out into a world so alien and different from their caged upbringing that they'd only venture as far as the nearest grain hopper to feed. Then in a few days, dogs and beaters would drive them towards the guns. The dead birds littering the floor of the release pen were just the start. Already there was enough carrion to bait every stink pit at Fairview and High Ridge, where the smell of rotting flesh drew predators into snares and cage traps. When the shooting actually started, the corpses piled high every day. Each client would take home a brace of partridge or pheasant and once the gamekeepers' chest freezers were full they'd need a mechanical digger to bury the rest.

Chapter 6

Raven heard the siren and then his wing mirror was full of flashing blue lights. He slowed to a crawl expecting the police car to speed past to an emergency. Instead, it swerved behind him. They wanted him to stop. As he waited he wound down the window. Two officers in bulky fluorescent jackets marched along the middle of the road, stopping all traffic.

"Can you get out of the vehicle, sir?"

Raven did as instructed. This had nothing to do with his driving. One officer motioned him to the rear doors of his van while the other officer waved on the traffic.

"We need to look in the back."

"Hang on a minute," said Raven. "You need to tell me what this is about."

The officer tilted his head towards a radio clipped to his stab vest. "Suspect stopped. Failing to cooperate."

The radio crackled. "Need backup?"

"Under control."

Raven felt his arms pulled behind his back, when he managed to straighten up a bit he was looking straight into a small camera fastened to the officer's other shoulder.

"I'm glad you're recording all this," said Raven and despite the camera he felt sure there'd soon be a fist in the side of his face.

The officer in front of him narrowed his eyes and leant forward.

"Vehicle of interest," he spat. "Now open the doors before I put you in handcuffs and call for backup."

Raven's arms were released and he unlocked the rear doors of his van. Inside were all the tools and equipment every tree surgeon would use. Three different chainsaws, helmet, fuel, hand saws, a step ladder, bags for cuttings, brooms, shovels, ropes and harnesses.

"I'm a tree surgeon, on my way to work and those are my tools."

Dickhead nearly slipped out as well but Raven managed to keep a semblance of calm.

The officers pushed aside the chainsaws and picked up some karabiners and a metal belay device. They spoke quietly to each other but Raven managed to hear the word 'snare'. The other officer was shaking his head.

"Got any small tools in here?"

Raven pointed at a frayed canvas bag which was upended sending all the contents onto the floor of the van.

"What are you looking for?" Raven asked, but he knew the answer and it was a good job he wasn't an electrician with a bag full of pliers and wire cutters. His question was ignored.

"You're suspected of theft and criminal damage and someone will come round to your house later to interview you."

"Well, you'd better make it after five o'clock because I'll be at work until then," Raven replied.

The officers turned to go back to their vehicle.

"Hang on," said Raven. "I've got plenty of my own stuff to report."

"Tell the officer tonight."

"No, you need to hear this." Raven felt more confident now. "Somebody dumped a dead badger on my doorstep at 5.00 a.m. And then I was followed by a gamekeeper in a pick-up truck. It was clear harassment. Are you not interested in any of that?"

The officer locked his eyes on Raven. "You shouldn't go stealing his traps then, should you?"

Raven held his gaze until he heard the buzz of their radios and then their aggression had gone.

"Another call's come in, sir. Drive carefully now."

Raven climbed into his van and gripped the steering wheel. His hands were shaking. There was a toot of car horn behind, he was holding up the rush hour traffic, so he set off to the first job of the day at Springvale Park.

The gates were open and Raven could see Colin and Mark waiting near one of the Council vans. They were looking at the ground pensively. Normally by now everyone would be laughing and joking.

"What's up?" Raven asked.

Mark tilted his head towards a council officer.

Raven heard the word *complaint* and how they wouldn't be allowed to carry on. This was his life right now, gamekeepers, police and now council officials, all with the same message. Nothing as obvious as a gun pointing at him, but someone was putting in a lot of time and effort. Somehow it cleared his head.

"Ok, I hear what you're saying. But we've got a proven record with you, including working in public places like this park. Just take ten minutes to check out this person who made the complaint, you've got the electoral register in your office, they won't be on that. Everyone has an online profile now, so do some searches and I think you'll find if they exist at all it'll be a profile created about a day ago." He paused. "Not a real person."

It took a while but the council officer agreed to do some searches back in his office. A large area had been taped off around an ash tree. The upper branches were bare with black tips. It was the die-back that had taken so many trees.

"I was bricking it there, Ray," said Mark. "I thought we were minted with the ash contract. That's my pension up in smoke, I reckoned."

"I think we've got it sorted lads. Doesn't take a genius to put two and two together to work out what's happening? If it gets stupid, you might have to disown me."

Raven felt a friendly slap on his shoulder.

"We'd never do that, Ray; we'd be lost without you."

Raven looked at his workmates. "Thanks, I'll explain why I was late when we stop for a brew."

They took the tree down in sections and sawed it all into manageable chunks. Then they moved on to the next taped-off area. It was heart-breaking to see mature trees lost in this way and it wasn't going to help climate change at all. But Raven had seen a few ash trees that seemed immune and that gave hope that the whole species wouldn't be lost, which had been the fate of elms, fifty years before.

Chapter 7

Logan managed about four hours of sleep before he heard Emma return. She worked at the farm shop at Midham Grange. They saw a spectacular volume of tourists who shuffled around the counters desperate to part with their cash for anything which bought them a tiny corner of the stately home. Most popular were standard tea mugs printed with a photo of the Grange on one side and the King's head and Saint George flag on the other. £7.99 each. And when it came to fresh food of course they were buying produce grown in the Duchess's own walled garden, with nothing to tell them otherwise. But in reality, it was one of Emma's jobs to drive along to the wholesaler each morning. There would soon be plenty of fresh pheasant and partridge on sale and visitors would pay top prices for those. Apart from shot birds, the only other local produce were jams and chutneys produced by some of the local families.

Logan heard her come upstairs and she soon put a mug of tea on the bedside table and then waited just as he'd instructed. She was learning, but it had taken a while. There'd been a time when her circle of friends had grown and she'd been dashing around doing one thing or another. It annoyed him and he'd made that clear to her. Now she knew that his needs came first and just to let her know he left her standing by the side of the bed as he took a slurp of tea.

"You can open the curtains now," he said at last.

She let the light in and waited at the foot of the bed, squinting against the brightness. She wanted to shield her eyes or turn her head away from the light, but he wouldn't like that. It was probably only one day a year when the sun was in this exact spot and she was seeing the room for the first time. Despite all her cleaning, the air was full of dust, dancing in front of her eyes. And there was the smell of dampness like she'd turned over a wet log. It didn't help he'd kept the window shut.

"Would you like a fry-up? I've got a lovely piece of gammon from the shop," she asked.

He nodded and she went back down to the welcome gloom of the kitchen.

As Logan finished his tea, he wondered if he should have told her to take her clothes off and kneel on the bed. He liked watching himself in the full-length mirror on the far wall. But there hadn't been enough fresh blood in his day to put him in the mood. One-shot badger didn't cut it. In a few days, he'd make sure the hounds were ripping apart a fox. That's what he needed. So he dressed straight back into his work clothes, shaking some dried mud onto the floor. He told Emma not to wash the trousers because he had to smell like a farmer's field so the badgers would come near.

He shovelled down the food and before he'd finished Emma put a flask and sandwiches on the table. He looked up at her.

"Jasmine asked if I'd pop around later. She needs some help with the fundraiser for the school," she said.

"Don't be long," he replied. And then he stared at her face, waiting to see if she disagreed. She tried changing the subject.

"Shall I leave you something warm in the oven?"

"This will be fine," he said patting the sandwiches. "Just as I've told you before, I don't know how things will work out tonight. I don't want to come back to the house and have to start wondering where you are. You need to be here."

She tilted her head down.

"Sorry, I'll be as quick as I can."

Then she turned and started wiping down the worktops even though they were spotless. Logan scraped back his chair and unlocked his rifle from the gun cabinet in the hall. He was ready for another night on the cull.

Emma waited until Logan's pick-up left the yard and then she texted Jasmine. *On my way.* But before she could leave, Emma pulled out the vacuum cleaner from under the stairs. Logan usually left a trail of dirt behind him and he'd check if it was still there in the morning.

Two minutes' drive or five minutes' walk? Emma felt as if she needed a walk, but taking the car meant she'd be home sooner. The options flipped back and forth in her head. It was exhausting. Until at last she threw the car keys onto the table and walked out of the door.

She expected them to be in the conservatory overlooking the garden around the back of Jasmine's house. The sliding doors were open and Emma saw Lily was there as well. They'd started a bottle of white wine and Emma joined them.

She meant to take a sip but ended with a large gulp.

"Looks like you needed that," said Lily.

Emma relaxed down into the wicker chair. "Well, you know, it's really busy this time of year."

"Tell me about it," said Lily. "Finn's out all hours. He's been running the grouse shoots and they'll be starting with the pheasants next, well partridges first." She paused and Emma pictured the birds rising in a wave towards the guns, the air full of lead shot then a brief pause in the shooting while the loaders passed a fresh gun to the clients before the repeated thump of shotgun blasts. The brief silence that followed the carnage always stuck in her mind.

Lily was the newcomer here. They'd moved down a couple of months before. Her husband Finn had been told he'd have plenty of help running a lowland and upland shoot together. But it hadn't worked out like that. Some help wasn't the same as plenty.

"Folk always want a day's work," Lily continued, "But they haven't got a clue and Finn has to explain everything three times."

Emma knew that was because every farm that came up for sale was bought by people who commuted into town. They might keep a paddock for some ponies, but for the rest of the land, there seemed to be a never-ending supply of cash from a few big landowners whose holdings grew larger every year. Not something to say out loud in this company.

Instead, Emma asked, "Are you settling in alright?"

"Yes, we're fine. I started at the school a few weeks ago, pretty easy really as an assistant. It's the teachers who have to do all the real work. And Logan?"

"He's just set off for work. I'm hardly seeing him at the moment and when he is there…"

Emma stopped herself, but it was too late. The last word she'd spoken sounded harsh and left a bitter taste in her mouth. She felt their eyes on her open mouth, then her neck flushing red with shame. The stares from Lily and Jasmine were like the shaft of the sun through the bedroom window, exposing her to the dust before she managed to continue, "Well, you know."

Then her throat scratched dry as she swallowed a mouthful of air. A top-up of wine came soon enough.

"We'd have to have another bottle before I told you what Finn gets up to," said Lily and that made them laugh, but Emma still held her embarrassment.

The others started talking about car boot sales and Emma looked across a manicured lawn to the river below. But she wasn't really seeing the view or hearing the words. She wasn't good enough for him, he kept telling her. It was in her now, proved once more by the flush of shame, made worse because of the attention of her friends. They noticed something was wrong with her as well.

Emma took in her surroundings once more. Jasmine's family were farmers, but not the sort that actually got their hands dirty. They were the ones who gave the orders and banked the rents with enough cash to snap up all the prime land at the auctions. Her own farmhouse came with Logan's job and as he kept telling her, no job meant no house. But was it worth it? Jasmine's clean, dry conservatory was something for other people, not her. She tried to enjoy the wine, but it was the numbness that comforted her and the hope Logan didn't return unexpectedly and find her missing.

*

Logan clattered over another cattle grid and pulled into the farmyard. Just about every farmer in the area was supporting the cull and they knew to expect him at any hour of day or night. It was a familiar routine: park the pick-up, reach into the back for a bag of peanuts and his rifle, then walk up towards their feeding grounds. The first year of the cull had been so much easier. They'd put baited mammal traps everywhere. Badgers would smell the peanuts and walk into the wire cage, leaving the door to spring shut behind them. And it was just a matter of doing morning rounds and an easy shot to the head. But there'd been photos and videos and people bleating to the government. So, the instructions changed and were now almost always free shooting with a night vision scope.

He could feel his boots squelching in the mud alongside a hedgerow and there by his feet, the oversized print of pads and long claws that told him he was in the right place. And just to confirm, there was a scrape in the ground and a pile of black droppings, a few inches in length. He'd found one of their latrines.

"Dirty little buggers," he said out loud.

He spread some peanuts and then walked downwind to a lumpy area of the field. It would make a good spot to lie up and wait for them to show. But that would be later after he'd checked some more farms. He was getting to know a much larger area, with every trail leading to a badger sett or fox earth.

Logan heard a shot from the buildings and returned to see the farmer leaning against the bonnet of the pick-up.

"All right, George?"

There was a slow shake of the head in response. George still had the strength to heft animals around but his fingers were bent over with arthritis and he'd been drawing his pension for a few years.

"That calf had been listless for weeks now. She wasn't clapping on any weight despite the feed."

Logan nodded his head. It would need very clear signs of TB for a long time before George would shoot the animal.

"You want us to dispose of it?"

A nod of the head, 'as soon as'.

"Right, we'll sort it, first thing. We'll come round with the flatbed. Put it down as a broken leg then?"

The hunt provided a fallen stock service. Dead livestock was chopped up to feed the hounds. It saved the farmer money and bypassed any vet asking awkward questions. But most of all avoided any testing for disease. It was mutually beneficial and also a big opportunity.

"You know we can help with all this, George, sort out those badgers and the foxes as well."

George had resisted the hunt for coming onto his land, but Logan wanted to expand their *country*, the area where they were welcomed. They'd follow a fox wherever it took them but it wasn't the masters who had to go round and apologise after horses and hounds had trampled someone's vegetable patch. That was left to Logan or one of the other helpers.

George wasn't biting yet.

"That calf's definitely got a broken leg. If the vet or the Ministry come asking we've got it covered."

Finally, a nod before George turned and walked away. Logan smiled, it had been the longest conversation he'd ever had with George. The badger cull and the excuse of Bovine TB really was working out well, a chance to rid the countryside of filthy, diseased vermin and a reason to be on George's land year-round to make sure there was plenty of sport.

Chapter 8

Edward Fraine, Duke of Midham stood at the head of the long table in the Great Hall. Midham Grange was his family seat and this part of the building had been constructed seven hundred years before. These days a stream of tourists trailed along roped walkways, necks craned upwards to see the vaulted ceiling, shoes polishing the stone flags. At £20 a head, he wasn't about to complain and that was before they paid heritage prices for cream teas in the restaurant.

There was just the right length of respectful silence before he opened proceedings. He raised his glass of supermarket red wine prompting a scraping of solid oak chairs across the stone as everyone stood and raised their own glasses.

"Welcome to the Annual General Meeting of the Midham Hunt." He paused and with a booming tone learnt from his father, he projected his voice down the length of the table and into the rafters, 'Pertemptant venandi!' the motto of the hunt since Henry VIII.

Everyone solemnly repeated the Latin and they all took a sip of wine. Those words were carved into the stone on the archway above the carriage-wide entrance to the hunt kennels. His family had chased and killed over centuries. As Chairman of the hunt, the introduction was all Eddie was required to do and one of the Hunt Masters, Jeremy Cockerill took over, but the wine left a bitter taste. His ancestors had owned large estates in France and would have had plenty of their own vineyards. But that was all gone. When this hall had been built, his family had owned the county but over the centuries the land had been sold off parcel by parcel and now they relied on tourists. He flicked open the accounts and saw the numbers, then looked down the long table, barely full. They were one of the most prestigious hunts in the country and they were struggling.

A week before Eddie had met with the hunt officials to decide the order of business and the outcome of everything that would be discussed with nothing left to chance if they could help it. Her Grace Sophie, Duchess of Midham had played the hostess and ushered them into one of the smaller oak-panelled rooms in the Grange, with tea and coffee laid out on a sideboard.

These days Eddie addressed his wife rather formally. There was a time when he would have added *darling* to every other sentence, but Eddie now lived up at Midham Lodge, on the edge of his grouse moor and Sophie took the Grange. A divorce would have been too messy with yet more land and property having to be sold. Sophie indulged herself in the heritage and gardens of the Grange while Eddie rode to hounds and shot game with Arabella. In days gone by, Arabella would have been his mistress, but now she was just his partner.

The AGM was all for show and hunt officials were now being re-elected. Jeremy Cockerill paused before saying, "And we have a proposal for a new joint Lady Master, Arabella Lievin."

He pronounced her surname in his best French accent and asked: "All those in favour?"

Eddie looked down at the table to see every arm raised. They all knew who she was.

Next up for discussion were the accounts. The hunt kennels and stables were located in a quadrangle of farm buildings in the parkland about half a mile from the Grange. A high stone wall kept out prying eyes. Rent, maintenance and stabling for Eddie's horses didn't appear in the accounts, but wages for the kennel master and terrier man were there, along with costs of quad bikes, feed for the hounds, horse transport, hound transport and more. The list went on.

As for income, every year they had a go with terrier and lurcher shows, the annual point-to-point race and the Midham Show. The real earner had always been subscriptions, but recently that was falling.

One of the newcomers raised his hand.

"If I may?"

"Please do James," Cockerill replied.

"I do have some experience in finance and I would like to help. But before I get onto that and I think I speak for a lot of people, I'm happy to hand over my £1500 a year, but I subscribe so that I can gallop my horse and leap over every hedgerow in the county. The point-to-point races are great but on hunt days sometimes we just trot around a couple of fields and stand in the rain while Logan digs the fox out of an earth. And then there's the sabs, sometimes they're everywhere, filming and it all ends up on social media. My clients are some very important people and I don't want them seeing me on a video." He shook his head. "And then the sabs always say they've sent a pile of evidence to the police…"

Eddie had to intervene. If James Ledbury and his pals upped and left, they were finished. "I understand, James," he said. Then he glanced at his Hunt Masters. "We'll sort out some stewards they'll keep the sabs out of the way. And as for the police, has any of that ever gone anywhere? No. And that's how it will continue. Now, as you can see, we have a shortfall of £50,000 a year. This hunt has been in my family for centuries and I won't let our standards slip and I won't let it fold." Eddie hadn't realised, but his voice had risen until it was booming through the hall once more. "For that, I need your help."

The hunt members rose as one and cheered. They banged their fists on the table until their glasses shook. Eddie smiled and felt the blood pumping through his veins. He'd managed what his ancestors had done over the generations—he'd called his men to arms, to preserve their way of life. But slowly over the meeting, that feeling ebbed away. Members weren't going to treble their subscriptions, there wasn't going to be any injection of cash. It would be down to Edward Fraine to fund the shortfall and he really didn't know how he was going to do it, especially with the added cost of stewards.

The meeting ended and there was scraping of chairs as everyone stood up and had a few words with their friends. Sophie came in and waited by the door chatting to some of the hunt members she knew. Everyone was drifting outside until Eddie and Jeremy Cockerill slowly approached.

"Looks like His Grace will be riding the Lady Master tonight," said Sophie her voice icily cold.

"And he's a lucky man, *Your* Grace," Cockerill replied, putting his hand on Eddie's elbow to usher him out of the door.

Eddie was furious it really was a cheap slur. "Thanks, Jeremy," he said as they passed through the door. "I really don't know what I'd have done if you hadn't been there." Then he looked around for Arabella before heading back to the lodge. His father had a chauffeur, but Eddie had to take the wheel himself.

Chapter 9

Raven realised he'd been staring into space when the chef coughed and raised a paper carrier bag above the counter. A takeaway curry, enough for two. Maybe he'd been asleep, so he forced himself to concentrate on the short drive home.

He was exhausted and couldn't work out what to do first. The badger remained in his outhouse projecting a message of failure. He couldn't save these animals and their killers were taunting him. He found himself scrolling through his contacts until he stopped at Matt from the Badger Group who answered straight away.

"Hi, Raven, can you make it quick? I'm out in the cull zone."

Raven explained what had happened in the night.

"The bastards," replied Matt. "You'd better report it to the police, but that'll be a waste of time. It's open season here. Every fucking sett destroyed. Just leave your outhouse unlocked and I'll collect the poor creature. It could be the middle of the night, so don't be worried if you hear some more noise."

Raven was shocked to hear the anger in Matt's voice. He was normally such a mild-mannered man. There was the door to un-padlock and a few tools to move inside the house. So, Raven slipped in the key and stared down at the small black eyes and blood-crusted mouth of a creature that led a complex social life as far away from man as possible, underground and in the night. But that wasn't enough to stop the government from ordering the extinction of the whole species.

Back in the house, Raven tapped through an online police report, not for a wildlife crime but for harassment. After typing in the details, he started ticking the boxes about welfare. The incident had affected his mental health and stopped him from sleeping and he'd like all the support they could offer. There wouldn't be any of course and it was all a paper exercise to make his local force look as if they cared.

He heard a key in the door and stood up as Becky came into the room. She stood on tiptoe and gave him a warm kiss on his lips. He blinked away the tears, it was the first bit of kindness he'd felt all day.

"Curry, my favourite," she said and bounced into the kitchen for some plates and forks. As they ate, he passed over the camera and Becky downloaded the footage onto her tablet. Raven had remembered to speak out loud as he videoed the geese being shot. An authentic soundtrack racked up the number of views. They didn't really talk and as she ate Becky was tapping the screen, editing the footage. Raven heard his voice over and over until she got it right. He could barely keep his eyes open and slowly realised Becky was staring at him.

"Have you read my blog?"

He shook his head but she wasn't letting go, sliding the tablet in front of him. There was a photograph of Becky standing in an allotment. Her skin was impossibly smooth, her teeth perfectly white and her cheekbones more angular than he'd ever noticed. He glanced at her face to compare.

"Don't you like it?" She asked.

"No, not at all, it's just a nice photo," he managed.

Becktivist was the title. *Activist Becky Vickers connects with the soil in her organic plot.*

"Didn't realise you had an allotment?" he said glancing through the text. His name kept popping up or rather his social media handle @RvnHarley. She was milking him and through his exhaustion, he felt a spark of anger.

"Yeah, just some friends," she replied casually.

He scrolled further to see another staged shot of her planting a seedling *in the autumn.*

"Great blog, Becky," he said trying to think of the right words to boost her. "You're building your profile then?"

"My followers need to know more about who I am. If they're keen to know what I'm doing they'll read and share every post."

Raven had heard the message before: profile, content and reach. It was the road to becoming an influencer. But Becky didn't have the content or the reach and Raven was starting to think that was his only purpose. He slid the tablet back to her.

"Aren't you going to share it?"

"I'll do it in the morning," he replied.

She grabbed his phone and started pushing the buttons on the side, but the login needed his thumbprint.

"Fuck," she said dropping the phone on the table.

Raven could feel the anger pulsing adrenaline around his tired body. He sighed and tried to relax his shoulders. "What's up?" He asked as calmly as he could.

"It's so important to me and you just don't get that," she said turning towards him.

Half her face was in shadow, the perfect image on her blog replaced by an ugly scowl.

"I'm knackered, Becky, that's all. No agendas. If you want to stay I'd love that, but I'm going to be unconscious in about five minutes."

It was like flicking a switch.

"Of course, I'll stay," she said warmly putting her hand over his.

Raven managed a smile in return before putting the dishes in the sink.

*

It was 6.30 a.m. when Raven woke and realised he'd slept right through. He glanced over at Becky, her face lit by the morning sun and he was taken back to that desire which had drawn him to her. She looked so young, with perfect half-moon eyelashes, blond hair with some pink highlights and soft smooth skin, all-natural and real, unlike the photo. She was studying Environmental Science at university: all part of the plan.

Raven swung his legs out of bed as quietly as he could and then pulled open a drawer for some fresh clothes. He glanced over to see Becky awake and tapping on her phone.

"Five hundred likes on TikTok," she shrieked. Raven couldn't take his eyes off her face, one second her mouth was open in rapture, then the next it was downturned when she realised it was only five hundred. She seemed to weigh something up in her mind.

"You don't need to go just yet do you?"

Of course, he didn't. Half an hour later, Raven was rushing around to bring her a cup of tea and a bowl of cereal and he sat on the edge of the bed to eat his own breakfast.

"I heard some clonking around last night. I nearly got up to have a look," she said.

Raven realised he hadn't explained what had happened the previous night, just that he had some footage.

"That'll just have been Matt, collecting the badger from the outhouse."

Becky put down her cereal and asked Raven to explain.

"Fuck," she said and he heard her disappointment in him just like last night, making his anger resurface.

"There was a dead badger in the outhouse all the time," her voice louder and exasperated. "I could have filmed you holding it in the twilight. Moody black and white, your voice just a croak and your face looking like you'd died a thousand times."

She paused and looked into his eyes. "That would have been ten thousand easily and another thousand followers, not just, you know, five hundred and forgotten."

Raven understood what she was saying: *Content and reach*, again.

She leant forward and punched him on the shoulder, not that playfully.

"You should," she said, punching him again, "have told me."

Raven realised she wasn't joking. He gathered his things and went out to the van, smiling when he realised he hadn't shared the blog. But shaking his head when he realised how much Becky's antics had taken out of him. He needed to work out what was going on and what he wanted.

Before he could consider any of that, his phone pinged. There was a Twitter message from @countryview987, not the first time, with information to follow up. He found himself thinking it was a trap. But then he realised he was being paranoid. He couldn't go on like this.

The police hadn't called around and now he didn't expect them. He hadn't even seen any snares and it had probably all been staged. It was harassment and collusion pure and simple and a mistake to think he had any friends in the *law*. Once more they'd chosen a side, evidence or not. Some solicitors had been in touch previously and offered to help; maybe he should contact them now.

Raven arrived on site and realised he hadn't thought about Becky at all since he left the house.

Chapter 10

It had been a long night for Logan. He did plenty of hands-on work for the Cull Company, shooting as many badgers as he could. But he also had the task of coordinating the other cull operatives in this zone. They all seemed to think that buying a cheap night scope for their rifles was a ticket to easy money. It required skill and patience to wait for the animals to come to you. If you moved around and they caught your scent, they'd be off. Before he had a chance to do any of his own work, his phone had vibrated and he heard the gasping breath of Mason, one of the young lads, trying to run up a field.

"Had a clear shot, killed the little bastard outright, I was certain. But it ran off and now the field is full of people in Hi-vis jackets quoting animal welfare at me and saying they're going to find the badger and take it to a vet."

Logan shook his head. "They're trespassing, right?"

"Of course, they're fucking trespassing, there's no path around here."

"I'll get onto the police then. Don't do anything stupid."

Superintendent Farlow had given him a number for the control room and assured him it was a police priority to make sure the cull went ahead uninterrupted. But when he phoned and explained that saboteurs were trespassing and stopping their lawful work he heard that all available officers were dealing with incidents already and it would be some time before anyone could come out.

Mason was about ten miles away so Logan abandoned his sett watch, packed up his rifle and drove over to see the chaos. After a few miles, a car pulled out of a lay-by and started to follow him. He could see their lights and they were with him left and right no matter how many turns he took. Mason's location became obvious as he drew near, there was a Discovery parked at the bottom of a field, headlights on the main beam, lighting up the slope. The car that had been following waited some distance behind. Logan wondered about walking down and getting the registration so Farlow could update his database, but they were a long way off, so he opened the gate and drove into the field, pulling up next to Mason.

"Come on," he said. "I've called the police. Let's see if we can get them shifted. Bring your rifle so we can finish up."

At the top of the field, they soon found one of the Hi-vis jackets. It was a woman with a very bright torch.

"You're trespassing. Police are on their way," said Logan.

"Oh good," she replied. "That Discovery has no road tax, as soon as you leave this field there'll be blue flashing lights pulling you over. Criminal."

Logan clenched his fists and snorted through his nose. No one talked to him like that, especially some smart-arsed woman. But then he looked around at all the lights. There were too many witnesses.

"Out of the way, we've got a badger to collect."

She planted her feet wider apart and stood with her arms by her side.

"Fuck's sake," he said, grabbing Mason by the elbow and walking around her. Beyond the field, the searcher's lights revealed an area of scrub. There was no point looking in there. So, they went back to their vehicles and waited for the police. Logan made a start on his sandwiches, but the bread tasted like sawdust and his stomach was a pit of slowly simmering rage.

After a couple of hours, they saw the searchers carrying a large wire mesh case. That was Mason's badger then, on the way to a vet somewhere, no doubt to be euthanised because of the wounds. He slammed his hand on the steering wheel. This was impossible. He'd be on the phone to Tranchard as soon as it got light. If the boss of the Cull Company couldn't get the police sorted out, then it really was a waste of time. He set off back to the kennels for the flatbed truck so he could collect the fallen stock in the morning.

*

George was up early, keen to dispose of the cow. All dairy farmers had a hoist, usually an attachment to a tractor. George's farm was old school the cows saw some daylight in summer. It was becoming the norm in this area that dairy farms were industrial units. Cows stayed in their stalls, summer and winter to produce their milk twice a day. Whatever the production method, they were big animals that never had a chance to develop their leg muscles so when they fell over they couldn't get up until someone came along to lift them.

Logan slid the webbing straps under the cow while George nudged the animal with a forklift. Then it was hoisted up and onto the flatbed before being tied down under a canvas.

Back at the kennels, Seth who was the whipper-in on hunt days was working in his other role of kennel man doing all that was needed for the hounds. Their abattoir was geared up to deal with large animals. The cow was hoisted using a tractor and Logan drove straight in dropping the carcass onto a huge butcher's block.

He changed into overalls, plastic boots, an apron, and visor and ear protection. Then he set to work with his boning knife, to slice off the skin and an electric saw to cut the carcass into manageable chunks. These went into a grinder, bones and all. The head and spine would be incinerated because of the threat of BSE and the skin would go in as well because of the lesions that Logan would find if he cared to look.

The grinder could produce a *superfine pulverisation* and no one would have any idea where that paste came from. But that took too much time. The dogs were happy to crunch their way through something coarser.

Logan finished up the skilled butchery and left Seth to feed the grinder and bag everything for the walk-in freezer. Gerald Tranchard was managing director of Midham Wildlife Services Limited, which had the contract for culling badgers in this zone, but he expected Logan to deal with all the day-to-day problems. Logan hated phoning because Tranchard never wasted an opportunity to denigrate him. One minute, Logan was tempted with a large bonus for completing the cull on time and the next he was about to be sacked because his marksmen couldn't shoot straight. Tranchard mixed with the aristocracy and all the big landowners. Logan would never be invited into those circles, it wasn't his *place*.

Tranchard answered his phone straight away and Logan explained what happened.

"We had some difficulties in the cull zone last night. Mason had a badger, but it wasn't a clean shot and in an instant, he had a field full of trespassers. There was no way he could finish up. I called the police, but they didn't show."

"Fucking hell, Porter, I've warned you about hiring every farm labourer who's borrowed a rifle. What kind of mess have you left me with?" Tranchard replied.

"They found it before we could and it's gone off to a vet."

"So, it's going to be all over social media and when that happens there's always a journalist on one of the nationals who picks up on it. We'll be a laughing stock and when the Ministry hears about it they won't be asking us to tender again all because of the sloppy work of some menial who couldn't hit a barn door."

Logan chewed his lip. Tranchard had interviewed and hired Mason.

"What do you want me to do?" Logan asked eventually.

"You get out there tonight and call the police at the first sign of any disruption. Kill as many badgers as you can. Is that clear? I'll call Farlow and tell him to sort out these terrorists otherwise he'll have the Ministry on his back."

With daylight, Logan felt wide awake. He wanted everything to be perfect for the hunt meet on Saturday and that meant all the hounds working together and obeying every instruction. He signalled for Seth to pause his work and told him to collect *Gunner*. The dog had looked promising but didn't have the temperament for a hunt. Seth held the hound as Logan fired a shot to the head. They lifted the animal between them and carried it to the butcher's block. *Gunner* would be another meal for the rest of the pack.

Chapter 11

Chloe had slept like a baby. It was still early so she pulled the quilt up over her head and then wriggled down into the warmth.

She was staring at the tattoo. Clever shading made it look as if the adder was wrapped around his spine and she followed the black diamonds up to the snake's head. Looking wasn't enough and she traced the coils with her finger, brushing the fine hairs on his back. She gave him a moment to wake then pulled his shoulder towards her.

The house was stirring as Chloe finally pushed herself away. She sat up, searching for her t-shirt.

"I need the bathroom."

"You'll be lucky," he said. "Jed's into grooming, he'll be hours."

"I really need to go."

"There's a toilet outside."

Chloe pulled on the rest of her clothes. He was lying in bed watching with a look that said *I want more*. It made her blush.

"Now that we've got to know each other, do I still call you Snake?"

He laughed and looked up at the ceiling.

"It's Jack." He paused. "In private," then he laughed again, "you know the drill."

She did. Back in the eighties, the Hunt Saboteurs were branded as politically undesirable and dangerous. Efforts were made to infiltrate their groups and they had to get real with their personal security and safety, so they could carry on. Using nicknames was simple and effective.

Sitting in the cold outhouse was like a basin of icy water in Chloe's face. But she didn't mind. He said *in private*, did that mean there was going to be more?

"Get a grip, girl," she said out loud and then she glanced down at her phone, in case he'd messaged. She groaned. And then embarrassed in case anyone was listening, she headed back to get ready for work.

The drive into the office was a crawl along car-filled roads but it gave her time to think.

Snake or Jack as she now knew him, slid into her life the day before. The last few months had been a blur and she eventually realised it was best to live a day at a time and to be somewhere she belonged. In the pub, the others had filled in the gaps and explained how hunts operated these days. Even the old established ones like Midham were teetering on the edge. It felt impossible to secure any convictions under the Hunting Act but the few successful cases along with constant pressure and publicity meant that support was draining away. The rural way of life had changed and backing the hunts no longer won elections. Farmers were sick of their fields being churned up and other residents were sick of a pack of dogs and even horses trampling their gardens. Time and again hunts strayed out of their *country*, where they had permission and onto land where they weren't welcome. They trampled over rural communities with their sense of entitlement. People had had enough.

Last night, she'd only exchanged a few looks with Jack, but it was natural to go back to his. She wasn't even sure she wanted another relationship and had no idea what he thought about it. But the best thing was she'd never thought about Raven once.

She was smiling as she walked into the office and in an instant that changed. Everyone stopped talking and turned to look at her. In a second, Siobhan was at her side, guiding her into the coffee room.

"I'm really sorry, Chloe. Leo Corbet has been found dead. There are rumours everywhere but it looks pretty horrific. The police are treating it as murder and HR are in Dave's office."

Chloe was shocked. Baby Leo was one of her clients and he'd been murdered. At first, she could only think about how much he must have suffered and how she'd let that happen. Then there was the unbearable guilt of having failed him, before finally trying to remember how she'd handled the case and what she'd done.

"But I only saw him two days ago," she replied.

Then Dave, the manager squeezed into the coffee room as well. He gave her a quick hug.

"Shiv's told you?"

Chloe nodded.

"You've done nothing wrong. I've read your notes and all the actions were agreed upon. But HR is here. They're like a bunch of fucking vampires after blood. They're going to suspend you."

She'd never heard him swear before. They moved to his glass-panelled box and she felt like a criminal being sentenced. Suspended from her job because a two-year-old boy in her care had died. The ten-tonne weight hanging over every social worker had just crashed on her head.

"Just go straight out, Ms Turner. If you have any personal effects on your desk, let us know and we'll get them to you."

Chloe couldn't look at anyone as she walked back across the office. On the stairwell, she grasped the handrail with both hands and slowly made her way down to the car park. She really wanted a coffee but worried they'd tell her off for leaving her car in the parking area.

"Fuck them," she muttered before heading into town for coffee and chocolate muffins. Life was going on in the coffee bar. No one was pointing at her and everything seemed normal. That was something to hold onto.

A couple of hours later back at the house, she didn't want to sit and dwell. Her best friend Siobhan had offered her the spare room after she'd split up with Raven, for as long as it took. Armed with the vacuum, cream cleaner, dish cloth, duster and furniture polish, she cleaned the house from top to bottom. Then she started preparing a meal for them all. Siobhan was back first and immediately gave Chloe a hug.

"How are you?" She asked.

"Depressed and angry. I just feel so useless. And I've dumped another thirty clients on you."

"Don't worry about that," said Siobhan, "Everyone is totally with you. It could have happened to any of us. It's an absolute tragedy for Leo, poor kid, but what can we do? We can't put them all in care. And HR? What a bunch of wankers. They treat you like shit and get off on it."

Chloe tried a smile but that just brought the tears. They hugged until Chloe broke away.

"Better thanks."

Siobhan looked down at the oven and all the clean surfaces. "Wow, you've been busy. Let's have a glass and chill for half an hour, Mark can catch up later."

After the food, they stayed at the table. Chloe told them about the day before with the sabs.

"This morning, I felt so happy and so alive for the first time after all that crap with Raven. And then this happens. It's like someone's telling me I have to be miserable all the time. And now I just have to pick myself up and get on *forever*."

Mark and Siobhan looked at each other. Raven had been an unmentionable.

"He looks like shit most mornings, Chloe," said Mark. "We're getting a bit fed up with him at work. Sometimes he's off doing his filming and other mornings he's just exhausted. Colin and I carry on, filling in the gaps when he's not really there."

Mark gathered his thoughts but he really needed to unload: "It's so hard not to love him, isn't it? And he brings so much. He charms the customers without trying and gets us all the work. And when I've had a few days off sick there's never any argument, he splits the profits evenly just as he always does."

He paused again. "But Raven's tortured, his mind is a complete mess and he wouldn't talk about it, not until today."

And then Mark told them what Raven had said, everything.

"He has nightmares, serves him right," Chloe replied. She shook her head, "I don't mean that." But his betrayal tore inside her.

"Becky's using him and I think he's finally managed to see that," said Mark. He laughed. "She's not after his body, it's his followers."

Chloe knew her confidence had been shattered. Raven wanted someone younger. She let herself feel angry, it was better than self-pity and blame. And now it was good to finally talk about everything: "She knows how to seduce, that girl. But Raven was more than willing. And those videos she puts out, *Becky Vickers and Raven Harley*, she soon managed to get star billing." She paused. "Do I sound bitter and obsessed?"

There was silence for a few seconds and Chloe started to think she was being unfair to her friends, they knew him as well and she couldn't ask them to choose.

"He is my mate but I think you were crapped on there, Chloe," said Mark and then he looked down at his phone. "Speak of the devil."

He tapped the screen. "Raven, how're you doing?"

"Might be in a bit late tomorrow, Mark, got some info to check out."

"No worries, mate, we're still on with those ash trees in the park. The next couple can be taken down from the base. Colin and I will crack on with it."

"Brill, I'll be with you as soon as I can."

Mark put the phone down. "Did you get that? Raven's on a mission. The world is back to normal," he said with a touch of cynicism.

Mark and Siobhan gathered up the plates and set about the washing up. Chloe guessed Raven would be out on a moor somewhere. And just like a descent from mountain fog her thoughts were clearing and she could see a way ahead. The anger remained but Chloe was surprised by a longing to be there with him. She pushed that aside and thought about Jack, his desire burnt a hole in her and that felt so good. It had been just one day and he'd probably be with someone else tomorrow. It hadn't felt like the start of a permanent relationship and she had no idea if that was what she wanted. But she didn't have to replace Raven with someone else and there were other ways of being with a partner which left her with more freedom. Maybe the Raven who everyone loved had been suffocating her. All these ideas were conflicting but it was a start.

Chapter 12

It had been a tortuous approach but Raven was now in place. He'd driven beyond his usual haunt—the High Ridge Estate and down into the valley beyond. He was no longer an anonymous figure, walking these hills along with so many others. He'd caused a vast amount of publicity that damaged the shooting industry and they were fighting back, changing the way they operated. And what better way than to call in the favours and carry on as if nothing had happened? Gamekeepers showed complete loyalty to moorland owners and in return, they were rewarded with a house, brand new pick-up and salary the envy of every other agricultural worker. Lawyers were provided to swot away accusations of illegality, but if the evidence was beyond dispute, gamekeepers were dumped and disowned as rogue operators, vilified by their protectors. The sudden departure of a long-standing head gamekeeper, mid-season had left one of the local estates scrabbling to recruit an inexperienced replacement, apparently the best on offer. Raven was starting to realise it was his job to turn that trickle of departures into a flood. And the way to do that was to get evidence of the inherent criminality of this industry.

He'd parked close to the Curlew pub, blending into the other vehicles. Then he made his way along unfamiliar paths climbing through woodland until eventually coming out onto the heather slopes of the High Ridge Estate. Walking here was easy because so much of the vegetation had been burnt recently. This was because grouse liked young shoots of their favourite plant and bare areas to collect insects for their chicks.

Crouching down, he made his way into a hollow before using binoculars to scan the slope below. Bracken dominated the sides of stream beds, but quad bike width paths had been mown through the ferns and these trails were dotted with grain feeders held in small wooden frames. It was a similar picture across the more open slopes; mainly rough grass, some gorse, bushes and low trees. Spread around these slopes Raven counted a dozen low enclosures with mesh sides and roofs, some writhing with partridges, others empty.

It all looked new, but how could he have missed this? Further down the slope, amongst denser woodland Raven caught sight of larger pens full of pheasants.

The number of birds was staggering. There was still too much daylight to explore more closely and no doubt early morning was the best time to find out what was really going on. So, he slid down into the hollow and made some calls.

Mark answered with a happy voice as usual and Raven heard Chloe in the background. Her voice was etched onto his brain, distinctive and this time quite loud. She was sometimes like that after a few drinks. It sounded as if they were celebrating and Raven was missing the party. That made him jealous. Then resentment crept in, he was crawling around on his hands and knees trying to expose the criminals and they were finishing a couple of bottles of wine. He shook his head and tried to focus. He wasn't doing this for the likes or any accolade or even self-aggrandisement. It was about trying to stop the rape of nature.

Next, he tried Becky and again there were voices in the background, male this time. *The friend with the allotment?* Raven pushed away the ache of jealousy. He was trying to see Becky for who she was but kept on being pulled back.

"Can you talk?" He asked. Then he heard a scraping of chairs and more background chatter. She was in the pub.

"Right, I'm outside now."

"I've got some info and I'm out there now, looks like it needs an early morning visit. Are you up for that tomorrow?"

"If you think it's worth it?"

It was how they'd met. She'd messaged him, offering to help. He was trying to get more people interested in his cause and they arranged to meet in a pub. He was wary of her at first. She could have been a shooter for all he knew but soon that didn't seem likely. She was very open about her social media accounts and where she lived. Most importantly she didn't probe for any information about his friends or what he was doing out on the moors. Before he knew it, her enthusiasm had spilled over. It was as if he'd been crossing a swollen river, one foot had been swept away and he couldn't stop the rest of him following.

"Yeah definitely. I'll pick you up at 4.30."

"I'm just writing an essay tomorrow, so that's a lucky escape. Better make this the last then."

He assumed she was talking about the drink in her hand. The light was fading and Raven poked his head above the edge of the hollow, camera in hand. There was a gamekeeper, dressed in camouflage with a peaked cap over his eyes and a gun over his shoulder. A crow was feeding on the ground and as the gamekeeper approached the bird flew up. Within a second, the shotgun had fired and the bird fell to the ground. As one, fifty partridges rose from the bracken and flew down the slope before settling once more. The gamekeeper ignored the partridges and walked over to the crow. He picked it up by the wing and threw it into the bracken, then turned and walked back down. He didn't seem to take an interest in anything else.

Raven waited until the light had gone before climbing over the fence and heading towards the pens. His video camera could cope with low-light conditions and even complete darkness. He started filming the writhing mass of birds in the covered enclosures and as they moved it became obvious the floor of the pens was covered in carcasses, decomposing, pecked and trampled with droppings. A couple of the pens were empty of live birds they were the lucky ones flying around for a few weeks. He asked himself why they didn't just flee, get away from this cesspool. The answer of course was the grain hoppers dotted around the slopes. Born in cages, crammed into pens with dozens of others before being dumped on a hillside, these birds had no idea of their natural habitat and no idea how to look after themselves.

Raven wanted to see more, but even in the dark, the partridges still rose up out of the bracken and the flapping of so many wings seemed deafening, advertising his presence. So, he turned back.

At home, he made some toast and looked through the video footage which showed the detail in black and white. Live birds moved in waves even within the pens, revealing ghostly grey carcasses everywhere. And in the background was a soundtrack he hadn't noticed at the time: hooting from a male tawny owl with the screech of a female responding.

*

Finn Sutherland drove his pick-up along to Brown Slack plantation in the last daylight. There was a small clearing near the centre of the wood and he dumped some dead pheasant poults onto the ground. Then, without lights, he followed twin tyre tracks between the trees to a spot about 30 metres away where he had sight of the bait. He scanned the wood with some night vision binoculars and propped up in the cabin of his pick-up was a rifle equipped with similar technology. He was waiting for a fox to catch the scent of the rotting pheasants but if a badger came along that would be dispatched just as well. This plantation on High Ridge Estate was outside the cull zone apparently because it was a conservation area and all sorts of assessments would be needed to kill here. But their tenant farmer Tony Bowden grazed sheep and cattle nearby and would only be happy when every disease-ridden badger had been eradicated. Finn's underkeeper Ryan was waiting near another pile of bait about a kilometre away at the edge of Carrlow Forest. This part of gamekeeping used to be called lamping—the animal would be dazzled and freeze for a moment when a spotlight on the roof of the pick-up was turned on, making an easy target. Now it could all be done in darkness away from prying eyes.

Finn couldn't settle. He needed to sit still and he needed to concentrate. He looked at his watch again and yawned. Taking care of the pheasant shoot and the grouse moor meant late nights and early mornings. He was only doing this because the previous gamekeeper had messed up with his traps. If these areas had been filled with snares he could be in the pub now, instead of staring into the dark. He gave himself two hours then he needed to sleep.

But it wasn't that long before he heard strong claws scratching the earth, searching for worms. The wind must have been carrying the scent of the bait towards the badger. Finn put the binoculars down and reached for the rifle, training the sight on the pheasants. Then the solid form of the animal came into view. It was an easy shot to the body. He watched for a few minutes as the badger died then drove back round. Logan had given him a pile of the clear plastic sacks that were being used in the cull and the badger slotted into one of these. It wouldn't be exploring his grouse shoot any more. His phone vibrated with a message, Ryan must have heard the shot. Finn told him to put in another couple of hours, the pheasant shoot was littered with carcasses and the whole area was flooded with foxes. Trying to keep on top of the vermin was a 24/7 job.

*

It was still dark when he knocked on Becky's door. She came out clutching a reusable coffee cup in one hand and balancing her rucksack in the crook of her arm, before gently pulling the door closed with her free hand. Raven had been driving for a few minutes, listening to her sipping the coffee before she spoke.

"Did you see much last night?" Becky asked before tilting her body away from him, concentrating on the blackness outside.

It was a reasonable question but he felt a stab of annoyance. She was straight down to business, no concern about his tiredness or lack of sleep and her words felt like lumps of wood in his ears. There'd been desire and lust, but tenderness? He tried to remember and felt again the sensitivity of her touch and soft words, that made him drop his defences and open up. *Falling for her.* But it had been a one-way street and she didn't reciprocate, not with anything that mattered, just the practicalities of her life. Whenever he tried to really talk to her, she always deflected the conversation back towards him. Had it just been an argument about the badger? No, there was much more to it. She hadn't been joking. He tried to tell himself it was still the middle of the night and not the time for any meaningful dialogue, but maybe the first rays of a watery sun would be enough to see her properly for the first time. Right now her words and the way they were delivered, felt like a fist slapping into an open palm.

He explained about the birds rising up and how that would be a fluorescent sign pointing at them. They'd position themselves outside the perimeter fence. Becky would monitor any gamekeepers checking traps, this was most likely to be in the trees and bushes towards the edge of the area, so predators could be killed before they reached the partridges. Raven wanted to see more of the lower slopes where there were pheasant pens as well. It might be a long wait before anyone showed up.

They parked and Becky followed Raven, moving quietly in the half-light of dawn, crouching sometimes, crawling over a few rises in the heather and running when they couldn't be seen. He pointed to a hollow where she could wait with her own camera near the top of the slope above the pens and he positioned himself to get the best view of the lower area.

His phone vibrated: *In place*

Then they lay and waited.

Slowly the native birds became active. There was hardly any singing at this time of year, just alarm calls and quiet flapping of wings. The partridges were another matter, restless with random movement. Those that were free moved constantly, racing in short bursts over the ground before flying up. And in the pens, it was agitated panic. Those birds were being tortured only alive by a reflex to eat the grain and drink from water bowls full of their own droppings.

Raven couldn't see Becky, which was good it meant she was lying still in dark clothes with her face and head covered. This morning his wardrobe was the same, he needed to blend in. But last night he'd dressed slightly differently, looking more like a rambler in Goretex and jeans and less likely to attract the attention of a gamekeeper.

After about an hour, Raven saw some activity at the bottom of the slope with the first one, older looking pick-up driving in and then a few minutes later a second, newer vehicle. The figure walking up the slope had the same gait as the gamekeeper last night. Becky should be keeping an eye on him. Meanwhile Raven concentrated on the newer pick-up and it looked like the one he'd seen at High Ridge a couple of days before. The driver climbed out and checked his phone before fetching a short ladder. He put this against a tree, climbed up and released a small flap on a box, pulling something out. Then he climbed down leaving the ladder in place. Next, he walked over to a wooden pole and pulled something off the top, placing it in his pocket.

Raven wanted to see what the other gamekeeper was doing but had to keep following his target. Now his gamekeeper jogged over to some other bushes. Raven sensed the urgency but the gamekeeper was partially obscured. Stepping back into Raven's line of sight there was the same routine of concealing something in his pocket but this time in his left hand, something was hanging down. The gamekeeper walked back to his pick-up and opened the rear door before throwing in the object. Next, it was back up the ladder to place something in the box before closing the flap.

Raven and the gamekeeper both looked around when they heard the shot and Raven's target man drove up the slope.

Becky had been filming her target pushing aside branches and walking into clumps of bushes and low trees. *Checking traps.* The gamekeeper disappeared into another copse then she heard the shot and it made her jerk the camera. A minute later the gamekeeper reappeared dragging a bright red fox by the tail. She watched the animal twist around for a second before its life drained away and its head was bumped callously on the ground.

It was like a punch in the stomach. Becky let go of the camera and clawed at her face covering before coughing bile into the bilberries where she was lying.

She panicked they'd have heard her, that they were coming for her. But glancing over the top of the hollow the two gamekeepers were chatting casually near one of the partridge pens, the dead fox at their feet. They untied and peeled back the covering of the pen. The birds were unsure what to do until one flew out. There was frantic flapping and a collision of wings as the rest followed. Becky watched and then realised she hadn't filmed any of the releases. One of the gamekeepers stepped into the pen and started throwing out carcasses. Becky grabbed the camera and started recording. The other gamekeeper walked through the vegetation and bent down, as he stood again there was a black shape in his hand, a corvid. He walked back to the newer pick-up and smashed the bird's head against the bonnet. Becky watched him repeat the movement. The dull thud amplified in her ears.

Eventually, the bodies were stuffed into a plastic sack, more rotting flesh for a stink pit and the gamekeepers left. Becky made her way carefully back towards Raven. He looked at her pale face and pulled a water bottle out of his bag, wetting a tissue, before gently cleaning her cheek. She sat in the heather and felt the bile rise again. This time, she dropped her head between her knees for a minute before letting Raven continue.

"Ok to head back?" He asked softly.

She nodded and followed.

Back in town, she pulled the memory card from her camera.

"Here, you take this, Ray. I can't face it at the moment."

Chapter 13

Nathan Parbolde waited outside the solid wood gates of Midham Lodge. The camera picked up his vehicle and the gates swung open. He followed the yellow sandstone drive up to the wide-fronted building, constructed of a darker, harder stone. There was plenty of room for his Range Rover and as he pulled the briefcase from the boot he took in the mature oak trees giving way to the heather of Haverstone Moor. A shooting venue he'd enjoyed more than once. The Duke was waiting for him by the door.

Nathan was ushered into the dining room for the full spread of an English Country House breakfast. He put the case down by the table and filled his plate with eggs and cooked meats. The housekeeper came in and poured tea, then left shutting the door behind her.

"You do spoil me, Eddie," said Nathan, spreading his arms wide. "Usually it's the *Peloton* followed by a bowl of muesli."

Eddie knew enough about exercise regimes to grasp that Parbolde was talking about a bike trainer.

"You need a lining on your stomach for field sports," Eddie replied.

Nathan nodded. He'd been introduced to country traditions that involved a gun and even that amount of blood had turned his stomach at first. But it was worth it for the connections he'd made. Not just Edward Fraine, Duke of Midham and his aristocratic chums but bankers, City traders and politicians, even a sprinkling of police officers just to add legitimacy.

Parbolde usually sent someone else with the briefcase, but Eddie had requested a face-to-face.

"You're coming on Saturday?" Eddie asked.

Nathan nodded. His apprenticeship hadn't extended as far as the hunt but that was about to change.

"I have a middleweight hunter for you. Jumps well and has a lovely temperament. I've graduated to the heavyweights I'm afraid," said Eddie patting his belly.

Parbolde's main UK residence was in Surrey and his wife Amelia rarely ventured this far north. They did ride together so he knew he wouldn't be a complete novice on a horse. And then there was the dress code.

"Don't worry, I'll look the part," said Nathan. "My tailor recommended a new country outfitter and they've fixed me up checked your livery, the works. We even worked out the etiquette for the buttons."

"You'll have to earn those, Nathan, but I do hope we see you more than once. It was the hunt I wanted to talk to you about. I can't tell you how important it is to me. It *is* my family and we've kept it going for 500 years. I know I don't have to give you a big speech here and I'm not putting the begging bowl out, but I do need to realise some capital, ongoing."

Nathan looked down at the briefcase and patted it. "A lot of people appreciate this, but my rule of thumb is we can't pump in more than ten per cent of your turnover without being noticed. Unless you're telling me things are looking up at the Grange?"

Eddie shook his head. The annual turnover was around £5 million but an additional £500,000 in cash was banked. Eddie's cut was £50k. But the trouble was he needed £50k more to keep the hunt afloat. Nathan had large amounts of cash that needed to be made respectable. Eddie had the impression it was done for friends, but it could have been down to Nathan's activities for all he knew. It was a world where people swopped favours and that at least was familiar to Eddie. Not so usual was the staggering amount of money involved. Eddie wanted a part of that and his reward had been an investment tip from Nathan: *RUsearch*.

It was a Russian oil and gas development company. Somehow Nathan knew before any other investor they'd found a huge gas field at the Arctic Circle. Eddie invested £200k and that turned into £2 million. Then before all Russian oil and gas companies were embargoed and sanctioned, Nathan informed him his investment had been sold and the money banked in an offshore account. Eddie wanted to go to the Caribbean to touch it but he had to satisfy himself with a series of passwords, codes, voice and facial recognition before he could see the zeros on his computer screen.

"My account in the Caymans," said Eddie.

"That doesn't exist as far as HMRC is concerned. If you want to hang on to all of it, we need to put some measures in place," replied Nathan.

"Go on."

"Well, easiest is the hunt is owned offshore and it's those offshore companies that inject funds."

Eddie was looking puzzled and Nathan was losing his patience. "A foreign investor props up a loss-making UK concern. In fact, I could get some investors who'd be willing to help out with that, a similar scheme to the Grange but it could all be electronic. No wads of fifties."

Eddie held up his hands, he was getting out of his depth. Nathan seemed to have an endless list of associates who wanted to launder their cash in the UK. It didn't matter that Eddie, Nathan and others all took a cut, so that only half the original amount went back to the owner. Those owners could now prove the source of their remaining cash as UK generated and were free to spend their legitimate pounds sterling without fear of prosecution.

"Just hang on a minute. I could never sell that to the hunt committee. I'd lose all the rest of the support I have. The hunt has to be owned by my family and people need to see that in the accounts."

Nathan sighed. "What about this then?" He gestured to the lodge around them and the grouse moor behind. High Ridge is owned by a myriad of companies.

"Fucking hell, I'd have to get Sophie to sign off on that, her name is on every document." gasped Eddie. And all he could think about was his wife's sneering voice. Her comment had ruined his planned celebration with Arabella. One of the local gastro pubs had a Michelin star and he'd ordered a rather special takeaway. His new Lady Master purred over her food but Sophie had a way of making him feel useless, *impotent* and that's what stayed in his mind.

Nathan could see the Duke was struggling, so he tried another avenue. "Eddie, I'm sorry. I'm not explaining this very well. How about I get Jonas to come over to go through all the options? You don't have to sign up for anything you don't want. If it comes down to it, we can get someone to sail over with a suitcase full of cash."

Eddie had met Jonas the accountant who now ran the financials at the Grange. Maybe he could sweet-talk Sophie to sign up for a perfectly legal tax avoidance scheme. She never said no to money.

"No, I'm the one who needs to apologise, Nathan. You have the patience of a saint. It's just we never learnt any of this at school and if they tried to teach me I don't think I would have understood a word of it. But I do have one last favour for Saturday I've seen some of your security at your shoots. Do you think you could get them to come along? I just want everything to run smoothly. Now, do tuck in."

Nathan made a show of slicing open a sausage.

"Callum and Sean? No problem, they love anything like that."

*

A dozen officers from the National Crime Agency sat around a large table in one of their meeting rooms. They stopped chatting as their Director Philip Bolton walked into the room. His appointment had been political. The agency had a large budget but rarely made the news for bringing down any high-profile criminal gangs. The government's need to appear tough on crime always came to the fore at some point in the election cycle and the headlines showed that was now.

"Some of you will have been briefed already but Whitehall has finally given the go-ahead to investigate all things oligarch, particularly the Russians and as you know their oil companies, weapons, financial services and most of their manufacturing is all embargoed, sanctioned. All those previously legitimate revenue streams are now officially closed, but we know the reality: it's business as usual in the UK and they can't do that without help. That brings us to their UK partners and fixers and our initial person of interest is someone quite familiar to you all: Nathan Parbolde. Most recently he shorted the Pound against the Dollar before anybody had even heard of Ukraine and that made him profits in the hundreds of millions. We can see that from his legitimate market activity. Then he's rumoured to have made even more, acting through intermediaries, going long on the Rouble as it bounced back after the initial crash."

Bolton paused to make sure the team understood and one of their recent recruits, Dew Foster raised her hand.

"So, he knew the war was going to happen before anyone else and he bet on the Pound going down. Then he had the info to tell him it would be drawn out and bet on the Rouble going back up. I think I'll be following him around Ascot, he obviously knows which horse is going to win before they've even set off."

There was some laughter and a shake of the head from most present before Bolton continued.

"You can't say we don't make dreams come true, Dew. You're going to be taking part in his pheasant shoot, all wired up so we get more of an idea of how he operates. I will say this though: his oligarch chums value loyalty and cement it by making sure their friends all get their hands dirty. So, I'd expect to see Parbolde walking around with a suitcase full of cash that's on its way to being laundered. Samantha will give you the details, Dew, and also fill us in on how far we've got with unpicking his spider's web of offshore registered companies."

Chapter 14

Gerald Tranchard sighed and scrolled through his phone once more. *#BadgerCull* was trending and it was his cull zone that was getting the hits, physically and electronically. He hated anthropomorphism. Evolution had created a simple planet: Man killed animals and ate them if they provided a good meal or dumped them in a pit if they were vermin.

But now there were constant updates on Barney the Badger, lying on his back with a fresh white bandage wrapped around his tummy, cradled by some schoolgirl and being fed milk out of a dropper. *Just until he can get his strength back after being shot by an evil gunman.*

And endless so-called experts saying *his* cull was causing untold cruelty and suffering, pointing to graphs and charts showing government scientists had lied and the cull hadn't stopped Bovine TB. There was so much noise the politicians had to respond and Tranchard expected more guidelines that he could ignore with the certainty that no one would check. That was the usual way of things. But now his cull zone would be full of do-gooders interfering.

He switched to his phone book and tapped on Jimmy Farlow.

"Superintendent, Jimmy, morning. Just wondering if you've been able to schedule any more resources for us. The cull has gone right up everyone's agenda."

For Farlow, there was nothing unusual in this request. His job was a constant shuffling of priorities and media coverage changed those day by day.

"I've had a word with the chief and she told me it was a public safety issue. We can't have anyone standing between a marksman and a badger, they might get hurt."

"I like it Jimmy, arrest them for their own safety, that sounds good."

"It's not quite as simple as that, Gerald. We don't want to get dragged into this media circus with everyone shouting brutality and bias."

"Best get your top men on it then. How many squad cars can we expect?"

"One. Unless there's an emergency."

Tranchard was quiet. He was used to people doing what he asked. One car wouldn't cover the hundred square miles of his cull zone. But he took a deep breath and swallowed his sarcasm.

"Appreciated! Can we have a phone number?"

"Ring the police control room. You've got the details. And can you make sure your lad's vehicles have tax and MOT? It makes us look like idiots."

*

Raven arrived on site more or less on time. He'd dropped Becky at her place and called in at home for his tools. They'd stopped for a tea break when his phone rang, Pete *the Journo* was a freelance who'd written very sympathetic coverage and had a knack for getting his stories into the nationals and these days that meant print and online.

"How can I help?"

"Barney the Badger, mate. Are you good for a quote?"

Raven had been following the story and he knew the kind of thing Pete was looking for.

"Great," said Pete. "Now here's the scoop: the government says it'll be seizing Barney to be tested for TB and is threatening to euthanise if he's positive or not."

"Over my dead body," said Raven.

"Cheers, pal, I knew you'd oblige."

Raven explained the call to Mark and Colin and then looked at Mark as he asked, "Do you think Chloe's going to be out there on the cull?"

Mark smiled. Raven was talking about her again.

*

The location of badger setts was a closely guarded secret because badger baiting still thrived in some rural communities. Participants dug out the tunnels and chambers and forced badgers to fight with dogs, filming and photographing everything so the horrific scenes could be shared. Chloe felt privileged to have a paper map in her hand so she could check if setts were active. Normally, badgers moved around and expanded their territories and young males, just like foxes used their energy to tunnel out new homes. But the cull had changed normal behaviour—killing a large number of healthy animals in a prime location encouraged other badgers into the area. But sometimes whole setts seemed abandoned. It was live, active setts that were of interest to the activists because those setts would be known to local farmers and that's where the marksmen would be found in the night.

Chloe had asked Jack how she could help and he'd given her the map. There was a big red circle at Nether Beck Farm and setts were marked in black felt tip. The farm was well known because that's where Midham Hunt terrier man Logan Porter lived and he'd been spotted almost every night at the cull. It was a small step from killing foxes to killing badgers.

Chloe had been told to keep away from her social work department. Her mind was flooded with guilt for failing to protect a young child, anger at the cruelty shown by the parents and anger at her department for the way she'd been treated. So, it was a relief to concentrate on trying to find badger setts and then searching for signs of recent activity. Her other instruction was to make sure she wasn't spotted.

The map wasn't very accurate, but when she arrived at Nether Beck, the badgers had been busy. This was clearly a major sett spread over a large area. There were numerous entrances all marked by a pile of yellow earth and rocks, dappled with paw prints. Chloe sat down and marked the map with a tick.

Lower down a broad, grassed-over ditch traversed the slope, edges marked by hawthorn and oak trees showing golden leaves, red berries and bright green acorns. A scene as pretty as any in rural England but this one was now a killing field.

Chloe walked down the slope to find a pile of peanuts in the grass and a short distance away more nuts in a shallow scrape, partially hidden by a flat rock balanced across the top. This was the bait and the gunman would be in the ditch below. She gathered up the nuts and went back to the path at the top of the bank.

A little further was a view down to the farm. Chloe sat with her back to a rowan tree and pushed aside some fronds of bracken opening a view of the buildings and courtyard. There was a pick-up truck and green quad bike parked in the yard along with a couple of large wire mesh dog crates, each with a small wooden shelter for the terriers. Logan Porter would likely be catching up on his sleep. After a while, a white van pulled into the courtyard and Chloe started filming. The driver backed up to a large door on one of the outbuildings. He fiddled around with a combination padlock and slid open the door, then started transferring clear plastic sacks inside. These were the victims of the cull and it was shocking how many badgers had died. They'd remain in the outbuilding until taken for incineration. None would be tested for Bovine TB.

Chloe packed up the camera and headed back. Jack had told her to rest and she knew she'd be back above Nether Beck with a bright torch to stop any more badgers being killed tonight.

Chapter 15

Logan stared at the wall beyond the foot of his bed. The wallpaper was peeling, but that was no concern to the Duke or his estate manager. Logan wasn't going to decorate, not on the money he was being paid. The afternoon sun had found a crack in the curtains and it was lighting all the faults in the dusty room.

He was angry. The cull wasn't going well. His marksmen had all said they were skilled with a rifle, even at night. But the wounded badger now in the news wasn't the first. The do-gooders were everywhere and the police never turned up in time. Tranchard had given him a dressing down and Logan now had to phone around everyone to tell them to take one lethal shot: that's why they were employed. His friends had signed up because they were happy to rid the countryside of filthy disease-ridden animals but now they were finding it wasn't easy money. He didn't have time to phone all thirty cull operatives as Tranchard suggested, he'd have to send them a message. Tranchard had told him emails were no good because anyone could end up reading those. But they had all signed up to the WhatsApp group and Logan could say what he thought on there. It was always the way: Logan or some other minion did all the dirty work for people like Tranchard or the Duke and *they* pocketed the money. He heard Emma climbing the stairs with his tea. He clenched his fists. It was about time she gave him a son.

An hour later, Emma heard him leave and she sat down at the kitchen table staring blankly ahead. In her mind was the image of Logan behind her, grunting with effort. She'd married a strong, muscled man who'd made her laugh and what she saw in the mirror was the apron of a flabby belly and the red face of a man who couldn't contain his anger. She couldn't bear to watch him and cast her eyes down on the bed. But he grabbed her hair and yanked her face upwards. She had to look at him but didn't feel anything. It was happening to someone else.

Years ago, she'd enjoyed sex with Logan but now he just looked as if he wanted to hurt her. And he did. She was dreading the hunt in a couple of days, the first of the season. He'd either be angry and drunk if it went badly or just plain drunk and violent if it went well. She couldn't be there for that.

Before he left, he'd been jabbing his fingers at his phone, cursing.

"How the fuck do you do a group message?"

He thrust the phone at her but her hands started shaking. In an instant, he'd grabbed her wrist making her drop the phone onto the floor. He picked it up and looked at the screen, checking for damage. She thought he was going to hit her, but not this time. Instead, he pushed the phone back at her and she tapped the message:

One shot to kill and no more fuck-ups.

"There, that's gone," she said, passing the phone back.

She was sick of the violence around her and knew he'd be the same tomorrow. This was her life and she pushed the thought out of her mind. He made her feel ashamed and she couldn't bear the thought of anyone discovering.

She needed a distraction and after a glass of water settled down to some admin of her own. The local police were always happy to get involved with crime prevention and educational visits to the school. This year, to help raise funds, Jasmine and Lily suggested the annual police visit could be expanded with gamekeepers giving demonstrations of quad bikes and short talks on the importance of their work to manage the moorlands. Parents and everyone in the local community would be invited and they'd think of ways to get the adults to put their hands in their pockets.

She scrolled through her phone for the sergeant in charge of rural crime. Paul Carson was working a late shift and answered straight away. Emma explained they were raising funds for St Mary's Primary and how they wanted to make a day of the annual police visit.

"No problem at all, I'm scheduled to work that Sunday," Carson replied. "Just email the details and I'll come along with one of the team."

Emma sent a quick message to Jasmine and Lily. They could sort out the rest of the activities. Emma needed a long soak in the bath.

*

Raven made himself comfortable on the sofa and started to look through the footage they'd taken. He hadn't heard from Becky and didn't know if she'd come round tonight. The nighttime and daytime footage conveyed the shocking reality of pheasant and partridge shooting. These birds were reared in their thousands and cost a few pence each. Their lives were cheap and those that reached adulthood could only look forward to being blasted out of the sky. It seemed even worse than grouse shooting because these young birds had never known any sort of natural life at all.

Raven looked closely to see what the gamekeeper was doing at the bottom of the slope near the pheasant pens. The ladder led up to a camera and they changed the battery and maybe the memory card as well. Some of these cameras connected to a mobile phone and there was enough of a signal for that to work. So, if he took a close look not only would he be captured on video but there'd be a gamekeeper there in minutes. Had they gone to that trouble just to stop thefts of birds?

The rest of the video gave a clue. There was the flat face of an owl in the gamekeeper's hand and Raven had heard Tawnys calling so it was likely one of them. The furtive activity around a wooden post was the gamekeeper removing a spring trap. It will have been the other trap hidden by bushes that killed the owl. It was a hideous death landing on a perch covered in a trap that slammed shut breaking the bird's legs and fixing it there until it died. These traps had been illegal for more than fifty years but how could he prove that had happened? The video on its own wasn't enough for a court.

He rummaged through a box of kit and pulled out another, miniature, camera. This one recorded in daylight and night with battery and memory lasting about 24 hours. It would fix in a tree behind the gamekeeper's camera so he would avoid detection. It had to be worth a try, someone had to stop them.

He felt exhausted but wouldn't rest until he'd done all he could. Dressed in black from head to toe he went back to the shoot.

Chapter 16

Chloe had driven out to Nether Beck with Jack and two others. It was dark when they arrived and they split into two pairs to check the sett entrances, Logan Porter was well known for blocking them on hunt days and the same strategy might be used here. Chloe and Ruby soon found a pile of rocks blocking one of the tunnels and that was illegal, cull or not. They heaved the rocks out of the way and down the slope. Not all the entrances were blocked and they guessed Porter had tried to work out which parts of the sett were most used and also to direct the badgers down towards his gun. So close to his home, there was no doubt they'd be seeing him sooner or later.

They met back at the top of the slope where Jed and Jack reported a similar number of blocked entrances. Jack was messaging all the time to find out where other groups were working and if they needed help. So far there had been little police involvement but that would probably change. The peanuts Chloe had found on the slope would have been replaced by now. Certainly, none of the entrances she'd seen had been blocked this morning. Porter had been busy this afternoon with a quad bike full of boulders.

Chloe was starting to get to know her companions. Ruby was a student and Jed worked night shifts on the help desk for a telecoms company, he was supposed to be resting before his next block of shifts but he said doing some nights out here was no hardship and better than trying to adjust to a few days of daylight living.

One person alone would be vulnerable. Four was the minimum number to see off violent cull operatives. And if the police turned up, witnesses were needed in case of aggressive questioning or accusations. They had no idea if Porter or anyone else would show up, but it looked likely so they sat down to wait in the dark. The wind was blowing up the slope towards them so any badgers coming out of an entrance wouldn't smell their scent immediately. But a marksman at the bottom of the slope probably would be picked up by them. Sitting quietly in the grass, torches off gave the badgers chance to get out and search for food.

After about an hour, they heard a quad bike in the distance. Porter didn't approach silently for his prey. They heard him stumbling into branches and cursing as he lost his balance. Before he had the chance to settle in the holloway, Jack turned on his lamp, illuminating the slope. Porter shielded his eyes from the light with his hand and tried to work out what was happening.

"You're trespassing!" he shouted.

"We're on a public footpath," shouted Jack in return and all four of them stood up so they were clearly visible.

"I'm calling the police," he shouted and made a show of putting a phone to his ear. He was on the phone for several minutes before he shouted that they were on their way.

They pointed their torches down the slope and agreed if the police showed then Jed would probably disappear into the night, he had the most respectable job. Chloe wasn't sure she had a job at all and agreed to see it out. It wouldn't be an easy site for the police to access given the slope and distance from the road. So, they waited in the quiet of the night.

After an hour, they heard a vehicle and Porter was joined by another shooter dressed in full camouflage. Eventually, they saw blue flashing lights and after a few minutes the fluorescent jackets of two officers walking carefully down the field.

It was all taking time and that meant no badgers were being killed. Eventually, the two officers made their way slowly up the hill. It was a man and a woman both wearing stab vests under their glowing jackets. Chloe thought she'd be sweating wearing all those layers and it took the officers a couple of minutes to get their breaths back. There were no body cameras poking out through their jackets so they obviously didn't want a record of what they were about to say. It was the female officer who took the lead:

"This is going to be a short conversation. You are disrupting the lawful work of that man down there. He's complained of feeling intimidated…"

Jack sniggered but didn't say anything.

"The Public Order Act 1986 gives me the powers to arrest you to prevent further disruption and intimidation."

Jack fixed his eyes on her. "We're only here because that man at the bottom of the slope as you describe him, blocked most of the entrances to this badger sett," he waved with his arm and held his phone up so the officer could see a photo on the screen. "That's an offence under the Protection of Badgers Act 1992."

Chloe saw the officer's jaw clench and Adam's apple grate up and down her throat.

"Report that on 101 and stick to the matter in hand."

"No," replied Jack. "That thug down there needs to follow the rules. It's an ongoing crime and I should be dialling 999. I don't know if you're recording this conversation but we are."

He looked at Ruby who nodded. She had a camera in the palm of her hand and that drew the gaze of the officer.

"Just a moment," she said moving away. She spoke into a mouthpiece on her jacket and then waited for a reply. Without meeting Jack's eye, she nodded to her companion and they walked slowly down the hill. The two marksmen at the bottom were soon waving their hands around and their swearing even reached the top of the slope. But within a couple of minutes, shooters and police were all walking away.

"Whoopee!" Ruby shrieked. "Own goal," and there were fist pumps all around. They turned off their lights and waited another ten minutes, but no one returned.

"I reckon we can call it a night," said Jack and they made their way back to the car.

*

Logan spat on the ground. He told the policewoman what he thought of her and he wanted to go round to Tranchard's *Manor House* to yank him out of bed. He'd driven the quad back to his pick-up and sat in the cabin having a cup of tea. He'd called Mason to help sort out the activists, but now he was on his own, there was work to do for the hunt.

It was Logan's job to make sure there were foxes to chase every time the hunt met. The Hunting Act lurked in the background but prosecutions were rare and if it happened to Logan he'd been told there was still a job for him and nothing would change. It wouldn't be the Duke in the dock that was sure. If anyone asked, they were following a trail and just happened to come across a fox. The old boundaries of hunting seasons and specified activities had all become blurred as had the dress code. The Midham didn't wear *rat catcher* tweeds to go cubbing, they just wore their normal black jackets, but some wore red if they wanted. And the end of cubbing leading to the main season happened as soon as possible. That was now. The pack was trained as much as it could be and for the hunt to survive they needed a paying field of riders who all had a good day's sport.

They didn't want to be wandering aimlessly around their *country* on the chance a fox was out during the day. No, they wanted to be sure of their fun.

It wasn't that difficult to find fox earths. Logan thought hunts should be paid environmental grants because they made sure hedgerows stayed planted and copses retained their trees. This was the image of *Merrie England* and precisely where foxes would be found. Many earths were historic, but foxes were always expanding their territories and Logan helped out with earths constructed from drainage pipes buried in the ground. These were easy to control.

At this time of night, all foxes would be out searching for food. So Logan went round the natural earths and blocked their entrances. That would lead the foxes into his artificial dens. It wasn't really that difficult a job. He knew the route he was taking and he made sure there were plenty of materials on hand at each earth—logs and boulders mainly but some concrete slabs as well. He'd go back for some breakfast and then see what had turned up.

Chapter 17

Chloe was back at her vantage above Nether Beck Farm in the morning. This place felt like the centre of everything and she wanted to film the transfer of dead badgers from the storeroom to the incineration van. A few hours' sleep had been refreshing and a flask of coffee along with teacakes and jam set her up for the morning. Porter's wife headed off to work and his pick-up was parked in the yard, maybe he was sleeping?

Logan had waited until it was light before going back to the fox earths. The metal box on the front of his quad held two of his Jack Russell terriers. There was another metal box on the back and that contained some netting. It was a two-man job and he collected Seth on the way. The first artificial earth had two entrances and Seth pegged the netting over one of them. Logan opened the box on the front of the quad to see two pairs of eyes gazing up at him, Spud and Billy. He grabbed Spud by the loose skin on the back of his neck and looked over to Seth who nodded, then threw Spud into the entrance. Usually, foxes didn't fight the terrier, not like a badger that would stand its ground and protect the sett. If there was a fox in there, it would come out quickly. Instead, they had to wait a couple of minutes until Spud trotted up to the net and barked. Spud was thrown back in the box and they drove to the next artificial earth again with no result. Logan had built three similar earths and if the last one was empty as well it would mean a lot more work for him on hunt day.

This time he threw Billy into the tunnel and they heard barking followed by a vixen running out of the other entrance and into the net, Seconds later one juvenile then another joined their mother trapped in the net. Billy the terrier stood in the tunnel barking and growling as the three foxes struggled to free their legs tangled up in the holes of wide gauge strong nylon net. Logan and Seth scooped up the net and carried the three foxes over to the quad dumping them in the box at the rear. The animals were still struggling until Logan slammed down the lid. He dropped Seth back at the kennels and headed home.

Chloe heard the quad bike chugging towards the farm and she assumed it must be Porter after all. She hoped she had the best viewpoint and started filming. Porter arrived on an ungainly-looking quad bike with large green-painted metal boxes front and rear. The courtyard building had several doors and he opened the room next to the badger store. He went back to his quad and unclipped the lid of the box on the back keeping his hand pressed on it before carefully lifting it up and gathering the edges of the net. As he pulled this out Chloe could see the ginger-red fur of a fox, but there seemed to be too many legs thrashing around. Logan struggled to carry the net into the outbuilding. The weight wasn't a problem he was trying to keep all the animals from escaping. A few minutes later, he came out and padlocked the door. Then he opened the front box on the quad and lifted two terriers by the scruff of the neck he walked over to their crate and shelter and threw them roughly inside.

Chloe filmed it all and was shocked by the way Porter threw his dogs around. The terriers fulfilled a purpose and beyond that they were worthless. From nowhere, Chloe started thinking about Porter's wife. Was she treated in the same way or did he somehow have a personality change when it came to human contact? It didn't seem likely.

He parked the quad behind yet another set of doors then went round to the main building. Everything went quiet and Chloe messaged Jack. She thought it was illegal to hold a fox captive so it could be hunted, but as always it depended on the exact wording of legislation. She'd leave it to Jack and the others to decide what to do but it didn't seem much of an option going to the police. She couldn't imagine those two officers from last night doing anything other than giving Logan a pat on the back.

*

Finn felt his heart racing as he drove up to the pheasant pens. He glanced up to pole traps and there was another bird dangling, legs broken. He could tell straight away it was a female sparrowhawk, much larger than the male, and capable of taking bigger prey. It had landed on the flat plate of the trap and the metal bar had slammed down breaking the bird's legs. It had obviously tried to fly away, but Finn had secured the trap to the pole with a short-length chain.

Excitement turned to anxiety and he looked around to see if anyone was watching. Of course, there wasn't. But he didn't want to push his luck and he'd stop using these traps now. He unclipped the chain from the post and removed the sparrowhawk from the bar and plate. The used trap went in his pocket as did the other one and he walked back to his pick-up, storing the bird in a sack. He slammed down the tailgate and looked around once more.

"Good work," he said out loud.

Then he inspected the pens. Two pheasants were squabbling over a carcass on the ground, taking turns to peck at the flesh. He noticed Jayden had joined him and was pointing at the carcass.

"Look at those dirty buggers, cannibals the pair of them," he said.

The two pheasants were eating one of their own.

"Better get that cleared up, Jayden, we'll be having a shoot in a few days and the punters will want it nice and tidy."

Jayden opened the pen and set about collecting the carcasses littering the floor. Finn could see some of the pheasants were now able to fly in and out of the open-topped pen at will. The breed they'd chosen was Bazanty, one he'd used many times before and the birds were moulting their juvenile feathers, revealing the black necks of their adult plumage. They were *stayers*, never venturing far from their feed. But on a shoot day, the beaters needed to make a lot of noise to make them fly high enough so there wouldn't be any human deaths from the guns. There was going to be plenty of sport and hefty tips from satisfied clients.

*

It was late evening when Raven went to retrieve the camera at the pheasant shoot. He replaced the whole unit with another and crawled back out of the wood. Driving back all he could think about was the footage. When he let himself into the house, he saw Becky's bag on the kitchen table, but she wasn't in the lounge. It wasn't that late. He found her sitting up in bed reading a coursework text.

"Looks exciting," he said.

She slammed the book shut.

"I was missing you…"

"Me too," Raven said automatically and he explained about the camera.

"Bring the laptop up if you want to check the footage. I could do with boning up on this," she said, lifting up the book to show him.

There were hours and hours to skim through. But Raven couldn't concentrate. He didn't know where he was with Becky. She seemed so desperate to produce killer videos that would get a lot of attention. And now he'd got something she was feigning indifference or had she really lost interest? Seeing the brutality of gamekeepers at work was enough to make any normal person throw up. Raven had seen so much he was hardened, at least at the moment it was happening. Later it hit him. But Becky, maybe her reaction didn't fit with her image as an influencer who risked distress and danger to bring a video to her followers. Raven struggled with that, he didn't do any of this for an audience he did it to stop wildlife suffering. Instead of Becky, an image of Chloe's face popped into his mind and he couldn't shift it. He remembered her lying in bed with her head on the pillow, eyes opening slowly and smiling when she saw him. But he'd messed up and lost it all.

He decided to find the footage from the morning to see if the gamekeepers had caught anything else in their traps. And there it was the same furtive activity around the posts and a different bird carried to the pick-up. So, he scrolled back to see a bird of prey swooping around the pens in daylight, making the pheasants frantic. The raptor headed towards the trap obscured by bushes. The camera picked up a shriek of noise and wings flapping frantically against the foliage. It seemed to go on forever before the quiet. And then two hours later the gamekeeper arrived.

Raven swallowed and now he felt sick. Becky was still engrossed in her book. He wouldn't show her, not yet. He copied the action into another file and closed the laptop.

"I'm glad you came over," he said and hated himself for it. He couldn't be genuine now.

Becky closed her book. "Any good?" She asked, nodding at the laptop. Raven nodded in return and Becky stared ahead avoiding his eye. She never acted like this. What could he think? It just seemed weird.

Eventually, Raven reached over and pushed the switch to turn out the light.

*

In the morning, Raven was getting dressed and trying to be as quiet as possible. He heard Becky yawn and turned to see her stretching her arms and back. Then her eyes drilled into him.

"You just don't get it, do you? You don't get me."

Becky seemed determined to carry on their argument. And then he realised he hadn't answered quickly enough.

"You called out Chloe's name last night and your arms and legs were all over the place. I thought you were going to punch me in the face," she continued.

"Oh God, sorry, Becky," he replied and some images from his dream came to him, he was choking again. And now he couldn't think what else to say.

"Are you regretting this?" She asked, gesturing *you and me* with her hands, her face set in a cold frown.

It didn't feel like a question. It was an accusation and he could tell she was determined to control the conversation. "I don't know," he replied. Honesty made him feel better than last night and now he couldn't remember why he'd fallen for her in the first place. She was taking charge, dumping him and he expected a comment that cut to the bone.

Instead, she smiled. "Don't look so glum, or, I don't know, panicked. I don't know about you, Raven, but this was never going to be happy ever after for me."

He sighed. How was she managing to make him feel deceived and exploited?

Then the dagger in his ribs: "I never said it was exclusive," she added casually.

This was happening so quickly, but it wasn't in him to throw hurtful comments back at her. "That's not how I looked at it," he managed.

Her face was difficult to read but he thought he saw pity. That made it worse.

"You *will* need some help with that video," she said, matter-of-fact.

Raven knew that was patronising. He'd had enough, "Fuck the video."

And that felt better. He went downstairs before she could say anything else. The kettle was boiling as Becky came down. She stretched up to try to kiss him on the cheek, but he recoiled. It wasn't a friendly farewell. *She was dumping him and then toying with him.* He held up the palm of his hand and looked away. There were no more words to be spoken. The sound of the door key dropping on the table broke the silence.

"I'll message," she said then let herself out.

He stared out of the window and realised he was on work time, it wasn't even 7.00 a.m. and it was Saturday. It felt like an empty day stretching ahead and for a moment that was frightening. Like the black void of his nightmare, where he was completely alone, choking and thrashing his arms and legs to escape. But in his waking world, the sun was rising, and he'd make sure he had some healing.

Before he finished the tea, his phone pinged—Chloe.

Really sorry, Raven, but I need some help. I didn't know who else to ask.

He phoned her straight away. It was her voice, the one he knew, but she sounded nervous. There was a problem with her car and she needed to do some filming. She started to explain, but he interrupted.

"I'll be with you in five minutes."

Chapter 18

Chloe was sitting on the wall in front of Siobhan's house. She looked alert but there were dark smudges under her eyes. Raven realised he wasn't a picture either and without thinking he ran his hand over his chin, he needed a shave. He wanted to look his best for her.

Chloe climbed into the passenger seat and she explained where they were going.

"I can help as long as you want today," he said.

"Brilliant. And how's things with you?" She asked.

It seemed a bit too jolly, a bit too polite. This was the first time they'd been together since they'd split up but he couldn't launch into some great analysis of what had happened. He wanted to say sorry, but then they would end up talking about everything. He needed to share something.

"I think I was dumped this morning," he said.

"You think?" It came out immediately but then Chloe slipped into the polite language of strangers. "Sorry, that's none of my business."

"No, it's over. I got the message." Raven paused. "Yeah, all about her...fuck, what an idiot."

They sat in silence for a minute, Raven staring at the road ahead.

"I called out your name last night," he said without making eye contact.

Chloe stared ahead as well. "So, I'm the stuff of nightmares now?" She asked before realising she'd betrayed Mark's confidence.

"The opposite," said Raven finally glancing to meet her eye. She didn't reply so he continued, "When we get there, shall I just kick the door in and rescue those foxes? That'd be about right for today."

Chloe laughed. Was he telling her she was the woman of his dreams? He'd have to try harder than that. If he wanted forgiveness, there was a mountain of hurt to climb first and she didn't know if she'd ever manage that. She concentrated on the animals.

"Let's keep you out of jail a bit longer, Ray."

*

They parked and made their way along the bank above Nether Beck Farm. Chloe recognised Jed even though there were only his eyes showing above his face covering. Raven was hovering a few yards away and Chloe waved him over.

"Porter's still in the house. There's his pick-up, quad bike and his wife's car parked in the courtyard," Jed told them. "I need my bed, I'm working tonight."

"Thanks," said Chloe and she sent Raven off to one side so they would have a better chance of a view of the doorway even if someone was in front of it. He didn't need any instructions on how to film the action.

They didn't have long to wait. Porter came out and looked at his watch impatiently until an old Discovery pulled into the yard. Chloe guessed it was someone from the hunt, Jack would know. They went into the room which held the foxes, leaving the door open. Chloe willed the foxes to escape. Instead, they heard a shriek of pain and another, then more. Chloe struggled to keep the camera still. The cries were like a punch to her stomach.

A few minutes later, Porter reappeared, cradling a sack, one hand firmly on the mouth of the bag. He dumped it into the rear box on the quad and slammed the lid. Then it was the same brutal routine for the terriers as they were thrown around and dumped in the front box. After Porter locked up, the Discovery and quad sped away, a convoy of cruelty.

Chloe looked at her phone. There was a message from Jack:

Upper Denling Wood you'll see us

It was the location where they'd been cubbing. Chloe ran over to Raven.

"Come on," she said.

They ran back to his van and he started to negotiate the narrow lanes towards the wood. Before long, they were behind a pick-up.

"Fuck's sake get moving," said Chloe helplessly.

Then the pick-up stopped. Chloe leapt out and looked down the lane. It was jammed with vehicles, all of a type. It looked like every farmer in the area was out to support the hunt. She leant in through the open door and told Raven what she'd seen.

"Just give me a minute to park and I'll come with you," he replied.

"They'll trash your van if you leave it here. I've got it covered," she said grabbing her rucksack.

Before he could say any more, she jumped over a five-bar gate and disappeared behind a hedge. Raven blew his cheeks out and wondered what to do. He looked in the mirror, at least he wasn't blocked in behind so he reversed and managed to turn around and drive away. A few minutes later he stopped in a lay-by. Chloe was right about his van being trashed but he didn't really care. She knew what she was doing and he'd just be in the way, she didn't need looking after. The sound from the outhouse was agonising and that was just the beginning.

Chapter 19

Nathan Parbolde stood in front of the full-length mirror in his dressing room at High Ridge Lodge. The black hunting jacket didn't really need any adjustment, but he still felt the urge to tug the sides straight.

He grimaced. Why did the old money of aristocracy make him feel like he was walking into the headmaster's study?

"Get a grip, they're just a bunch of fucking inbreds," he said to himself.

He stood tall and walked out into the yard. Callum opened the door of the Range Rover for him. Sean was behind the wheel of the pick-up they sometimes used, though judging by the number plate it was three years newer than the last time Nathan had seen it.

"You've had your briefing?"

Callum nodded. "They'll be filming everything, but need to be taught a lesson. Maximum damage with a minimum of fuss."

Nathan smiled. He loved the privilege that money brought. In this case, owning people to do his dirty work, whatever that involved.

*

Edward Fraine, Duke of Midham sat astride his horse and surveyed the *field*, all friends who paid their subscriptions and fought to keep the tradition alive. Porter had sorted out a fox so there would be a kill today, choreographed so the hounds caught their quarry after a chase over the hedges and through the pasture, his *country* where *his Duchy* had hunted for centuries.

Vehicles and horse boxes were parked neatly and riders had climbed on their mounts. The hounds were excited but the whipper-in had them under control. Sixteen *couple*, the ideal number just as his father had always said. The Hunting Act had made no difference and they were following a trail if anyone asked. Eddie had plenty of people to shoulder the responsibility if by chance they ended up in court. That wasn't going to happen as the police never attended for breaches of the Hunting Act, Superintendent Farlow made sure of that. But Farlow was eager to ingratiate himself so he sent a squad car or two if the sabs interfered. The field were eager for the season to start properly, but Parbolde looked out of place trying to be nonchalant when his nervousness betrayed him. He probably wanted the chance to get used to his mount but was surrounded by people needing to introduce themselves, seeking contacts and favours. Eddie had loaned him Samson who knew exactly what to do without any prompts from his rider, so there wouldn't be any embarrassments.

But in the distance, there was the figure standing on the roof of a minibus. *A saboteur*, dressed in black, face covered, radio in one hand, camera in the other, waiting for it all to start. His ancestors were brutal with anyone who upset the order. These days Edward Fraine needed to be more subtle and that's why he had Parbolde and Farlow, the modern-day equivalent of bankers and bailiffs. Eddie would keep his hunt going until his dying breath and nobody was going to stop him.

*

Chloe made her way around the field boundaries, mainly tall hedges. It was obvious where the hunt was going to start by the throng in the distance. Hunt supporters and spotters were all looking that way so she could move unnoticed. Then she heard the chug of a quad bike and looked through the hedge to see Logan Porter swing the vehicle around in a wide circle with the box at the back facing into the centre of the field. Porter stepped off the quad and made a call. Chloe started to film. Within a minute, she heard the short blasts of a hunting horn and lots of shouting.

Samson started to move before any instruction from Parbolde, a walk at first then a canter. Some of the other riders had hunting whips and they were *rating* the hounds, cracking their whips in the air. Nathan heard the breath of the horses and smelt damp earth as the ground was churned. The hunt narrowed as they approached an open gate and all of a sudden there were three black-clad sabs to the side blowing a horn with long mournful notes and shouting "Come hounds!"

For a moment, the dogs looked confused and started to peel off before being whipped and ordered, "On!"

Chloe heard the noise and knew it wouldn't be long. Porter opened the box at the back of the quad and pulled out the sack. He untied the top but held it closed in his fist until the hounds were in the adjacent field, then he tipped the sack upside down.

Chloe saw the vixen fall to the ground, looking dazed. The vixen started to run, limping badly on all four legs. It must have been adrenaline that made her pick up speed away from Porter. Within seconds, the hounds had caught the scent and were in full cry, they appeared through another open gate as the vixen tried to reach the hedge at the far side of the field. Chloe panned the camera capturing the fox then Cockerill the huntsman urging the hounds on. *Intent and orchestration.*

Most of the hedge was over six feet high but a small section had been cut back to around four feet just next to a stile. Two thickset figures had appeared and were waiting to one side.

Nathan knew when the hounds had the scent of a fox. He could taste bloodlust in the air. It oozed from riders and animals. They charged through another gate then straight on towards a hedge. The horses in front leapt over and he followed. Samson landed safely, but Nathan was caught off balance and lurched to the side. He grabbed the saddle and managed to stay on.

The sabs were running to keep up and Chloe joined them near the stile. Jack was first but Callum grabbed him and spun him around towards Sean who delivered a short powerful punch to the stomach. Jack crumpled to the ground. Chloe tried to squeeze past the thugs but this time the punch came from Callum. Chloe felt burning in her chest and she doubled over unable to breathe. She started to fall, but someone grabbed her arm and they were running again for a gap under the hedge.

In the next field, the riders had stopped and the hounds were trying to force a way into a patch of brambles. Before the sabs could get there, Porter drove up on his quad and skidded to a halt. The vixen had recognised her surroundings and headed towards an earth but Porter had blocked the entrances. The only chance of safety was dense vegetation but the hounds were inches away and eventually one was able to grab enough of the vixen to drag her out from the thicket. Then it was over in seconds as thirty-two hounds ripped the fox to pieces.

Chloe looked on in horror through the barking and yelps of the hounds, the cheers of the hunters and the stench of death. Then she watched the figure in black stand tall and stride into the throng of hounds.

"Back!" he roared and the dogs paused for a moment. Jack bent down and grabbed the front leg of the vixen, now severed from her body and then he walked towards his friends and held the leg up to a video camera.

"Look," he said. "The pad has been sliced with a knife."

And then Chloe knew. Porter had taken the vixen and sliced the pads on all her paws, those were the screams of pain from the outhouse. The hounds smelt the blood and the severed scent glands. The poor animal didn't stand a chance.

The whipper-in was calling the hounds and Porter was proudly holding the remains of the fox, his hands covered in blood. Astride their horses, the huntsmen were laughing and joking. It had only taken a few minutes.

Chloe was feeling nauseous with shock and the pain in her chest. She wasn't really taking in her surroundings and started to pull down her face covering. She needed air. A hand grabbed her wrist. It was Jack.

"Best leave that on for a bit."

Then he was staring at her, she thought her face was white as a sheet, but not that much of it was exposed.

"Are you ok?" He asked.

She shook her head. "That punch from their *security,* I think he broke my ribs."

And then she felt a tender arm around her shoulders, but it only lasted a moment. The hunt had moved on.

"And you?" She asked. "You hit the floor first."

"I don't know what he hit me with but it feels like he's ruptured my stomach."

Jack's eyes were following the hunt as they cantered away, Porter following on the quad with the vixen draped across the back. "Come on!" shouted Jack, "they're carrying on."

Chloe tried to jog but the pain in her ribs was too much. The hunt was moving quickly and soon disappeared from sight. All the sabs had left was the distant sound of barking. Jack stopped and radioed back to the vehicles, but the minibus was soon blocked by hunt supporters.

"Fuck," he said before calling everyone together for the slow trudge back. There was no buzz of excitement now, just anger the hunt had got away with it.

But then Chloe told him about the morning at Nether Beck Farm and catching Porter releasing the vixen. "And I think I filmed the fox with Cockerill urging the hounds on," she said waving the camera.

"Bloody hell, great work, Chloe." He shook his fist in the air. "That must be enough for a prosecution."

"Let's have a look at all the footage, but yeah, should have nailed the bastard," she said.

Then Chloe realised she didn't want to spend the afternoon making a police report. Jack was already one step ahead.

"Let's put together the evidence, but we need to get the other foxes out before we go telling Plod anything."

She could barely think about what Porter had done to the vixen, but the image had set in her mind. It was churning and she fought the urge to scream.

"How did you know about the pads?"

"Porter's got form on that one, but we've never had any evidence before." He paused. "Pretty blatant what he did. I reckon they're under a lot of pressure to provide a quick kill for their subscribers, so the money keeps rolling in."

Sitting in the back of the minibus, Chloe felt each bump and pothole. Everyone was subdued, they hadn't stood a chance and a poor animal had been ripped to pieces, but there was an air of determination. Next time, they would save a life. A few pints in the Dragon would ease the pain.

*

Emma was sitting on a sofa in her sister's house. They were watching Saturday evening television, eating a takeaway pizza and drinking wine. Emma had told Debs about Logan. It was really hard to talk about him because she was *conditioned* to take the blame, for *everything*. She was at fault and was failing him.

"You've done nothing wrong," Debs repeated.

When Emma finished speaking, she stared down at the floor. Debs took her hand.

"You don't have to put up with it, Emma. You can stay here if you like."

But somehow that wasn't an alternative. They were waiting for the phone to ring and when it did Debs muted the television.

Emma jabbed the speaker symbol on the phone. Her fingers were trembling.

"Where the fuck are you?"

Emma could picture him. He would have been in the pub all afternoon, everyone buying him drinks because he'd made sure they'd had good *sport*. Then as the huntsmen and women departed he would have sat around a table with his mates, drinking steadily for another few hours. Now he'd be leaning against the dresser in the kitchen, face flushed, spitting the words into his phone.

"There's a note on the kitchen table, Logan. A pie in the fridge just needs a couple of minutes in the microwave. I'm with Debs just for the night I'll be back tomorrow."

She tried to make her voice steady. They heard the intake of breath. Emma expected an explosion. Instead, Logan's voice was soft.

"Look, Emma, I picked you out of the gutter. Made sure Deano never showed his face again. You were in bits and I put you back together again. No one else would have done that."

Their relationship started with her owing him for that and he made sure her dependency grew. He wanted to control her, completely. Delivery driver Dean had been violent and Emma couldn't see any way out until Logan came along. She had been in pieces and soon Logan was telling her what to do because she couldn't manage for herself, could she?

He let the silence hang a little longer.

"I work so hard for you, Emma. Aren't I allowed a couple of pints with my mates on my only afternoon off?"

He always did this. She had to agree with him. And that meant she'd failed him in some way. She took a deep breath.

"You have a lad's night, Logan. I'll see you tomorrow."

It took a couple of goes to hit the off symbol on the screen. Then she shut the phone down.

"How did I do?"

Debs twisted around on the sofa and gave her sister a hug.

*

The grouse moors were full of gamekeepers, the woods were full of pheasants and more gamekeepers and the fields were full of packs of hounds and huntsmen on horses. *Merrie England.* Raven caught the bus into town for the last day of the Spanish season at the art-house cinema. A couple of hours later he blinked into the daylight and turned his phone back on.

There was a message from Chloe.

Could I ask a big favour? Today was gruesome. Feeling bruised and battered. Any chance you could keep an eye on Nether Beck tomorrow morning?

Raven didn't want to seem too keen but Chloe had already waited a couple of hours for a reply.

No problem. I'll get out early and stay until midday. Got something planned for the afternoon. Hope you are ok?

The reply came straight back.

Thanks, really worried about those foxes. Been soaking in the bath for an hour! x

Wow, a kiss. That got him thinking. The evening seemed brighter all of a sudden.

Chapter 20

Raven listened to the autumn bird calls and felt the life around him. Then he looked down at the farmyard with fresh eyes and saw neglect and decay. The quad bike had been abandoned, leaning over with one wheel on a pile of rocks in the yard. Empty plastic sacks had been tossed by the wind until they jammed against splintered wood pallets and a couple of empty plastic drums had toppled over. Raven wondered how that scene gelled with the countryside code.

Eventually, Porter came out and filled two bowls of food for the terriers. Then he filled another two bowls and unlocked the door that they'd been watching yesterday. He closed the door behind him and then reappeared a few minutes later without the bowls.

About an hour later, an old hatchback pulled into the yard and a woman climbed out. She opened the back and pulled out a holdall and then he was on her grabbing her shoulders. He looked as if he was going to head butt her and she jerked her head back. He let go and shrugged his own shoulders as if it was some kind of misunderstanding. She slammed down the hatchback and brushed past him into the house.

Raven had the feeling he was intruding in somebody's private business but it looked like a marriage full of violence. The way Porter had grabbed her shoulders showed a practised aggression. It was a familiar dance for both of them. For Porter, people and animals were there to be *used*. Then Porter went into the house and it wasn't long before his wife came out carrying a cardboard box which went into the car before she drove away.

An hour later, Raven glanced over to see Chloe walking towards him along with a blond-haired man who looked to be in his mid-twenties. They were dressed in hiking gear. Raven shuffled back out of sight of the farm buildings and the three of them sat on the grass.

"This is, er," said Chloe making half an introduction.

"One of the sabs, er Snake," her companion said.

"You know Raven," she continued.

They all nodded. Then Raven explained what he'd seen.

"There's definitely more foxes in the outbuilding. The law's probably useless for getting them out. Porter will say they're his pets or he's rescued them or something, but they'll end up in front of a pack of hounds. Trouble is the padlock is fastened securely and it's a solid door. You'd need a crowbar to get in and it would make a lot of noise."

"They'll be the juveniles and we saw what happened to the vixen yesterday," said Snake. Then he explained about Porter slashing the feet.

Raven wanted to put his hands over his ears. "So, that was the screaming?" He asked.

They went through the options. The juveniles would suffer the same fate as their mother at the next hunt which could be anytime in the next few days. Snake didn't trust the police and neither did Raven. The evidence was compelling, but the police would find a reason not to search the building and would likely just warn Porter to get rid of the young foxes. Breaking into the outhouse would make a lot of noise. Porter was out most nights on the badger cull but his wife would always be there and she'd call the police. But they had to do something.

*

A crowd had gathered in the field next to St Mary's Primary School. Raven drove slowly through the gateway and parked in a line of saloons, SUVs and pick-ups. There were a couple of large vans parked to one side which looked as if they'd been converted into campers.

It felt like a long time since breakfast and several stalls were selling tea, cakes and jars of homemade jam. But one in particular caught his eye: organic regenerative smallholders, he could have a sandwich and cake from there without being poisoned by pesticides.

The gamekeepers were obvious from their clothes; waistcoats and rolled-up shirt sleeves with neckties pulled up to the top button, trousers and jackets in country brown or green, some with a ludicrous check. They were generally thickset men, ruddy-faced; standing legs apart, strutting as if they owned the place. But one carried himself differently. He was quite wiry and had restless eyes that kept scanning the crowd. Raven recognised him from the camera footage of Fairview where he'd acted as if he was in charge. He'd heard a name for the new head keeper; Finn who'd come down from Scotland. Raven did his best to blend into the crowd, but his face had been all over social media and he expected all the gamekeepers to recognise him.

Some of the pupils were sitting crossed-legged on the grass as one of the keepers gave a talk, illustrated by photos of purple heather, male grouse perched proudly on rocky tors and men dressed in breeches and checked shirts striding through the heather accompanied by black Labrador dogs. Another keeper was taking one of the gun dogs around the young audience and offering the children cubes of roasted grouse flesh. Raven heard a voice in his ear.

"They start them young around here. Not sure I'd want my kids to get a taste for grouse. The lead content must be a killer."

Raven turned to see Paul Carson, the sergeant in charge of rural crime. Hovering behind was a younger man wearing the same bulky stab vest. "And this is Constable Philips, Xan."

Raven nodded but felt on his guard. The aggression of the officers who'd pulled him over was at odds with these smiling faces.

"Looks like you're on, Xan," continued Carson. His companion left to take over the talk from the gamekeepers and Carson explained it was all part of community policing and making people feel safe. Raven thought the whole gathering was legitimising a bunch of criminals, but there was no point picking a fight with the police just now.

Carson looked as if he'd noticed Raven's mood.

"I've time for a chat. If you're interested, we could sit in the car and won't be overheard."

"Ok," replied Raven, glancing at the police vehicle. "You go first and I'll follow in a minute, I don't want those gamekeepers taking too much of an interest."

Carson looked over at the crowd and even though Xan had started his talk a couple of the keepers were looking their way. Carson made his way to the patrol car, a four-seat pickup in fluorescent green. Carson sat in the driver's seat looking at the fete and jolted when Raven suddenly appeared, opening the passenger door.

"Don't think they can see you there," said Carson. "I'll just make sure this is off," he added as he fiddled with the bodycam on his shoulder.

Both men stared straight ahead out of the windscreen. Raven wasn't about to share anything until he thought he could trust the officer.

"I saw the report about you being pulled over…"

Raven felt his jaw tightening. There still wasn't any eye contact. Carson sighed and turned towards Raven.

"I'm in charge of all wildlife policing day to day. But I've been told by on high that I'll be transferred into another role. Something more urban and I doubt anyone will replace me. I thought things had changed with us but now I'm not sure."

Raven twisted round to meet Carson's eye. He thought *us* meant the culture of policing.

"So, it's just like it's always been. That lot…" Raven pointed to the gamekeepers, "can do whatever they like."

Carson was quick to respond, "You bring us the evidence and we'll prosecute. We have to."

Raven was shaking his head and wondering how it had become his job to provide evidence and nothing to do with the police.

Carson seemed resigned to it, keeping his head down so he could hold onto his job.

"Look, Raven, I know it's crap. But if you've got anything now, send it to me and I'll pass it on to the Crown Prosecution Service. But I expect you know how difficult it is to meet their threshold for prosecution."

And Raven knew that was the problem, the CPS and police deciding between them that yet another case wasn't going anywhere. But the video he'd taken with Becky would be ready in a few days and the cameras had been removed. It would all be public as soon as they posted online. As far as Raven could tell, Carson was being honest. It was time to offer him something in return.

"The pheasant shoot at Fairview Mill…"

Carson knew his superintendent would be there, lined up with the guns in a couple of days but he couldn't tell Raven, not directly. After Raven went through the details, Carson realised this might be an opportunity for some leverage to keep him in his post.

"I won't be able to look at it for a couple of days but send it to me directly. The great and good will be shooting there very soon and they'd be shocked to find out what goes on to provide their sport."

Raven realised he'd been given a big hint about the shoot and he needed to find out more.

"And my situation?" He asked Carson. "Are you lot going to pull me over every five minutes?"

"Those officers were just following instructions. Not from me. All I can say is make a complaint, that incident on its own won't get you very far, but if it happens again you've got a case. It's the one thing that makes the higher-ups sit up and pay attention. Lawyers, publicity, compensation, they hate it."

There it was Raven needed a lawyer.

"That morning someone dumped a dead badger on my doorstep. The poor creature had a snare around its neck. Bit of an obvious message, then the police pulling me over a few hours later, looks like you're all working together."

Carson shook his head again and took out his notebook.

"Give me the details, Raven, and send me a photo. You've logged it already?"

"I have logged it and no response."

"Well, you should have had one. Harassment of a person gets way more priority than wildlife."

Raven gave him the date and there were even enough signals to send the photo. Carson had confirmed what Raven already knew. He left Carson in the vehicle and walked back to the stall for another tea. Raven took his drink and pointed at the police officer next to the gamekeepers.

"Look a bit cosy, don't they?" He suggested.

The stallholder glanced over and pulled a face. "They do and they're not well liked. Mind you plenty will take their money. They were looking for beaters the other day."

Raven feigned an interest, "Oh yeah, when's that?"

"Tuesday, Fairview Mill," came the reply.

Then they all heard an announcement. The children had written poems about their lives in the country and as they were being recited someone would come round to collect donations for the school. Raven handed over some cash and heard about country life through the children's innocent eyes. Last up was ten-year-old Willow with her poem. She had the words on paper but spoke from her heart:

85

The Last Crow

I live in the tallest tree.
We chatter all the time
but no one understands.
A community safe together
even the buzzard stays away.

In the spring I have four hungry mouths to feed.
I love a puzzle and the wire cage leads to a meal
but now I'm trapped can't stretch my wings.
With rancid food and mouldy water
death is all around.

My purpose is to call my friends
they come day after day.
Go away I shout but they explore inside
and the trap door shuts behind.
My children starve when I don't return.

He comes with a club in his hand
to splinter the bones of my brothers.
Vermin he spits.
And I wish he would drown
in his venom

The sun brings life
and a girl wearing a mask.
She tips the trap upside down.
I am released but feathers cut,
flight is lost.

Still not free
He ripped my beating heart
and took my soul.
I am The Last Crow.
And wear the curse of man.

There was a moment's silence and then a barrage of vitriol.

"Fucking antis should be locked up!"

"She's one of them van-dwellers up on Moor Lane. Always crapping on the verge."

"No way had she written that poem. It's her dad, bloody terrorist. Criminal damage, disgusting!"

The poem had split the audience in two.

"Show us where the Larsen traps are officer."

"About time you arrested your pals."

Willow stood tall and stared down the hecklers. Both police officers moved closer to her but it was Logan Porter's wife who took charge with a clear steady voice, "We're here to raise funds for the school, the centre of our community. And in this valley, we respect our neighbours," said Emma. "Now dig into your pockets, it's your children who benefit, without having to be bussed into town."

As she spoke, Finn Sutherland stared at her shaking his head. *More disapproval.* And then he turned to the other gamekeepers who'd gathered closely in a group. What did he expect her to do? Tell the police to arrest the girl for conspiracy to commit criminal damage.

Emma looked around for Jasmine and Lily but she was left on her own to shame the crowd into emptying their pockets. "Come on, we're doing this for everyone," she shouted, rattling the bucket of coins and notes.

Raven watched on, inspired. It took the courage of a primary school girl to decimate the sanitised message of the gamekeepers with a poem about the suffering of a crow in a Larsen trap. A mutilated bird spends months in a small cage with the sole purpose of attracting other birds through one of the trap doors. And the recommended way to dispatch the birds was to club them to death. He hoped her parents had videoed the recital because it needed to be out there. Carson had some work to do with this community if his overtures were at all genuine.

*

Willow and her parents had driven away in their van with no vehicles following. But Carson read the reaction of the crowd. There was a frightening aggression in some of the audience and groups of men were talking themselves into violence. He looked at his watch. There wasn't time to follow up on any of this because they had clear instructions from the superintendent.

"Right, Xan, you're on driving duties," said Carson. "You'll be taking the superintendent back home and picking him up in the morning. Make sure you don't scratch his car now."

They drove along to Midham Lodge and waited for the gates to open. Carson drove up to the house and Xan hopped out. Farlow was enjoying his Sunday roast with the Duke and Arabella was playing the gracious host.

"More vegetables, James?'" She asked.

Farlow had quietly dropped the 'Jimmy', it wasn't grand enough for his new status.

"I'm fine thank you, it's delicious. I will have a drop more wine."

Then Arabella frowned. "Do you think we should invite your officer inside? He could sit in the pantry."

"No, it's a test of initiative to see if he sits in the car especially if it comes on to rain."

As the first drops fell, the diners gave a little cheer as Xan opened the car door and settled in the driver's seat.

*

Lily and Jasmine appeared when they saw the success of Emma's fundraising and together they tidied everything they could at the school. It would take a while to count all the cash, but it looked like they'd make over £500 and that would pay for welly boots and waterproofs for the children so they could explore outside and learn about nature.

Emma didn't really want to go home. Someone would have reported back to Logan and Emma could imagine feeling his fingers around her neck as he spat at her: *You don't respect scum like those van-dwellers.*

She'd heard the gamekeepers today saying they were helping nature for the benefit of the community, providing jobs and helping nature keep in balance. But from what Emma could see it was just a few people who gained. The Duchess had her stately home while Emma had to be grateful for a damp rented cottage. Emma knew animals lived and died, but she was sick of the brutality around her, it was so *unnecessary.* And she couldn't sit back and do nothing.

It had really helped to talk to her sister so she could snap out of the closed loop that was her rural life. And today she'd been moved by Willow's poem. She was the crow. Duped into a trap and used. And even when the physical barriers had gone she still wasn't free. Debs had offered an escape, but she'd gone straight back to Logan, hoping he'd be different. She needed to change her life but her curse was that change seemed impossible.

She let out a long sigh and suddenly felt exhausted. Trying to get Logan to hear her would take all her energy. It would drain her completely and make no difference.

This morning he'd grabbed her shoulders in the yard and she knew: *he's going to hurt me.* And of course, he insisted he just wanted to kiss her because he'd missed her after a night away. He couldn't leave it at that, she'd overreacted and it was all her fault, again. She needed to understand so he could *put things right.* And as soon as those words had been spoken, he was on his phone and obsessed with everyone else who was ruining his life. The sabs of course tried to disrupt every meet of the Midham Hunt. And his latest mania: "Raven Harley, how do I get into his Twitter?"

Looking at her watch, if she left now he'd only be at home for another twenty minutes or so until he left for the badger cull. She didn't think he could do much at that time.

Chapter 21

Raven had dragged a series of video clips into the editing App. But he was struggling to create any sort of narrative that would grab the viewer and keep them watching to the end. Attention spans on social media were incredibly short. He leant back in his chair and clasped his hands behind his head, staring at the screen.

There was a knock on the kitchen door and he glanced through the window to see Becky waving. He noticed her key was still on the table.

"Wondered if you needed a hand?" She asked as he opened the door. They'd split up the day before and here she was again. Immediately he was guarded.

"What is it you want?" He asked.

"Nothing hidden with me, Raven," she stated. "I did some of the filming. Putting out a good video is good for me and good for you as well."

He knew it was never that simple with Becky. Eventually, Raven gestured to the table strewn with leads and notes scribbled on paper. "I do but..." he replied.

They sat down next to each other and she started making notes of her own, asking him what each file showed. As they scrolled through the most likely ones, she pulled her chair closer to his until their thighs were touching. They laughed as he offered her the mouse, "No you do it," she said. And they leant into the screen together. She smelt fresh, if she'd used a scent Raven couldn't tell.

Before long, Becky was splicing scenes together and typing a summary of what they'd say in the voiceover. It took about an hour and they had a draft. Becky took a copy of the file.

A day before Becky had been treating his house as if it was her home, now he wondered if he should offer her a drink.

"That should do for now," she said and then she looked at him with wide expectant eyes and a hint of a smile. "I don't have to go."

"You dumped me yesterday." *What's this about?*

She shrugged and Raven wondered if this was practised, a slightly puzzled look, a touch of hurt, letting him speak his mind, making him think it was his idea.

"You don't have to analyse, live in the moment," she urged.

Raven felt himself falling again. He took her hand and led her up the stairs. He felt as if he was cheating on Chloe but that was over as well and it didn't stop him.

An hour later, they lay side by side facing each other.

"What's happened?" He asked.

She raised her eyebrows and looked at him with her large blue eyes. Raven thought she was trying to look innocent but now her pupils had shrunk down to points. Half an hour ago they'd been wide pools drawing him in.

"I got some replies to my emails. One definite and two possible companies interested in my work. I heard nothing for months and then it's as if they all know what their rivals are doing. Anyway, Kerbstone Streetwear, they're interested and they're willing to pay. They want to expand from purely urban to more outdoors. Don't know if you've heard of them. Their image is all about being risky, a bit edgy, anti-establishment with a conscience."

It was a *greenwashing* sales pitch. "And they want to use this video?"

"It's us they're interested in, for different reasons. You've got the right profile and reach. You're good-looking…" She broadened her grin and waited for his reaction. But he didn't reply, so she pushed on. "Advertising in magazines is ancient history. Brands need influencers. It can all be very subtle but if you associate yourself with them they'll pay you a lot of money."

"Is that what this is about, Becky?" He leant on his elbow and looked down at her naked body.

She tried changing the subject, "I've never heard you cry out like that."

She'd *consumed him* for a moment that stretched out. But now he felt revulsion.

"I wasn't faking," she continued. "Look my neck is still flushed, itchy as hell."

But that moment had gone. "You had no use for me yesterday and here you are back again when you want something," he said. And as her face creased up, he knew he'd really hurt her. But she soon bounced back.

"You've been part of my life, Ray, but not all of it. I'm twenty-one and I don't want to be chained to one person for the rest of my life. This is brilliant, but there's more out there. You want to get your message out and you want to do that as a hobby in between chopping down trees. I want to monetise it. Kerbstone and that video is the start. There's more to relationships than settling down like mums and dads. Have some fun. Use me and I'll use you and we'll both get what we want."

Raven rolled onto his back. It was more than she'd ever said. Ending with him had given her the freedom to speak her mind. He had his followers, thousands of like-minded people but that hadn't grown. Maybe he could use Becky and Kerbstone to make more happen. But for any kind of relationship, he couldn't trust her anymore and he wasn't going to be left dangling.

"I do want to make more of a difference," he said. "So, as you describe it, I could use Kerbstone and you to do that, but I need to think about what's involved. Any kind of relationship between us, that's over, finished, and dead."

He was surprised to see her sit up and pull on her clothes but then thought she'd try again in a moment. She needed to get her way. When they were both dressed, they went downstairs and sat on opposite sides of the table this time. Becky outlined the Kerbstone deal as much as she could and Raven explained there'd probably be more footage to add to the video next week, all very grown up and business-like.

When Becky left, Raven felt a wave of tension leave his body. For the first time in months, he felt his life had direction and it was up to him what happened next.

Chapter 22

Chloe and Jack hadn't stayed long at Nether Beck Farm. They decided the juveniles would be kept in the outhouse until the next hunt and they usually had a tip-off about the dates. Later that evening, Chloe was getting ready for bed when her phone buzzed with a message. It was Jack.

Are you free?

He wants sex? Now? She just wanted to curl up in bed. Then another message:

For the animals

That changed everything.

I'll be outside in ten minutes.

Ruby was driving an old Mazda and Chloe sat in the back. Jack twisted round to explain.

"We didn't know what to do about the juveniles, only that leaving them there wasn't an option. Then we had a bit of a cryptic message on our tip-off line. Logan Porter's birthday 230582."

"It's a combination padlock on the outhouse, big chunky thing, probably six digits to open it," offered Chloe.

"Yeah, just what I thought. It's worth a try otherwise we'll have to go back with a crowbar. We've had some messages, Porter's out on the cull. We've got a couple of pet carriers in the back. I couldn't get anyone else at short notice. Are you up for it?"

Chloe had already thought this through. "Yes."

Ruby took an out-of-the-way route along narrow lanes then pulled off the road through an open gate, parking next to a hedge. She stayed by the car as Jack and Chloe walked through the fields without torches, eventually ending up on top of the bank above the farm. There were no lights showing. Jack checked the farmyard with some night vision binoculars: all clear.

They walked down the bank and into the yard. The code was correct and they were in. Jack stood by the door and shone a light inside. Two young foxes were cowering at the back of a large metal dog crate. They were hardly bigger than a cat. Chloe opened the door and knelt in the entrance, whispering to the foxes and coaxing one then the other into the carriers.

She could manage both cases back into the yard as Jack replaced and reset the lock. Then Jack took a case and they made their way back up the bank. The walk back to the car seemed endless but they concentrated on keeping quiet. Ruby was waiting in the field and opened the hatchback for the cases. As they drove, Chloe and Jack stripped off the dark tops swopping them for brightly coloured t-shirts and fleeces. They looked like they'd been for a night out.

It was about an hour's drive to the animal rescue and they were expected. The juveniles had a large room for themselves. They'd swopped one closed space for another but they seemed to know the difference and Jack filmed them tucking into two bowls of food. After being checked over, the young foxes would be released into an area free from hunts and traps. Chloe was cosy in bed at 3 a.m. and sleep came easily.

*

Logan Porter was struggling to keep the badger cull on target. He'd been interrupted a couple of times tonight by people shining bright torches towards his bait and eventually, he'd given up. The shooters who'd signed up had started to moan about the time and effort it was taking for a kill and the lack of money they were being paid. He needed to phone his boss, Tranchard in the morning. As soon as Porter drove into the yard, he sensed something was wrong. There were muddy patches on the broken concrete base and his lights picked up footprints. He left the engine running and checked the lock on the outbuilding where he kept the foxes. It looked secure but he wanted to be sure so he opened up and went in.

They'd gone. How the fuck had that happened? The door was the only way in and there was no sign of any damage. He picked up a food bowl and threw it against the wall in a rage. How could someone get in here without making any noise? He'd trained his terriers to stay silent so they wouldn't have alerted anyone.

Porter turned off the engine of the pick-up and killed the lights. He stood in the dark for a moment, remembering everything Tranchard and the superintendent had told him. He unlocked the other doors to the building that held his quad bike then drove it round to George's farm. Half an hour later he was back. He rummaged around his tools for a crowbar then locked all the doors to the outbuildings. Each padlock he levered off made a loud screeching noise but it only took a few minutes. Torch in hand he looked at his handiwork and then dialled the number of the police control room.

"Logan Porter here. I'm in charge of the badger cull. Superintendent Farlow told me to call directly if there were any problems. I've had a break-in and my quad bike has gone…Nether Beck Farm. There was a van parked nearby…"

*

Raven was dreaming. He was in a club and the bass was vibrating through his body. He was happy. Then he slowly became aware the banging was coming from outside. It could only be the police. He pulled on some clothes and grabbed his wallet and phone. Two officers stood outside his kitchen door.

"Raven Harley, I'm arresting you for criminal damage and theft of a quad bike. Can you come with me, please?"

Raven didn't say anything, he was holding it in. He turned out the lights, locked up and followed the officers to their patrol car.

"Which one is your van?" One of the officers asked.

Raven pointed to the dented red Volkswagen. Immediately the officers were shaking their heads.

"Can you open it up for us?"

Raven did as they asked and he went through the same routine as the last time he was searched.

"Some tools in there. I'm a tree surgeon. The valuable stuff is in the house."

The officers had a quick scan and Raven heard one muttering about no room to hide a quad bike.

At the station, the custody officer took his name and address.

"Do you want a solicitor?"

Raven nodded.

"Ok, you can make a call then we'll have your phone."

Raven hadn't expected he'd actually find himself in this situation but he had put a number in his phone book. It was 5.00 a.m., but criminal defence solicitors had a 24-hour answering service.

A couple of minutes later, Raven turned back to the officer, handing over his phone.

"It'll be 9.00 a.m. before my solicitor arrives."

He was told to wait on a chair in the corridor.

*

Four hours of sitting on hard plastic made every muscle in his body ache. He found himself wanting to agree to anything they said just so he could get out. At last, there was someone making eye contact. Cory Fuller had the solid presence of a rugby player and Raven thought he wouldn't like to meet him on the wrong side of a scrum. Fuller turned to the officer by his side.

"Can I have a word with my client?"

They were shown in the interview room. Client and brief introduced themselves and Raven explained the background as best he could, including the harassment over the last few days.

"Ok," said Fuller. "I'll do the talking and I'll see what evidence they have. I expect there's nothing in which case you don't need to say a word. If they've got something concrete, go no comment to everything. It's up to them to provide proof of an offence."

PC Lewis Callaghan came in with a slim folder which he placed on the table. The offences were apparently damage to three doors and padlocks and theft of a quad bike worth £10,000 between 9 p.m. last night and 4 a.m. this morning.

Callaghan started to ask Raven where he'd been last night, but Fuller butted in.

"What evidence do you have of my client's presence at these alleged offences?"

"Mr Harley's van was spotted nearby."

Fuller soon found out that Callaghan couldn't specify a time when Raven's van was nearby, there were no eyewitnesses, and no CCTV and Raven's van wasn't big enough to hold a quad bike.

"So, you've no evidence linking my client to these alleged offences."

This time it was the police officer who stayed silent.

"If you'd be so kind as to return my client's phone, what I can show you there is an intervention from Sergeant Carson to action an incident of harassment where a badger was dumped at my client's door, something that your colleagues failed to follow up. Then my client was stopped and searched by your officers without a shred of evidence for criminal damage and theft and now these allegations again with no evidence. Quite a pattern."

"I'll get his phone," said Callaghan.

"Hang on. I want you to de-arrest my client," insisted Fuller.

"I need to speak to my custody officer about that."

"You do that, we'll wait."

Half an hour later when they made it out into the car park, Raven looked up at the sky and felt his lungs and the pores in his skin open up.

"I can't thank you enough, Cory. You'd better sign me up and I'll pay your bill," said Raven.

"This one's covered by Legal Aid; thank God, we've still got a bit of it left. I've seen quite a few cases like this and I think the only way you'll stop this harassment is by getting a legal firm to make a complaint. We can do that but we charge £300 an hour."

"That's what credit cards are for," replied Raven.

"Come on, I'll give you a lift home, you look done in."

On the way back, Raven phoned Mark who told him they'd secured more work with the council. It was larch this time, affected by phytophthora and Raven wondered if there'd be any trees left standing.

Chapter 23

Raven stayed another two hours on site after Mark and Colin left. He felt a need to pull his weight but there was also a need to lose himself in some simple physical tasks: sawing, lifting and sweeping up.

Back home he forced himself to cook some proper food, slicing a pile of vegetables to go in a stew. As it was cooking he leant on the work surface and stared out of the window. There was a familiar figure and Chloe was knocking on the door before Raven had a chance to move.

"Come in," he said. "You should let yourself in, it's still yours."

Chloe looked around the kitchen, it was familiar and alien at the same time and she felt like an intruder.

"I didn't know if you had company?"

Raven laughed which was a welcome interruption to the thoughts stuck in his head.

"Have you eaten?" He asked.

Chloe wasn't expecting the offer but maybe it would be ok. They sat at the table with two plates of stew.

"I'm really sorry, Raven. Mark told me about the police arresting you."

He took a while to reply. His skin looked grey and the life had gone from his eyes.

"I just feel exhausted, Chloe. There's nothing to be sorry about. Nothing you've done, but I don't know what that is anyway?" He managed another laugh and relaxed a little.

Chloe didn't know where to start. Then she was saved by the beep of a notification on her phone. She felt her eyes flickering between the phone and Raven.

"Go on take a look," he said.

It was a message from Jack with a link to YouTube.

"You'll want to see this," she replied and moved round to his side of the table.

Logan Porter Terrier man with Midham Hunt

Chloe had captured it all: the sack of writhing animals bundled into the outhouse, the shrieks of pain from inside the building and Porter releasing the vixen into the path of the hunt. The long knife wound that had sliced open the pad on the severed leg was gruesome.

Jack had worn a bodycam and there were the juveniles cowering in the back of the cage. Raven would know Chloe's whispered voice anywhere. She was dressed in black from head to toe including gloves, just a slit for her eyes. Then Raven saw the padlock being replaced.

"Fucking hell, I don't believe it, Porter ripped those locks off himself!" he shouted.

Chloe paused the video.

"We got a tip-off for the combination. There was no damage to anything."

"I don't care if you did damage anything. It's spot on what you did," replied Raven. Then he continued, "You know Porter accused me of stealing his quad bike?"

"He was out on the cull on that night and made up the story about the quad theft because it's a police priority and would get their attention. That's what they'll do to have a go at you."

Raven was quiet for a moment then shrugged his shoulders. "Let's watch to the end," he said.

And there were two young foxes at a rescue, bouncing around, eating, play-fighting and full of life.

"That's just brilliant, Chloe, how did you do it?"

"Well, I got over my phobia of fox scent, that's for sure."

Raven put his hand over hers, but couldn't quite meet her eye.

"Let's have some food before it gets cold," he said.

They'd nearly finished when Chloe's phone beeped again.

"Porter's just been spotted trying to shoot badgers. He's driving that quad bike you stole Ray."

Raven pushed back his chair and started to stand. He had to get out there for the evidence. *To clear his name.* Chloe put her hand on his shoulder.

"Just calm down, Ray. You're knackered; you need a good night's sleep. There are plenty of people out there who want to help. You're not on your own. We'll prove he's a lying bastard."

Raven sat back down and Chloe made some tea. They moved into the lounge with their drinks. He hadn't rehearsed a speech but had to say something.

"I'm really sorry, Chloe, for how we split up. It was all me, you weren't to blame at all. For some reason, I got it into my head you didn't want me."

Chloe didn't reply, Raven needed to say more.

"Then there was Becky and I was tempted. More than tempted, I fell for her with every cliché you could imagine."

"You really hurt me, Ray. That night you didn't come home, I was really angry but that soon turned to hurt. I felt betrayed, all that trust I thought we had, all gone."

She looked at him.

"I really wanted you to suffer…but that hasn't made me feel any better."

It was Raven's turn to remain silent.

"You can't take all the blame, Ray. My job had taken over my life, so I don't suppose I was there for you. But you could have cut me a bit of slack. You could have talked to me. You're not the only idiot, Ray, where's my all-consuming job got me now? I'm suspended and I might even be prosecuted."

They were both quiet for a minute. Raven realised it was nothing to do with winners and losers. *The mess of life.*

"I don't know where you are with the rest of your life but I want to try to get your trust back," he said, waiting for something from her. A big rejection really would mean no going back, but Chloe skirted around that.

"I'm still paying half the mortgage, Ray. Does that mean I can't let go?" She didn't expect a reply. "There's all that to sort out and how am I going to pay any bills if I've been sacked? Siobhan and Mark will get fed up with me squatting at theirs eventually."

Raven explained about Kerbstone.

"I would have said keep well clear," replied Chloe. "But I don't know now, maybe I'll be tapping them up for a job myself. Look I do owe you, Ray, I've made you public enemy number one as far as the police are concerned. So, let's see what's happening on the badger cull and try to nail Porter driving around on his stolen quad bike."

He told Chloe about the pheasant shoot and tried to find out who attended.

"That's one for you and Becky," she said. "The cull gets going after dark. If we want to find out what Porter is up to we shouldn't need to be out all night."

*

Emma managed to avoid Logan after the fete. But the next day after she returned from work he grabbed her arm and pushed her into one of the chairs at the kitchen table.

"Did you hear anything last night? Those fucking sabs broke into our house."

"Just a lot of noise, a kind of scraping, screeching sound a couple of minutes before you came in. I heard you on the phone then I must have fallen back asleep."

"Right, this is what you're going to tell the police." He held her chin between his finger and thumb, squeezing. It hurt. "About two o'clock in the morning, you heard a noise outside. Then it sounded like the quad bike was being driven off. Got that?"

Her head was gripped solidly but she tried to nod. Eventually, he let go and wandered around the house cursing. Then he went into the lounge. The door didn't close properly because it was warped and she could hear him on the phone.

"I reported it all, laid it on thick…the police let him go, not my fault they're fucking useless…I'm going to need a new quad bike…what do you mean it will take a while, I need it every day…don't worry if they come around, it's not here, I've got it tucked away…I know he's a fucking problem, you tell me what I should do to him…a video? What's on that that? For fuck's sake!"

"Emma! How do I find a video?" he shouted.

She took his phone and searched *Midham Hunt YouTube* and top of the list was *Barbaric Cruelty at Midham Hunt*. She pushed the red play button, un-muted the sound and handed the phone back to Logan. She hoped that would absorb him and turned to go, but he only watched a few seconds before jabbing his finger at the screen to pause the action.

"I haven't finished with you yet."

She sat back down and realised her hands were shaking so she knitted her fingers together and leant her elbows on the table.

"Finn told me about the fete. That Lily of his puts big words in his mouth. He said you were an *apologist* for those fucking antis, those saboteurs that wreck the cull every night. And Raven Harley was there lapping up every word you said."

Emma took a deep breath. "All I said was we respect our neighbours round here. What did Finn want me to do? Tell the crowd to string up a ten-year-old girl and her dad. That would have gone down well with the police."

She was surprised by Logan's silence but soon worked out what it meant.

"What do you know, Logan? Are Finn and his mates going to go round to sort them out? For God's sake, Willow is one of the pupils at that school which has been threatened with closure because there aren't enough kids. And you're driving a family out?"

"Just enough will happen. They'll get the message. And you," he said leaning over and jabbing his finger against her lips. "You'd better not say anything like that again."

Logan went back to his video and Emma could taste the blood in her mouth where the inside of her lips had jagged against her teeth. She went to the bathroom and rinsed her mouth, staring as the crimson liquid swirled around the white sink.

Chapter 24

Dew Foster climbed out of the bath and dried herself on a soft white towel, monogrammed *MS*, Midham Stables Country House Hotel. It was Midham everything around here and she wondered if she'd see the Duke at the shoot. She'd taken the trouble to wear her new outfit a few times at home so it looked creased and worn in. It was a mix of country green and brown with a faint red check, loose-fitting trousers, a brushed cotton shirt and a loose waistcoat. She'd fit the buttonhole camera later and there were plenty of real buttons and pockets to hide the surveillance equipment. It would be interesting to see if anyone was wearing a similar outfit at breakfast, she hoped other shooters were staying so she could start to get into character. Her credit card said she was Dew Exton, divorced and in the area to enjoy some country sports.

*

Raven had slept well. It had been an early start but that wasn't a problem. He'd crept into the wood opposite Fairview Mill and found a spot with a clear view of the car park, on top of a small mound. He was stretched out on the ground and glad the weather had been dry.

The gamekeepers were first to arrive, all wearing the uniform of jacket, waistcoat and tie in matching country green. Next were the beaters. Some had taken the trouble to dig out similar clothing, but their outfits didn't match the crispness of the gamekeepers. They parked their 4×4s amongst the trees. Soon the head keeper was giving instructions and the underkeepers were handing out poles about a metre long with white cloth pennants attached. The beaters practised flicking their wrists to snap the flags open with a crack. They chatted for ten minutes in the car park until the underkeepers led them in a long looping line up the hill. The partridges Raven and Becky had filmed would be driven back down towards the guns.

The car park started to resemble a luxury SUV showroom full of Range Rovers with a sprinkling of Mercedes. The VIPs all had drivers. Raven had worked out that the owner of High Ridge grouse moor was Nathan Parbolde and he owned the pheasant shoot as well. He had a guest in the back of his Range Rover and they were accompanied not just by a driver but by two minders; the thugs who'd floored Chloe.

Raven soon had what he wanted. Superintendent Farlow drew up in a spotless Mercedes and pulled a pair of shotguns out of the boot. Raven knew Farlow had overall command of rural crime and here he was at the very place where gamekeepers were killing birds of prey. With that cosiness, there was zero chance that Raven's evidence would lead to any prosecutions.

Last of all to arrive was a dark-haired woman in a Range Rover. There was something about her that was slightly odd and Raven realised she was turning her whole body to take in the scene rather than just swivelling her head. Maybe she had a stiff neck, but it didn't look right.

Porter's wife was circulating through the crowd, handing out stirrup cups; brandy Raven guessed. It didn't matter if they were all half-cut, the guns wouldn't need any skill at all to put down a dozen birds, when the sky was full of them.

In the distance, the beaters were spaced across the hillside, waiting for the signal to move down.

*

Dew felt her jaw and cheeks aching from constant smiling when introducing herself to her shooting companions. About half were visitors like her and the rest seemed to know each other already. Parbolde and his guest had disappeared into the mill building. She was sure the guest was Russian; they'd be on the vodka and caviar in there. And she couldn't wait to get her camera footage back to her colleagues. After a while, one of the minders came out and the Duke accompanied him back inside. Interesting, that alone made the trip worthwhile and Dew thought she might be extending her stay to take a closer look at the Midhams.

The cabal emerged from the mill, gave the signal and everyone strolled up the open ground. The Duke was the only one wearing plus fours ending just below the knee, where green knee-length socks covered the rest of his spindly legs. Dew had been assigned a loader, Hudson who looked like he should still be at school. He was as eager as a gun dog and more than happy to carry her shotguns and a large box of cartridges. They were walking towards a line of shooting hurdles, simple wooden barriers that looked like pallets tipped on end. The prime locations were in the centre, where the beaters aimed to drive the birds. Dew was right at the end, Parbolde, the Duke and the Russian right in the middle. She was sharing the hurdle with Justin a retired businessman who was trying too hard to look part of the country set. He kept talking about being invited to the Grange for tea with the Duchess, but his sycophancy washed over her.

Dew had spent a lot of time working on her cover story. She was the only woman with a gun in her hand today and every man she'd met only heard the word divorced before their eyes stuck on her chest. At first, she thought they'd seen the buttonhole camera, but it was just one lascivious man after another. Maybe it just went with the killing spree that was about to begin. All very primaeval, she was in a cloud of testosterone surrounded by huntsmen strutting their stuff. Baggy waistcoat, shirt buttoned to her neck and baggy trousers were hardly her sexiest outfit but that didn't make any difference.

At last, everyone concentrated ahead. The shouts of the beaters and the cracks of their flags grew louder. There seemed to be too many birds for this small piece of land. Dew raised her shotgun and fired into the throng, one shot then another. Then Hudson was handing her the second gun and she killed more. He reloaded quickly for more killing. There were more shouts from in front and another wave of birds. The bodies piled up on the slope, many still twitching in the last moments of life. Gun dogs collecting corpses would be woefully inadequate; a mechanical digger was needed. Soon the gun barrels were burning her skin and her ears were ringing. She had thought about ear protection but didn't want to miss any snippets of conversation. She felt disgusted by the slaughter but had to appear jubilant.

"Good shot, Justin!" she exclaimed, slapping him on the shoulder.

She turned to thank Hudson.

"I expect you'll be taking a load home with you?" She asked.

"Not allowed," he replied. "You get a brace each and they'll dig a pit for the rest."

She'd take her brace of partridge back to Midham Stables and have to crunch through the lead pellets tonight. But the day hadn't finished yet. They were to be fed and watered in the restored mill building.

*

Parbolde and his friends made their way upstairs for a gourmet lunch. Everyone else was shown into the ground-floor dining room. As the food was being served, Dew decided to explore. She climbed the stairs up to a landing to find one of the minders blocking the doorway. She couldn't even see beyond that because of a second door. They didn't want to be disturbed.

"Thirsty work this morning, I'm gagging for some champers," she said in her best Surrey accent.

Before he spoke, she had to endure the same look but this time it was more menacing. Callum slowly slid his eyes down her body as if he was undressing her. But he'd learnt his lines.

"Sorry, ma'am, it's a private party in there." He turned to his companion who was standing in the space between the two doors. "Sean, get some champagne for the lady here."

Then he stared at her. She'd been dismissed.

"Thank you," she replied with her best smile.

*

Raven drove back into town and stopped at home. He took a quick look at the video files to find he'd captured Farlow in his tweeds, a shotgun in each hand. The slaughter of the shoot was more long distance but showed everything well enough. He realised it would be better if Becky added the files so he sent them along with a message:

Do you have time to add these? You can put the Kerbstone logo at the end of the video. Just that and nothing more.

Chapter 25

Paul Carson had been enjoying a bottle of wine with his wife. The kids were in bed and he was due to work an afternoon shift the next day. Then his work phone rang.

"Sorry, no escape," he said as his wife collected the dishes. He didn't recognise the number but it must have been one of his colleagues so he prodded the green button.

"Sergeant Carson, it's Madelaine Chatton here."

"Yes, ma'am." It was the chief constable.

"I need you to do some work for me starting tomorrow. Someone else will take over your normal duties. Come to my office at nine and you need to be wearing some well-worn hiking gear. Bring a bag with something slightly smarter, still casual. No uniform. Don't worry, you'll be back home in the evening."

The chief paused and Carson thought it best to keep quiet.

"I don't normally touch social media with a barge pole, but my PA thought I'd better take a look."

Another pause.

"It looks like our superintendent has blotted his copybook."

Then the line went dead.

It didn't take long for Carson to find the grisly footage from Fairview Mill where protected birds of prey had very obviously been killed. Less raptor meant more pheasants and partridges. And there was Superintendent Farlow enjoying the spoils.

*

Carson had expected some wildlife-related work but it wasn't that direct. He was to assist the National Crime Agency. Not all their officers were serving police but there might be a call for police powers including arrests. He was driving an unmarked car to a rendezvous at a lay-by to meet Dew Foster.

A few minutes later, Carson was sitting in the passenger seat of a three-year-old Range Rover. After rather formal introductions, they agreed to use first names. Dew had served twenty years in Military Intelligence and was weapons trained. Paul thought she had quite a posh voice and carried an air of entitlement. She'd fit in well at a pheasant shoot.

When it was Paul's turn, he explained how he'd helped on an operation to break up a dog fighting ring before being promoted to sergeant. He'd built up quite a knowledge of the area and people who worked here. Some would recognise him, but it would be easy enough to explain he was enjoying a few days' leave, walking and sightseeing.

"It's the local knowledge we need. Your chief thought you were a straight bat and we could trust you," said Dew.

Paul didn't quite understand the cricketing analogy, but everyone thought he was honest which must be a good start.

"Yesterday we had hedge fund manager Nathan Parbolde meeting a Russian oligarch Sergei Yvprestov and the Duke of Midham. Those three along with your superintendent and a couple of other businessmen were all very cosy in the VIP lounge afterwards. I tried to get in there but the minders wouldn't have it."

"The newspapers tell me everything Russian is sanctioned. Sorry, I can't get my head around his surname, but what was Sergei doing there?" Paul asked.

"As far as we know, he's a second-generation oligarch involved in oil and gas exploration. One of his companies is called RUsearch which shot to prominence when they discovered a new gas field. And that meant the share price went through the roof, making *some* people a lot of money. The government hasn't quite decided but Sergei might be blacklisted in the next round of sanctions."

Paul was trying to figure out what a gas field on the other side of the world had to do with rural policing in the north of England when Dew continued.

"Of course, it depends if he's made any donations to the right political parties and those might be hidden by proxies as well, to make them look as if they're sourced in the UK."

"Right," said Paul still completely confused. "What are we looking for?"

"Because of the sanctions, any profits from Russian deals result in dirty money which is of no use to anybody. So, we're looking for ways that money is cleaned up. Where it's placed, how the origin is concealed and how it's extracted. Parbolde hasn't paid any UK tax for years but he's just bought a pheasant shoot and they're all best pals with the Duke. A lot of this is down to shuffling money around offshore bank accounts but sooner or later it has to come down to earth. I've got a feeling there's something really dodgy around here and that's what we want to find."

"We're looking for ways to hide suspiciously large amounts of cash, is that right?" Paul asked.

Dew nodded.

"You're making me think for this early in the morning," said Paul. "I suppose the way to hide a suitcase full of bank notes is amongst a lot of other cash. Maybe that's where the Duke comes in. Midham Grange is a gold mine it must generate a massive amount of money every year with car parking, entrance fees, gift shops, farm shops and events."

"What about Parbolde's pheasant shoot and grouse moor?" Dew asked.

"The pheasant shoot is recent but there are plans to have a cafe and restaurant in the mill year-round. You should know about the shooting fees at the mill. Up on the grouse moor they pay about £3000 a day. But when we looked at the books for another operation last year apparently it all runs at a loss and only survives with big injections of cash."

"Yes, that's what I paid for my sport yesterday. We need to figure out where the money has come from to buy the mill and set up the pheasant shoot. But let's start with the Grange, your car I think."

Paul pulled in at a kiosk and paid his five pounds for the car park. Then they queued at the entrance to the Grange itself. When they came to pay their entry fees, they both noticed a discrete sign: *We accept all major cards but cash payments reduce our transaction fees and help us maintain the house and grounds.*

They followed the roped walkway through the house and wondered which sections led to the private quarters. It was an open secret that the Duke and Duchess led separate lives and Paul imagined they were following a long tradition in the aristocracy. Of course, it was history and tradition that drew visitors in their thousands. Paul soon had a sense of a building which had evolved over the years. The Great Hall looked medieval, all interlocking stonework and other parts were Victorian with wood panelling and carpets. Lots of paintings of course and the most prominent were the male line of Midhams. Pride of place was the fifteenth Duke who had extended the Grange and doubled the land holdings in the mid-1800s.

"Paid for by the slave trade," whispered Dew.

It didn't feel like the kind of place for a loud brash conversation. The open display of centuries of wealth and privilege was intended to cow everyone into subservience. At least that's how Paul saw it.

Soon they were in the gift shop, with other signs encouraging cash payments. Beyond was the restaurant.

"Coffee?" Dew asked.

Paul felt drained already. "And a sit down. Why is it so exhausting trudging through these places?" He asked.

*

Superintendent Farlow was sitting in the waiting area outside the chief constable's office. The phone rang and Madelaine Chatton's PA told him to go through.

"Good morning Jimmy, take a seat," she said brightly.

He didn't have the courage to tell her he preferred James these days.

She locked her fingers together and stared him in the eye.

"I was brought in to clear up a mess. Nothing to do with all the important policing we do, nothing to do with the safety of our communities. It was all about a few people who wanted to go shooting. Some of our own were very keen apparently. I thought we'd put all that behind us. But no, my PA is sending me videos of a pheasant shoot which you attended at a location which seems to be a cess-pit of wildlife crime. Not one of our priorities as you know, but it's all about perception."

Chatton looked down at her desk, gathering her thoughts. Farlow didn't think he had permission to speak and in a moment the chief continued.

"And a considerable overlap of clientele hunting mutilated foxes in a clear breach of the Hunting Act and God knows how many other pieces of legislation."

Another pause.

"How far have you got with investigating these incidents?"

Farlow shifted in his seat. The honest answer was that he wasn't going to be doing any investigating at all. But that's not what the chief was going to hear.

"We're making progress," he replied.

"Progress?" Chatton reflected sarcastically. "Ah yes, Professional Standards have just informed me Fuller & Wainwright have submitted a formal complaint on behalf of their client who was de-arrested by the custody sergeant because of a lack of evidence. They're claiming the evidence from the hunt operative was fabricated. Shame you didn't corroborate that before dragging the suspect out of his bed."

Farlow had worked hard to create his little empire and reap the rewards he justly deserved. But now he was in free fall.

Chatton took a more conciliatory tone:

"I know these are problems faced by every force in the country. But this is what you're going to do: make some arrests and search some properties. Do it today, both the shoot and the hunt. I'll get our media team on it and we'll have some proactive, very public policing."

"But the CPS will be telling me there's insufficient evidence."

"I'll deal with the Crown Prosecution Service for now. You've got a lot to learn Jimmy. If we don't do what I say, this mess will be in the news for months. My way we shut it all down because they're ongoing investigations. If there really is no evidence, the CPS can tell me in a year but by then everyone will have forgotten about it."

Farlow started to stand up.

"Not so quick, Jimmy, there's more. Another video in fact. Your team attended a school fete in the same area, some nice community policing. And a young pupil recited a poem which caused a bit of a stir. My PA tells me social media has gone to town over a report the family's campervan had its tyres slashed in the middle of the night. So, we have serious criminal damage and a terrorised family. Get it sorted."

She paused and he felt her eyes drilling into him.

"All this was brewing when you were having lunch with the Duke of Midham and you were so pissed one of our officers, who was keeping an eye on the situation at the fete, had to spend half his shift chauffeuring you home."

He could only stare at the chief's desk.

"I'm not doing any of that HR bollocks Farlow but let me make it clear. This is your first and final warning. Now build some bridges with your team and show everyone some professionalism."

"Yes, ma'am."

The PA was smirking as Farlow marched out and that added to the heat in his face. He needed to grovel to his sergeant who was the only one with any expertise. Carson was on some secret deployment for the chief and Farlow would have to plead for some of his time. It was humiliating and a cold anger grew inside him. Fuck the chief, he had plenty of support and they all wanted Raven Harley to pay.

Chapter 26

Raven had time for some hot food after work. He was collecting Chloe at 7.00 p.m. which meant they should get into the cull zone before it was properly dark. The zones were not publicised but there were so many people involved in the slaughter that details leaked out. Apparently, badgers were safe on the grouse shooting moors probably because these were all protected areas. The whole rationale of the cull didn't stand up to independent scientific scrutiny and it would have been even harder for the government to justify on so-called conservation sites. Several years of culling had not reduced or eliminated bovine tuberculosis in cattle herds but the government had plenty of tame scientists to justify extending cull zones and killing tens of thousands of badgers every year. Tonight Chloe and Raven would be searching the rolling fields, lanes, hedgerows and copses for active badger setts and shooters hovering nearby and in particular any sign of Logan Porter.

Chloe was waiting outside Siobhan's house and she made herself comfortable in the passenger seat of the van. The tension of their last conversation had gone.

"Have you heard any more from work?" Raven asked.

"Nothing at the moment," said Chloe. "But I expect to be hauled in at some point. When there's been a death, they usually set up an inquiry run by someone external and a big part of that is making sure everything has been documented, decisions agreed and all agencies kept informed." She paused and looked at the outline of the hills where the sun was setting behind. "Psychologists, medics, police and ourselves are all supposed to talk to each other. It's easy enough to copy them into an email but I'm sure those never get read. To be honest it seems a million miles away now so it's going to be a shock to go in for a grilling. Mark said you've got plenty of work rolling in?"

"Yeah, it all seems simple and straightforward compared to this stuff. Mind you one of my trolls put in an anonymous complaint to the council which caused a bit of a panic. So, I suggested they take a closer look at the complainant and they'd find it wasn't actually a real person. Parks and Woodlands who we deal with, know we do a good job and we're safe so they're keen to have us."

"Did you send anything to the police about the pheasant shoot?" Chloe asked.

"I emailed the sergeant with some of the details and sent a video file. I really don't think they'll do anything with it, but you never know. The biggest reaction was from the close-ups of the shooters. Managed to get a good crop there; hedge fund manager, police superintendent, the Duke and someone identified a Russian gangster at least that's how they described him."

"Jack sent them everything on the fox hunt. It's a totally blatant breach of the Hunting Act but getting them to do anything about it is something else. Oops, let his real name slip there."

Raven wasn't going to tell anyone. He did want to know more about Chloe and Jack and was trying to think of a casual way of finding out. Then Chloe's phone beeped.

"Looks like most folks are heading down to the southern end of the zone, there's a lot of shooter activity down there. Porter has been seen around Catchbrow Hill, there are several copses around that area."

"Not one I know, Chloe, so just tell me where to go."

It wasn't that much further than Nether Beck Farm and the light had gone by the time they arrived. They climbed out of the van and listened. There were far away sounds of fast-moving cars on the main roads and closer, a few sheep bleating.

The sound of the quad was unmistakable. A chugging thumping noise that grew louder as the engine revved up a slope. They both had bright torches and night-vision or low-light cameras. Chloe jumped over a gate and stood in the cover of a hedge and Raven remained on the roadside, leaning against the same gate.

Porter was above them and traversing a large open field with clumps of trees at the top of the slope. He'd drive along then hop off the quad to pour a mound of peanuts every fifty metres or so. He was coming closer. Through the camera, Raven could see it looked like the same quad Porter had used before, with large boxes fixed front and rear. Some clearer footage would help so Raven turned on his head torch and Porter looked straight at the light and was immediately on the phone. There was no conversation, Porter just turned on his headlights and left the engine chugging. And that's how they stayed for five minutes until Raven saw some headlights come closer and the flickering of blue lighting the lane.

The police car pulled up onto the verge in front of Raven's van and two male officers wearing fluorescent jackets climbed out. Raven turned his head as they approached.

"Would you mind pointing that torch somewhere else, sir?"

Raven obliged by taking the torch from his head and pointing the light at the ground.

The officer continued, "We've had a report of intimidation and disruption of lawful activity, preventing that person," he signalled towards Porter with his thumb, "from going about their job."

"That person, as you describe him, is driving a quad bike he reported as stolen. That's why I'm here."

It was as if he hadn't spoken.

"Are you the registered owner of this vehicle, sir?"

Raven gave his name and address and the officer questioning him went back to the police car to call in the details. Raven could hear some of the conversation.

"VRM...vehicle of interest and person of interest...he's had a warning already?"

Raven heard the quad bike engine and saw Porter come out of another gate and onto the road before heading back towards Nether Beck.

The two officers had a whispered conversation and turned towards Raven, but the person of interest got in first:

"He's lied to you about a quad bike theft and he's driven down a public road without a licence plate. What's he got to do before you arrest him?"

But it soon became clear which way this was going. The two officers loomed in front of Raven until he could smell their breaths.

"Are you going to cooperate or do I have to handcuff you?"

Raven wanted to shout and scream, but he made himself calm down.

"There's no need for that," he said quietly.

"Raven Harley, I am arresting you under the Public Order Act 1986 for suspicion of intimidation and disruption of a person going about their lawful work. Further, I am impounding your vehicle by the power given to me under Section 59 of the Police Reform Act 2002. You have received a warning previously and you continue to drive your vehicle causing distress to a person going about their lawful work. I am taking you to Central Police Station where you will be processed."

"I haven't had any warning. This is a wrongful arrest," said Raven as calmly as he could.

Then his arms were grabbed and his wrists clamped into rigid handcuffs. Immediately one of the officers twisted the cuffs and pain shot up his arm. He'd had worse but screamed for the benefit of the bodycams both officers were wearing. No doubt that footage would be lost. Then one officer held his upper arm as the other demanded his keys.

"In the ignition," he said.

Finally, he was led to the patrol car and shoved into the back seat. One officer drove him to the station and the other followed behind in the van.

As the vehicles drove away, Chloe straightened up behind the hedge. She'd seen it all and filmed it all through a gap in the foliage. Then she found herself on the grass shaking as if she was having a fit. She gasped for breath and all her senses seemed heightened; the traffic which must have been a mile away, the touch of wet grass on her hands and the rich smell of fresh cow dung. After a few minutes, she managed to sit up and hoped she wasn't covered in it. Then she made a phone call and within fifteen minutes Jack had arranged a car to take her home.

She hadn't finished yet, not by a long way and she made herself concentrate. Porter's quad bike was identifiable by the twin boxes, but also because one of the tail lights was out and half the rear offside mudguard was missing. She'd seen those features tonight and before. The quad had disappeared into a dip in the road but she hadn't seen it climb out of that hollow towards Nether Beck. Porter could have driven it off-road anywhere, but he would definitely have it stashed somewhere away from his farm.

Ruby was driving her back.

"Are you ok, Chloe?" She asked. "You're very quiet."

"Yeah, I'm all right, just working out what I need to do."

"It's shocked me what's happened to Raven. I don't know if that's what we've all got to look forward to?"

"Not if I can help it," said Chloe.

Chapter 27

The plastic chair in the corridor hadn't got any softer and the whole police station had an air of chaos. One of the custody officers explained prisons were full and police cells were being used as overspill. Raven had his handcuffs removed, made his phone call and settled in for a long wait. There wouldn't be any interview until the morning and they wouldn't let him go home. He tried to doze in the chair, but it was too noisy to sleep. It became an impulse to rub his wrists and scratch his arms, his eyes were gritty and he just felt grubby. Eventually, he should have been looking at the dawn but he found no natural light anywhere. He imagined he was on the windowless top floor of the Lubyanka imprisoned for crimes against the state. But this wasn't a dream, it was all too real. And pounding in his head was that image of gamekeepers and police officers at the fete when the mood turned ugly. Willow's poem had made it onto social media along with photographs of slashed van tyres. All planned with the police looking on. It would be another unsolved crime and no gamekeeper would ever be pulled over for driving a *vehicle of interest*.

*

Chloe hadn't slept either. The low-light camera had collected Raven and the officers. You could pick out the audio at full volume and see the twisting of handcuffs was gratuitous. Raven's torch had illuminated Logan Porter's face and when he spun the quad bike around there was the broken tail light. She found some daylight footage from the farmyard to link the quad to Porter and put the footage together with captions and loaded it onto a tablet. Finally, she phoned Raven's solicitors and left a message asking to meet in the Costa opposite the police station at 8.30 a.m.

Mark would be getting up at six and she needed to tell him what had happened. Meanwhile, she had an urgent need to wrap her hands around a large mug of strong coffee. She sat sipping her drink in the lounge, lights off and curtains open and let her thoughts drift to what Raven meant for her.

*

Paul Carson had fist-pumped the air when Superintendent Farlow's call had come through the evening before. Farlow was asking for Paul's help.

"I've been having a rethink about the rural crime team, Carson…"

And it turned out that visible policing was needed with a raid on the High Ridge Estate. But Farlow couldn't find any officers who could identify Fenn traps, never mind determine if they were used illegally. Instead of ordering, Farlow had to ask politely if Carson could be spared from his secondment. On top of that, there was the fallout from the school fete: Willow's family had reported criminal damage to their vehicle and a complaint of bias about the officers who came to interview them.

All this led Paul to try and understand what was happening. Rural crime such as theft of farm machinery had always been a priority, but intimidation from the rural community? He hadn't investigated that before. Wildlife crime was an afterthought and any incidents that were reported were seen as an inconvenience rather than a priority. Put the two together and it created a very ugly picture of organised criminality and a police force that looked the other way. A police superintendent rubbing shoulders with a Russian oligarch was not a good look at all and Raven's video was bound to lead to more press interest. This initiative had to come straight from the top and the chief could see the best way to deflect criticism was to get in first and set the narrative with proactive policing. But there was very little chance of a conviction unless the dead birds of prey had been left lying around somewhere in which case an x-ray would reveal their legs had been snapped by the bar of the spring trap. Paul was going to Keeper's Cottage with two colleagues and Xan was heading to Fairview Mill with another team.

*

Cory Fuller was a welcome sight especially as he was carrying an extra-large coffee.

"Oat milk cappuccino, Raven, heard it was your favourite. The custody sergeant made me peel off the lid, but I made sure he didn't gob in it."

118

Raven tried a smile, but it was a struggle. It was the same routine as before, they had a word in private before the interview. Raven catalogued what had happened as best he could.

"I'm sorry, Cory, I'm finding it very difficult to concentrate and I expect that's deliberate. I've been in that corridor for twelve hours with one plastic cup of water. I'd sign anything to get out of here."

"Just like before, leave the talking to me, Raven. The Public Order allegation, there was no warning, no request to move on?"

"Nothing," replied Raven. "He just laid it on me."

"And you've not had any warning about your vehicle use in the last twelve months?"

"Absolutely nothing, no idea where that came from. And when I told them, that thug whipped on the handcuffs and it felt like an electric shock shooting up my arm."

"Can I take a look?"

Raven rolled up his sleeves and they looked down to see an ugly red welt on grey skin. Raven sighed. A couple of minutes later, they found themselves facing the same officer, PC Callaghan who looked wary.

"Don't worry, constable, I don't bite," said Cory. "I'm here to see my client gets justice."

Raven drank his coffee and listened to his solicitor speak in a quiet but no-nonsense tone. Callaghan went off to check if any warning had been given under Section 59. He returned five minutes later with another officer who introduced himself as Sergeant Ferguson, Custody Officer.

"There's no record of a Section 59 warning," said Ferguson.

"So, my client will have his vehicle returned."

It wasn't a question.

"Your officers allowed no discussion about what my client was doing in that location…"

Ferguson interrupted, "I'll have to ask them and they're off shift now."

"Perhaps I can save you the trouble, sergeant," said Cory as he pulled a tablet and memory stick from his case. "I have a witness and a video of the arrest. As you'll see my client was trying to identify the quad bike he was alleged to have stolen and it was indeed that very same vehicle and the person driving it was the one who made the allegation of theft."

Cory Fuller held the tablet at the end of the table and they all watched the arrest and listened to what was said. Raven winced when he heard his scream. Chloe had added some footage of the quad bike in Porter's yard which showed the distinguishing features of the vehicle.

There was a hush as the video finished. Cory pushed the memory stick towards Ferguson.

"Can you show us your injury?" Cory asked.

Raven rolled up his sleeve. Both solicitor and custody sergeant photographed the wound and Cory requested the bodycam images from the arresting officers. They agreed the arrest would not constitute a warning under Section 59 and Raven had good reason to be in that location. But given all that, Ferguson was still reluctant to 'de-arrest' because they were now looking at the conduct of his officers. Eventually, Cory was satisfied, for now at least the incident would be closed under *No Further Action*.

Pleased with his morning's work, Cory made it clear he'd be in touch with Professional Standards and he'd be pursuing a case of assault and misconduct in public office. Raven let it wash over him and he was just glad to get back in the fresh air. Chloe was leaning against the back doors of his van. Then she had her arms around him squeezing as if she never wanted to let go.

"Give me the keys," she said. "I'll drive you home."

*

The gate near Keeper's Cottage was open, so Paul Carson drove into the yard by the buildings. He had a quick word with his colleagues Alex and Beth and made sure the paperwork was in order. Paul noted the registrations of a covered pick-up and Corsa which were parked in front of the main dwelling. Before he could knock on the door a tall, slim, dark-haired woman came out. She had a large document bag on her shoulder and a bunch of keys in one hand.

"Oh, what's going on?" She asked, looking over at the three officers in stab vests.

"Mrs Sutherland? We have a warrant to search your premises," said Paul, waving the documents in a clear plastic folder. "Is your husband here?"

"He's out," she said moving her arm in a wide arc across the moorland view behind. "Somewhere over there like he is every morning."

"Except when he's at Fairview Mill?" Paul asked.

"Aye, well, that's just down there," she said pointing at some trees in the distance.

She was quiet for a moment and Paul was about to ask her to step aside when she put the bag down on the doorstep and pulled her phone out.

"I'll call him," she said tapping the pin.

Paul could hear the chug of a quad bike even though her phone wasn't on speaker. Her Scottish accent grew thicker as she spoke to him.

"Polis is here to do a search. Yes, but I'm going to be late for work. Ok quick as you can."

She turned back to Paul. "Did you get that? He's heading back and I'm not to let you in until he gets here. I just need to phone the school and tell them I'll be late."

She phoned St Mary's and turned her attention back to the officers, shaking her head.

"A couple of days ago you couldn't do enough for us at the fundraiser." Her accent thickened once more. "The big man is *not* going to be pleased," she said nodding at the Range Rover pulling into the yard.

Parbolde drove right up to them and wound down the window but remained in his elevated driving position. Just like the gentry had done for centuries, astride their horses looking down on the peasants. Paul could see Parbolde was dressed in his casual outfit; only a sweatshirt was visible, but there'd be discreet designer labels somewhere, a clear enough message about power and wealth. Parbolde took his time looking through the warrant before handing it back to Paul.

"I'll be phoning your chief constable, Sergeant. This is intolerable. And you'll be hearing from my lawyers with a *substantial* claim for disruption to my business. Lily here has had to deal with a deluge of cancellations, since you let that terrorist creep around with his camera invading everyone's privacy."

"It was the chief who sent me sir. And just to let you know a similar warrant is being served at your Fairview Mill premises."

They heard a quad bike and Finn Sutherland pulled up next to the Range Rover. Parbolde had a whispered conversation with his keeper before heading back to the luxury of the lodge. Sergei was waiting for him in the lounge and Parbolde joined him at the floor-to-ceiling windows overlooking the moor.

"All sorted?" The Russian asked.

"They won't be bothering us," replied Parbolde. "Now, you were talking about an increased investment?"

Sergei was in his late thirties and had attended school in Edinburgh but he hadn't picked up that accent. Instead, he spoke in monied, home counties tones that didn't betray his roots. He was a second-generation oligarch and rarely in the news: his father had carved out an energy conglomerate from post-soviet chaos and sent his children to the safety of American and British schools, preferring to keep his family out of danger. In Sergei's world, all police officers had a price.

"Finn knows how to deal with them, I've seen that before," Sergei said.

Parbolde was surprised that Sergei remembered their shooting up at his Glen Fowthing estate, interrupted briefly by some allegations of poisoning wildlife. Parbolde had moved Finn and his wife south because he needed a safe pair of hands at High Ridge. And he took lessons from Sergei about how to ensure loyalty from his *troops*. Remember their names, ask after their families and be free with bonuses which meant everything to them and nothing to you. Parbolde hadn't seen Sergei switch from *benefactor* to *man betrayed,* but over the years he'd heard how problems had disappeared and was sure the minders, sitting in the back with Sean and Callum, would stop at nothing.

"The boom in energy prices has generated plenty of capital I need to disperse," Sergei continued. "About £100 million needs a steady and boring investment. And in case I get too much attention and end up being sanctioned there has to be no way to link it to me. My hard-earned money will not be snatched by the US or the UK."

"I've given it some thought," said Parbolde. "London property is in the spotlight, but around the rest of England, land prices only ever go up. I'd suggest a wide portfolio of farmland and forestry. There are lots of new opportunities in carbon offsetting as well as boring run-of-the-mill agriculture. £100 million will be noticed but not if we split into ten or more shell investment companies, registered in the usual havens, Virgin Islands, Caymans, Mauritius, Belize and so on. And you'll have ultimate control of all of them. I know who can do the leg work: Tranchard is well-connected. He hired my gamekeepers, runs the badger cull and knows what to look for in property. And he knows he has to deliver. He'll want a cut and we need to work out what that's worth."

"What about shooting estates like this?"

"Probably doesn't fit your profile. As you've seen over the last couple of days, they can end up in the news. It doesn't bother me too much but you really do need to keep quiet. These moors probably have more carbon than one of your oilfields and people are starting to pay for keeping that in the ground and sequestering more. That's the post-fossil fuel world for your grandchildren."

Parbolde wasn't sure if he should say more but he was becoming annoyed by their links to *The Duchy*.

"And we need more than Eddie's world of hunting, shooting and tourism," he added.

"There's a lot more money to come from my *fossil fuel world* before then. And I don't think it's time to give up on the Duke of Midham just yet," said Sergei who looked as if he was weighing up how much to share. "Eddie might look like a buffoon in his plus fours and stupid hat but a lot of that is an act. When it comes to *krepostnoy krestyanin* his backbone is *Sankt-Peterburg* steel, just like any Tsar."

Parbolde hated it when Sergei slipped into Russian, it made him feel like a peasant, gawping at his master, not knowing what had been said. Sergei helped him out, "The serfs old boy, those who are bought and sold."

Parbolde thought he owned the Duke of Midham and now he was being told about a business enterprise where he'd been totally excluded. Sergei was playing with him and he gave another crumb:

"It's in Eddie's blood. The Midham Shipping Company built the Grange and bought all the land, with profits of the Caribbean, Mauritius and Cape Colony."

Sergei was talking about slavery. Was the Duke really involved in people trafficking? Parbolde sensed there wouldn't be any more. But it was always a game with Sergei, to show Parbolde could never be equal, could never be a party to all those secrets. And Nathan felt a constant need to assert himself, to show his importance.

"Eddie's been hard work recently. He's panicking about getting his hands on his RUsearch gains. My accountants are going to have to take him to task on that."

"I owe a thank you for keeping him sweet, Nathan. Those suitcases of cash don't come from me. I've been told to recycle them and Eddie's doing me a big favour. It's how the world works."

Now Sergei had slipped into co-conspirator, the confidante where Nathan would be fed a few crumbs. *We're all in the same boat, Nathan, we all have to deal with unpleasant stuff so we can earn a crust.* Nathan didn't want to think about where the cash came from. Drugs would be one of the more palatable options although this conversation was telling him there was money in trafficking. It was funny to think Sergei took orders from anyone but maybe even with their billions they were all just small players.

*

The search hadn't yet revealed anything obvious. Paul had stood on tiptoes to pull the smooth fitting stone from above the door lintel in the vehicle shed, something he'd discovered on a previous search but the cavity behind was empty. Then Beth called him over to a coal bunker and pulled back the lid. Inside it had been cleaned thoroughly and instead of coal there were several large bags of rat poison in different brands. Paul knew the common ingredient was Brodifacoum an anti-coagulant. At first glance, it was legal if used indoors. But this had become the poison of choice on estates, apparently within the law but used in large doses on bait outdoors would result in birds of prey dying slowly from internal bleeding.

Paul called over Finn Sutherland. "What's this?" He asked.

"We have a rat problem," said Sutherland.

"And at the mill as well?"

"You've got it."

Paul would generate an alert for poison bait but he knew no officer on duty would ever step foot on an estate like this to chance upon a rabbit laced with Brodifacoum. And that's why these crimes were never detected.

He called Xan who was conducting a similar search at Fairview Mill. They'd found a similar stash of rat poison.

"The search warrant is too restrictive," said Xan. "There's a laptop up in the office, but the underkeeper Ryan Walker snatched it away as soon as I saw it. I've checked and we can't seize it."

Paul had no say in the wording of the warrant. He expected laptops, tablets and phones at Keeper's Cottage as well but there was no way he could access them. Maybe that was the intention? The search was for appearances, not to get to the bottom of any criminal activity.

"You'll have to stick to the letter of it," said Paul. "I'll come down in a while and review what you've found."

"I've got a shed full of Fenn traps, Larsens, snares and other spring traps but there's nothing to suggest any of them are illegal."

"It's the same up here. I'll be about half an hour."

Paul gave his colleagues instructions to take samples from the open bags of poison along with some of the traps and provide Sutherland with a receipt. He arrived at the mill to find Xan's team doing the same. Paul gathered everyone around.

"When you finish up here head back to the cottage, make sure everything is sealed and labelled and give Alex and Beth a lift back to the station. Xan and I are going for a little walk."

First of all, they checked the pheasant pens. Paul was trying to orientate himself to Raven's video footage. There was the pen at one side and at the other some bushes, still in leaf. He could see one pole about four feet high with a small flat piece of wood nailed to the top and they walked over to take a look. A second pole was partially obscured by branches. It was this one that birds obviously favoured because the leaves provided cover. There were no traps there now. DNA analysis was available to identify the presence of birds of prey but they would need the trap itself not a piece of wood. Paul had no doubt the trap and raptor would be buried somewhere he'd never find.

In the report, Raven had said the estate had a camera on these pens. He asked Xan to take a look and a couple of minutes later he was called over to take a look at a trail cam tied to a larch tree. That camera would have recorded all the illegal activity. Surely they can't have been stupid enough to keep the footage? But of course, their search warrant didn't cover cameras or other electrical devices and Paul was sure after today any digital evidence would be long gone. He didn't have the energy to take it up with his superiors.

Next, they took a supply of clear plastic evidence bags and walked up the slope. The number of birds was astonishing, there must have been thousands. And they all congregated near the feeders which were blue plastic drums full of grain running into a small tray underneath. Giant versions of the feeders Paul had in his garden for the sparrows, but these were so heavy they each had to be supported by three sturdy wood posts.

Paul had seen the statistics: only forty per cent of these birds lived long enough to be killed by the client's shotgun pellets and he expected to see lots of carcasses, which Raven's video had revealed. But they'd all been tidied away apart from the flattened birds on the tarmac of the approach road. They needed to raid this place before any publicity. But without the publicity, there wouldn't be any police interest. The thicket where the fox had been killed was surrounded by a standard-height wire fence of around one metre. That would stop any pheasants wandering in but of course, now they could fly over. Within the thicket, every animal path had at least two snares. The wire loops were set close to the ground and would catch a badger but the legislation was vague so the snares were probably legal. The wire loops were attached to metal posts hammered into the ground. As they moved into the thicket the stench of rotting flesh grew stronger until they were looking into the stink pit filled with dead pheasants and dead foxes. Any foxes new to the area would head towards this and be caught in the snares. They took some photos but it was unlikely anything here was laced with poison.

They followed another snared path to the far side of the thicket and just inside the fence was the small wire cage of a Larsen trap. In one compartment, a forlorn crow was agitated at their approach. Paul was taken back to the poem he'd heard at the school fundraiser. A mouldy water bottle and some disgusting soggy pellets were the only food and drink. And this bird couldn't fly. There seemed to be some feathers missing but Paul wasn't an expert. It certainly looked as if the bird had been mutilated and the general conditions would be in breach of animal welfare regulations. The corvid they were looking at was the 'call' bird used to attract other crows and had probably been in this tiny cage since the spring.

"Ok, Xan," Paul said. "Let's get some photographs and some video on our phones and we'll try and get the bird and the trap to a vet for an assessment."

Once they'd gathered the evidence, they hauled the trap over the fence and carried everything back to their vehicle.

Chapter 28

Chloe popped into the supermarket for some fry-up ingredients. Raven hadn't said much and she left him in the van. Back at the house, she set about cooking hash browns, sausages, baked beans and toast. Raven was leaning back in his chair with his eyes closed as she brought him a cup of tea. A few minutes later, she put a plate full of food in front of him and joined him at the table.

"Eat," she said and he did as instructed.

The hot food and drink revived him to a degree. As they were on their second cups he turned to her. There was a bit of colour in his cheeks but folds under his eyes were filled with black and yellow smudges.

"Thanks for everything, Chloe. I'd still be in there if it wasn't for you. I'm glad you didn't get dragged into it. You just seem to disappear behind those hedgerows, I don't know how you do it?" He asked.

"I think there was a bit of instinct and a lot of luck there."

Chloe did want to say more. She wanted to say something about them. But Raven was exhausted and she wasn't sure what she felt. Guilt and protectiveness were in there somewhere and all combined it wasn't the best basis of a conversation.

"Anyway," she continued, "I've got an idea where Porter might have stashed that quad bike. You've used a buttonhole camera, haven't you?"

"Not in anger, but I did try it. Should be in the spare room, all charged up. I'll show you how to turn it on."

The garage around the corner had been in touch about her Fiesta. The cylinder head had been reground and it was all ready to go apparently. She packed a rucksack full of cameras and headed out towards Nether Beck Farm.

She decided to start at Catchbrow Hill where they'd had the encounter with the police. Porter had driven towards Nether Beck but didn't go as far as the farm. The engine temperature in the Fiesta was behaving and she set off to explore the area. The road dipped down into a hollow and at the bottom, a wide unsurfaced track headed left. She stopped for a moment and read a new sign on a post: George Carter Quality Beef. It looked promising but parking further away would be a better idea so she carried on up the hill. The map on her phone showed the farm buildings were called Middle Beck Barn and there was a footpath running right through the buildings. She set up the buttonhole camera, grabbed her rucksack and started her hike. Even with the phone in her hand, the path was difficult to follow. The stiles at hedgerows were overgrown so it was difficult to spot the route across the next field. Under her feet was lush green grass and nothing else. It will have been the best part of a hundred years since these fields were wildflower meadows. And there wasn't much sign of badgers or any other wildlife, those animals were squeezed into token areas that chemicals wouldn't improve.

At the last hedgerow before the farm, Chloe took some time to scan the buildings. The path veered off to the right but there were modern barns and sheds to the left. Chloe approached at a casual pace and made a point of looking around as if lost before heading left.

Around the back of the buildings, there was Porter's quad bike, parked in an open-sided shed. Chloe walked past the vehicle then retraced her steps for more footage and did her best to look lost.

"What do you think you're doing?"

An old man in overalls with a weather-beaten, leathery face had appeared from one of the sheds.

"I'm terribly sorry," she replied holding up her phone. "I seem to have lost the path."

"You're not the first love. Back there," he pointed with his thumb, "then straight on. Bloody Council needs to get those signs sorted."

"Sorry," Chloe replied and she quickened her stride in the direction he'd indicated.

It took a while to loop back around to her car. She phoned Cory Fuller and left a message, "I've found the stolen quad bike. It's actually at the farm next to Porter's, but it's quite a distance. I need to film him collecting it."

She was fairly sure Porter would only appear around dusk to start his work for the night. So, she spent the afternoon looking for badger setts and then found a cafe for some food. The service was pleasantly slow and she hoped it was a sign that everything was prepared from scratch. And it gave her time to think about Raven. It sounded as if he was finished with Becky and he wanted to be with her again. But vagueness and half-truths were no good to her. She wanted certainty and maybe she could get that despite the chaos of the last few days.

He was a good catch as her Nan would have said. But they'd been together just long enough to take each other for granted. Maybe they'd both stopped trying, but that was no reason for Raven to destroy their relationship. If she thought about meeting him for the first time now, she wouldn't hesitate getting together. But she knew the reality of him, he could betray. That betrayal really hurt and he'd been completely callous. With a click of his fingers, she was out of his life. But maybe that was Raven surviving his own guilt. Before they'd met, she'd had relationships which morphed from friends to partners and back again until she didn't know what she felt for that person. And now she was approaching thirty she really didn't know if she wanted a child or if he did. Would Raven be a good dad, for sure, he would. But having a child to mend a relationship never seemed to work and she didn't want to be a single parent.

She stopped and looked out of the window for a minute, surprised where her thoughts had taken her. She was suspended from work, didn't have a partner and wasn't sure if she'd ever be back in that same job. She'd somehow evolved into a full-time activist and everyone said she was great at it, but it did feel as if she could be arrested any minute and then her professional life would come to an end.

She decided to trust her instincts. She didn't want to see Raven begging on his knees, but he hadn't proved himself yet. She wasn't going out of her way to make it hard for him but needed patience to see how things worked out.

Her food arrived. A bite to eat and then it would be time to nail that bastard Porter.

*

An hour later, she was behind the hedgerow opposite the entrance to Middle Beck Farm. The low-light camera captured Porter arriving in his pick-up and five minutes later he roared out on the quad bike.

Chloe messaged Jack: *Porter's on his quad again. Catchbrow Hill area. I've got some video to sort out so I'm heading back.*

She'd put together another evidence pack for the solicitor and that would form part of the complaint against the police. She was doing their job for them but a terrier man falsifying a claim of theft was obviously not on their radar at all.

*

Raven dragged himself out of bed while there was still some daylight. When Chloe had left, he crawled under the duvet and found himself shivering at least that's what it felt like. And then he realised he was shaking as the stress left his body. He concentrated on his breathing and thought about the help and support that had been there for him. The solicitor cut through the bluster and the police knew when they'd messed up. There was no argument when Cory got hold of a mistake.

And Chloe? She'd been there for him and probably done an all-nighter to put the evidence together. He did manage to laugh at himself. It had been a hell of a performance to get her attention.

He stepped in the shower and scrubbed the stench of the police station from his skin. He needed to get his blood flowing and set off for a brisk walk around his neighbourhood. After fifteen minutes, he rounded the corner back into his road. There was a pick-up cruising past his house. The spotlight mounted on the roof of the cabin was a give-away. He took a photo and tapped the registration number into a notepad on his phone. Was he going to get another visit? It seemed likely at some point. Back home he managed another smile, the box of cameras was getting plenty of use and he set a trail cam in the back garden to cover the door. Then he got some insurance from the tool shed.

A bit more toast and he was ready for bed. Whatever they were up to, they wouldn't stop him sleeping tonight.

Chapter 29

It had been a deep, dreamless sleep and Raven was awake at 4.00 a.m. He was wondering about making himself a drink when he heard the crash and then a grunt as someone forced open the kitchen door. The footsteps vibrated through the house, coming closer. He leapt out of bed and nearly stumbled over the object on the floor. It took more seconds to pick it up. Then he stood at the top of the stairs. Someone was climbing up to meet him.

Raven flicked on the light and pulled the cord to start the chainsaw. The figure below him had climbed two steps, a long-stem sledgehammer in one hand and a bin bag in the other. It looked like a man with his face covered by a balaclava.

Raven revved the chainsaw and stared for a second at the startled eyes looking up at him. The man took a step back but he stumbled, unable to grab the banisters. Even above the noise of the chainsaw Raven could hear the crunch of bone as the back of the man's head hit the wall at the foot of the stairs. But he wasn't down for long. He pulled himself up and staggered out of the house.

Raven was left staring at the sledgehammer and bin bag at the bottom of the stairs, wondering what had just happened. He slowly walked down the stairs and checked the rooms on the ground floor before shutting down the chainsaw. He went back up to the bedroom for his phone and called the police. Sitting on the bed in his t-shirt and boxers he was shaking again. After a couple of minutes, he pulled on some clothes and waited. He expected blue lights immediately, but it soon became clear that wasn't going to happen. So, he went down, careful to step over the sledgehammer and bin bag which was stinking now.

The trail cam in the back garden had captured the man smashing the door and a couple of minutes later the same person staggering out. Raven copied the files onto his laptop and onto a memory stick. Then to make sure he had another copy he sent them to Chloe as well. Finally, he added the photo of the pick-up to the memory stick.

He put on the kettle and took a look at the door. The lock had failed but the wood was still reasonably intact. He had bought a more secure lock but hadn't had a chance to fit it yet. That would be this morning's job. He was halfway through his tea when the police finally arrived.

Raven was shaking his head as he realised it was the officer who had handcuffed him just one night before. He waited for the officer to speak.

"We were the first available." Then a long pause, "Shall we start again, I'm PC Colne and this is my colleague PC Singh. Can you tell us what happened?"

Raven couldn't speak for a minute; all he could think about was this officer responding in five minutes to a complaint from a terrier man on a badger cull. And Raven had to wait an hour after someone broke down his door with a sledgehammer in the middle of the night. He took a deep breath and explained what had happened. Then he showed them the video and photo on the memory stick.

"You didn't see his face at all?" Colne asked.

"No, but you just need to look for someone with a large bump on the back of the head."

Raven took the two officers a few steps to the foot of the stairs.

"I haven't touched the sledgehammer or the bag, but I can guess what's in there from the smell."

Colne pulled on some gloves and took a look at the contents of the bag. "Looks like a decomposed fox to me."

Raven went back into the kitchen for a torch and shone the light at the wall opposite the foot of the stairs. "Look, some blood on there from his head."

Colne nodded. "And you were waving a chainsaw around at the top of the stairs, up there?"

"Yes. If I'd waited for you to turn up, I'd have been stone-cold dead for an hour."

Colne looked up the stairs, imagining the scene. Eventually, he said, "Let's hope it was just a warning, not a murder attempt." He turned to his colleague. "Gaj can you get the largest evidence bags we have, we'll bag up the sledgehammer and the fox." Then he turned to Raven and started to explain about victim support.

Raven cut in, "I'm not bothered about that. The pick-up truck I saw yesterday afternoon is the same one I reported to you, let me see, was it just a couple of weeks ago? You still haven't given me an incident number for that. It's one of the High Ridge gamekeepers. From his build, I'd guess it's Ryan Walker, not the Scottish one. Go and interview him and take a look at the back of his head."

Again Colne went quiet and considered his words. "I'll report it all and we'll get scene of crimes out here to take a DNA sample. And we can get someone to fix the door for you."

Raven explained he really needed to get to work today so they agreed that scene of crimes would call to arrange a time to come over. Raven was already installing the new lock by the time the officers had bagged up the evidence.

"We'll be in touch," said Colne.

Raven wasn't holding his breath.

*

Gerald Tranchard had better things to do than an urgent early morning meeting with Ryan Walker. Tranchard had carved out a role as a fixer with a finger in every pie and a slice of every bit of money that was being made. But the badger cull was one bit of hassle after another. Today he had to view three farms, or rather estates, for Sergei's portfolio and that meant a lot of driving. But before he could get on with that he had to sort out this gamekeeper. He'd hired Ryan Walker for Parbolde because of his record of assault and Walker had assured him of his skills in that area.

The pick-up stopped behind Tranchard's Range Rover and Walker approached the passenger door. Tranchard beckoned him in. Walker looked nervous.

"What happened?" Tranchard asked.

"I smashed the door in just like you said, then I was going up the stairs with the fox and he just appeared and put the lights on. Then he was waving the biggest fucking chainsaw I've ever seen in front of my face. I fell backwards and cracked my head. Then I legged it."

Tranchard sighed. "I told you to smash the door then just throw the fox inside. That was simple enough. Warn him, nothing more."

"I was going to stick it in his bedroom."

Tranchard thought there was no point arguing. Raven Harley needed to be warned off but he wasn't listening. And now Walker had left enough evidence for the police to investigate.

"Right, just stay calm," said Tranchard. "All you've done is damage the door. The police are not going to spend much effort on that, trust me. But we don't want them interviewing you."

Tranchard reached into his jacket for a wad of banknotes and gave Walker £500. "Get yourself up to The Scottish Estate, Glen Fowthing. I'll tell them to expect you. Pay cash for everything and go on the train. Leave now."

"Yes, Mister Tranchard."

Tranchard's contacts in the police told him Finn Sutherland would be arrested for killing a sparrowhawk. It wouldn't go anywhere but it was a nuisance and Tranchard had wasted more time sorting out a lawyer. He hadn't signed up to be Parbolde's estate manager but he was being sucked into it. It seemed Sergeant Carson was acting on the instructions of the chief constable so there was no way to intervene. And next on Carson's list was the Midham Hunt. It was all far too messy and the person behind everything was Raven Harley, he was sure of it. If Harley couldn't take a hint, maybe a more permanent solution was needed.

*

Raven enjoyed an uncomplicated day at work with Mark and Colin. They'd asked how he was but Raven didn't say much about the nocturnal visit, he just wanted to get on with his life. Scene of Crimes was coming at 6.00 p.m. and the new lock had slotted into place, simple things. He'd have to remember to give Chloe a key. She'd obviously downloaded the files.

Wtf, Raven, are you ok? Shall I come over?

He wanted to make light of it.

Yeah, all good. That nice copper who arrested me the other day is now sorting this one. I'm having an early night and will help tomorrow x

See you then x

Chapter 30

Paul Carson had left his colleagues to work their way through the evidence gathered in the search of the shooting estate. In the end, it had been easier to get a private vet to examine the crow rather than involve a government agency. Almost immediately, they'd called back to say the bird's wings had been mutilated so it would never fly again and the crow was in such a poor state that it should be euthanised. The fate of the bird touched everyone in the office and there were a few offers to re-home the crow but that was never going to work for a wild bird.

The next morning, he was back on money laundering. Paul met Dew Foster close to her hotel. This time he was driving and they stopped down the road where it was quieter and Dew gave him an update:

"We've had a closer look at the Midhams. My office asked HM Revenue to request a VAT audit using a snapshot of current documents. So, we've got detailed account documentation, don't look so bored Paul. Usually, the accounts take a couple of years or more to be published and they don't contain much detail. We told HMRC to make it clear it was routine, but they wanted the paperwork as soon as possible. And we've flagged up a few things to look at."

Dew brought up a map on her phone and gave Paul directions. Soon, they were driving down a broad flat bottom valley away from the moors.

"All this is owned by the Duke?" Paul asked.

"A lot of it," replied Dew. "Whoa, just pull in here."

Paul braked hard and they pulled into a lay-by where a couple of large potholes bumped them out of their seats. They looked across a large flat field with the river bank in the far distance. There was a line of people bent over pulling some sort of vegetable out of the soil and into plastic crates. A tractor and trailer followed slowly. The significance was lost on him.

"We're on a flood plain here with nice sandy soil. This time of year, they'll be pulling up carrots. Look at all those workers, Paul, I doubt any were born around here," said Dew.

And then Paul listened to a resume of seasonal workers and their visas. They needed £1270 in a bank account to get a six-month agricultural visa or at this time of year leading up to Christmas, a poultry workers visa. That was to demonstrate they could look after themselves but were open to exploitation with some workers never able to pay back money loaned to them by Agents who held onto passports as well.

"What we're looking at could be perfectly legitimate or some gang master modern slavery?" Paul asked.

"Yes," replied Dew. "It's something to note. If everything else is dodgy, this will be as well. Can you find out where their lodgings are Paul? We might need to take a closer look."

They carried on and after a mile, Paul turned off the main road on a surfaced track marked as a dead end. Soon they were creeping around potholes until they stopped by some large double gates with a sign.

Paul took a photo: *Riverside Hagg—A Forest Recovery Project* and there was the government logo.

"They don't miss a trick when it comes to grants, do they? What are we looking for?" Paul asked.

"We're looking for a large tree felling operation. The accounts tell us Midham paid £250,000 for specialist conservation tree felling, opening the canopy for biodiversity gains."

"So, it's not a clear fell, but plucking out trees here and there to let in more light?"

"That's it," said Dew.

They ignored the large *Private* sign and climbed over the gate. Luckily, they'd both packed wellies, within a few metres they were wading through several inches of mud and deep ruts from heavy vehicles.

At first, they could see some thinning with freshly cut tree stumps and there was a pile of logs by the gate. But within a hundred metres they were in a dense plantation of Sitka spruce and the vehicle track they were following became much drier and less rutted. After a few minutes, they came to a fork and they split up. Fifteen minutes later they met back at the fork.

"Any sign of conservation felling?" Dew asked.

"Absolutely nothing," replied Paul, "just dense forest. I took plenty of photos. Who pays £250k for work that hasn't taken place?"

"Precisely," replied Dew. "Are you getting the hang of this now?"

"I think so. Where next?"

They drove back towards the hills and the Duke's grouse shoot at Haverstone Moor. The building at the edge of the moor, Midham Lodge was sheltered by a fold in the hillside and surrounded by a high stone wall. The grouse moor was relatively small at 1500 hectares, but it was still easy for the two officers to explore without being noticed. There were a couple of neatly painted gates adorned with the Midham, crest but locked with very obvious chains and padlocks.

"They don't like hikers around here," observed Dew.

The only other means of access were climbs over barbed wire fences or scaling one of the endless dry-stone walls. They opted for a gate at the foot of Haverstone Clough and started up a smooth track of crushed stone.

The note in the accounts described more conservation work: gully blocking using peat dams, heather mowing and sphagnum planting.

"You're going to have to explain, Paul. I really don't know what I'm looking for," said Dew.

Paul stopped at the edge of the track. At his feet, a large drainage ditch carried brown, frothy water down the slope. "The peat soils here are full of carbon and the aim of the restoration work is to make sure that carbon remains stored here. It obviously hasn't worked because the water run-off is full of peat and we shouldn't see that much water unless there's been very high rainfall. The peat dams should mean water oozes off the moor rather than pours off and the sphagnum they've planted should soak up a lot of the rainfall anyway. If it's anything like the forest we'll find a couple of neat examples near this track and nothing else."

They carried on up the track, quickly gaining height. It didn't appear to be a natural landscape but one that was heavily managed. All Paul could see was heather in patches of different heights with blackened stems of previously burnt plants mixed in with newer shoots. Soon they were walking past shooting butts and Paul explained what these shelters were used for: just like the pheasant shoot, they were stations where the 'gun' and a loader waited for the birds to be driven close enough to kill.

At the end of the track, they found a turning circle and as Paul expected some examples of the work that had been 'completed'.

"This has been mown, you can see where the heather stems have been cut and there's no soot or charred vegetation." They walked onto the patch and Paul pointed to some small green and red plants at their feet. "This is sphagnum moss, planted in a grid," and he pointed to other plants nearby, "and it should get established. When it does, it will help to keep the water back and help new peat to form."

This time Dew was looking bored. "And that's another £250k of work?"

"Er, no," said Paul. "I could have done these four patches here with a strimmer and a tray of plants in an afternoon. It would make a good photo though." He took a few shots on his phone then walked to the edge of the patch and waved over Dew. "At least they've managed one peat dam." They looked down at an earth barrier across a small dry stream bed. It did look natural with some transplanted bilberry plants across the top of the dam and some water had started to accumulate behind. It made another nice photo, but only one.

Paul slowly swung his arm across their view of the hillside. "It's a harder call this one. They could have done that work somewhere up there but I doubt it. These mown patches are very clear and I can't see any up there. If you like, we can walk up one of these stream beds for a bit, then down another, looking for these dams."

An hour later, they were back at the turning circle. As expected, they hadn't seen any more restoration work. Paul was feeling weary and his feet were aching as they trudged down the hill.

"Thanks for all this, Paul. I would have really struggled without you, especially the last bit. Give or take a few quid, it looks like we've found half a million pounds worth of money laundering over the last year. That cash was not legitimately earned, but having gone through Midhams accounts it's *bona fide* now. We need a lot more documentation to prove it, but that's a great start. A couple of local contractors might have been involved with the small amount of work we've seen but that £500k went to offshore companies, layer upon layer of them and I don't know if the team will ever uncover the ultimate ownership. It's frustrating, I've had my eyes on Parbolde for years and what we've found here is all about the Duke of Midham. I'll report back to my office and see what else they've dug up. But I expect I'll be up again next week."

"Ok," said Paul. "That suits me. The chief has given me a pile of other stuff to do and it's all about how these boys have their fun."

"Yes, I did see the video of the shoot. I'm glad I didn't appear."

Dew took in the view of heather-clad moors, green fields, hedgerows and a winding river. Archetype bucolic *Olde Englande*. It was a pretty picture but not such a green and pleasant land when you scratched the surface.

"And I'm glad I'm working with you and not your super. He's one of the *boys* for sure," Dew continued.

*

As the two officers made their way off the moor, Edward Fraine, Duke of Midham was sitting in his armchair in the lodge, looking down over the river valley. He had the phone to his ear and was listening to a nervous Superintendent Farlow explain how rural policing was now being run by a sergeant at the direction of the chief constable. It had been taken out of his hands, stripped from his purview. And as far as Farlow knew, there would be more arrests and possibly charges next week.

Eddie had seen the videos and had heard about the search at Parbolde's estate. Tomorrow the hunt and his way of life would go on. It was time to gather his troops. His family had ended up backing the right side in the Civil War. That's what he would remember. Cromwell's rule was painful because they were royalists but the Midhams prospered, just like they always had. He phoned Logan Porter.

*

Paul Carson dropped Dew Foster back at her vehicle. It felt like a long day with two evidence-gathering walks but it was still only 3 p.m. And that gave him time to get over to St Mary's Primary before the school day ended. There was no field to park in this time so he added to the line of vehicles on one side of the narrow lane. A few minutes later, children started spilling onto the road to be greeted by their parents or carers. He recognised Willow chatting to a man and they were making their way towards their van. Paul strode over with his ID tucked in the palm of his hand.

"Mister Torsen? I'm Sergeant Paul Carson, sorry I'm normally in uniform," he said showing his badge.

Willow and her father looked warily at Carson. Paul tried to gain their trust:

"I'd like to apologise for my colleagues. The superintendent sent me to try and sort things out."

"Well, Sergeant, I'm Mal and I expect you recognise Willow from the fete? You were there, weren't you? Couldn't you tell something was going to happen? And when your colleagues had a chat with us after the damage, all they were bothered about was checking my tax and insurance and asking if we had the landowner's permission to park on the verge overnight. They might as well have spelt it out: we deserved what we got."

"I can only apologise again. It's my job to protect everyone in rural communities. If those officers fail to uphold the standards we expect, they'll pay the price for that."

It was routine police speak but enough to get Mal to explain what damage had occurred and that following the social media post there was now a crowd funder which had already covered the cost of the damage.

"We want Willow to have a safe, stable education, somewhere she's welcome. The school have given us their full support. But probably the best thing to result from this is one of the farmers Erik Sanford is letting us use some hard standing on his land. There are an awful lot of people who are sickened by what happened and they're sickened by a bunch of thugs who are above the law."

"And you didn't see or hear anything?"

"There's always some noise at night when you're parked on top of a moor and the van is buffeted in the wind. If I checked everything, I'd never get any sleep. But I thought I heard some footsteps and an unusual sound, the digital clock was showing 1:57 a.m. I wish I'd gone out, but I thought the noise was probably the wind catching the roof rack."

"Did you put that in your statement?"

"Your chums didn't ask me for a statement."

Paul shook his head. "Ok, we will need that in writing."

They swapped phone numbers and email addresses and Paul said he'd send someone over to look at the slashed tyres which were at the farm, possibly look at the van as well and someone would come out to take a statement. He also explained ANPR traffic cameras were only on the main roads and were unlikely to yield any suspects and unfortunately no witnesses had come forward so far. "But we'll do our best; you have my word on that."

*

Logan was still in bed and trying to sleep after another night working on the badger cull. He rolled over and picked up his phone from the bedside table. When he saw it was the Duke, he sat up and tried to shake the sleep from his head.

"Your Grace," he answered. In his twenty-five years of working for the Midhams, he'd learnt to use the formal address until the Duke signalled otherwise. When Edward Fraine had succeeded his father a few years before there had been no drop in standards.

"We need to put on a good show tomorrow, Porter. Farlow has arranged for some officers to be on hand in case there's any trouble from those terrorists. We'll carry on just as we always have. Now Logan will you be able to find us our quarry?"

That was the signal he could relax the etiquette slightly. "I'll do my very best sir. Once we're out of sight of the Grange Seth will direct the pack towards the most likely coverts. I'm sure there'll be some good sport."

"As far as everyone's concerned we're following a trail," said the Duke.

"That's right, sir. I'll get one of my cull operatives to make a big show of laying the trail from his mountain bike. I'll be following behind everyone on the quad."

"Good. That should satisfy Farlow's men. But he did say there might be some interest in last week. All beyond his control apparently."

Logan wanted to reply immediately but held back. The Duke had just dropped him in it. Last week Logan had been told to produce a fox which he'd done. And now he was being told he'd be the one to pay the price for that. He had to suck it up and not answer back because the Duke owned him. He tried to keep his voice level.

"If there's any trouble, sir, I'll call Procter and Hargreaves, they're in my phone."

"Good man," replied the Duke then the phone went dead.

They'd only had to call on the solicitors a couple of times over the last fifteen years and the accusations had melted away. But public attitudes to hunting were hardening. It added to his paranoia and aggression: everyone was out to get him.

He heard Emma come in from work and that brought another surge of anger. If he wanted a cup of tea, he'd have to go down to the kitchen. He needed to put things back to how they were but there wasn't the time for that now. When he was dressed, he found Emma had left him some tea on the kitchen table. She was unpacking some shopping.

"Shall I make you something to eat, love?" She asked.

Her voice was cheerful but it was clear she wanted some distance between them.

"Give me an hour," he said, "I need to meet Seth at the kennels."

She turned around and caught his eye.

"Are you going to be disappearing off again?" He asked, "To your sister's?"

"Not this time, Logan, but we need to talk."

Those words, every time he heard them he wanted to spit on the floor.

"I might be in the spare room," she added.

"When are you going to give me a son?" It was an accusation. She didn't reply.

"Aye, well no point rushing home then is there."

He scraped his chair back and went out to the pick-up. The drive to the kennels only took five minutes and he found Seth was feeding the hounds. As always the bowls were emptied in a minute. They chatted about the Duke's call.

"I've got Mason to look as if he's laying a trail from his bike but there won't be any scent to confuse the pack," said Logan. And then they went through a list of locations: Farriers Hollow, Park Brook, Wet Sitch, Copper Fold and more. Some of these names were on the map and others were just known in the community of people who'd lived there for generations. They described a loop around Catchbrow Hill that they'd followed many times.

"We should have a fox in one of those coverts. So, cast the hounds around there until they pick up a scent," said Logan. "And I'll be using your quad," he added.

Seth nodded. He knew what to do. He'd be on horseback, the long whip in his hand. He'd keep the hounds in a tight bunch for the parade past the Grange a respectful distance behind the Masters and the Duke. Then they'd take the lead and let the hounds go when they had the scent of their quarry.

Chapter 31

Edward Fraine fastened the last button on his hunting jacket and admired himself in the full-length mirror. There wasn't space for a dressing room each in the master bedroom of the lodge and he was sharing with Arabella. Still, their wardrobe space was bigger than most people's guest rooms.

"The red one doesn't get much of an airing these days. You look good in it," she said.

The hunt had agreed to look a little less brash, more toned down in the era of trails and the Hunting Act. Black jackets hadn't been much of a sacrifice but today it felt like their very existence was under threat. Despite their carefully cultivated connections, *it's out of my control* meant they were at the whim of powers that didn't understand. Eddie had no doubt some of the field would baulk at the publicity they'd had. But those that remained were of one mind: they were fighting for their way of life. So, Eddie had a word with Jeremy Cockerill: stand proud in your red jacket. The male masters wore red and as a gesture to equality joint master Arabella was allowed a red collar on her black jacket.

They went down to a cooked breakfast. Unusual for a hunt day, Eddie was nervous.

"You've told everyone to bring their children?"

"Yes, darling," she replied, placing her hand over his reassuringly. "Even accounting for no-shows we should have a field of fifty. And the support? Everyone for miles around will be out. Her Grace even assented to the staff at the Grange coming out to see us off."

Eddie envisioned cheering crowds in front of one of England's finest country houses celebrating a centuries-old tradition. He tucked into his eggs, bacon and sausages. Some of the field had probably been up for hours, preparing their horses, getting them into trailers and driving to the Grange. But Eddie had people to do all that, it was his job to lead.

It had also been an early start for the sabs. As well as the local group two other groups were coming over to offer support. Midham was one of the biggest hunts in the country but there were rumours it was struggling with a lack of riders and local people starting to become vocal in their opposition. Jack had a good idea of the route they'd take from the Grange. His phone was beeping constantly and he passed the binoculars to Chloe so he could answer the messages. Once the field set off it would be difficult to keep up on foot as they'd found last time. So, Jack had given locations for his colleagues to wait and intervene if needed. Driving around the lanes wouldn't work as there'd be plenty of hunt supporters to block their progress.

Chloe looked down at the Grange, surrounded by fine parkland all planned by Capability Brown. It was a landscape that drew hordes of visitors, but for Chloe it was *unnatural*. The eye was drawn to follies and man-made ruins in the distance along with a few strategic mighty English oaks. It was all to send a message: look how much land I've got and how much money I must have to keep it looking so neat.

"Porter's arrived early and he's on a different quad bike, a red one with just the one box on the front," she said.

"Let's hope he hasn't got any bagged foxes in there," replied Jack. "I know there's a while to go but I don't see hundreds of riders down there, despite their desperate efforts to drum up support on social media. It looks more like a kindergarten with all the kids on ponies."

Chloe could see what he meant. It was all part of their education, straight from Pony Club to ripping foxes to pieces. Those who were there just for a day's riding would soon split leaving the hardened Hunt to do the killing.

"Look," she pointed, "they're getting a police escort."

Jack took the binoculars for a closer look at the fluorescently marked pick-up.

"That unmarked Discovery they've stopped alongside, they'll be the liaison officers. That's a joke they're just here to get evidence on us. Bloody hell, the masters have got the red coats out, they must mean business."

Jack explained the dress code and how Midham had changed to black until today. Unnoticed by the crowd below a man on a mountain bike rode onto the manicured park dragging a ball of rags on the end of a length of string.

"That's supposedly the trail layer for the benefit of the police," said Jack before sending a group message to tell everyone whom to identify.

Down below, Nathan Parbolde was getting more used to his attire and his horse. Eddie looked like he was bursting with pride and was busy greeting everyone who arrived. Eventually, the Duke made his way over. Their horses were used to the commotion and paid little attention to the jostling.

"Jonas said he'd had a word," offered Nathan.

It hadn't been an easy conversation for the Duke. He'd asked the accountant to repeat everything in simple terms. Eddie nodded and Nathan leant over so he could lower his voice.

"Straightforward really, Silver Shore Trading will send you £50k for the timber you supplied from Riverside Hagg. There won't be any tax liability because of the losses incurred in the conservation work."

"It's needed," said Eddie, still not quite understanding the transactions. "The field scrubs up well but everything else is looking shoddy and people need to be paid. If we rely on volunteers, it makes all of us look amateur."

"I'll be happy if I don't break my neck leaping over those hedges Eddie."

Emma was making her way around the riders carrying a tray full of small glasses filled with brandy, the stirrup cups, which were solid silver for the Masters and the Duke. Eddie raised his cup to Nathan.

"Your health. Pertemptant venandi!" he said repeating their motto and hoping to leave Parbolde struggling for a translation. But Nathan had been to the best schools and knew his Latin. He raised his glass.

"The thrill of the chase, Your Grace."

They heard a few rapid notes of the hunting horn and the dogs were gathered together. Emma appeared at exactly the right moment to take the glasses. The Duke made his way to the front. Arabella was in the centre, flanked by her joint Master Jeremy Cockerill on one side and the hunt Chairman the Duke of Midham on the other. They moved off the parkland and onto the road in front of the Grange, blocking all traffic and causing vehicles to pull onto the verge. A van driver was revving his engine, edging to get out but that just resulted in the police car following the parade to stop for a stern word. The police chose not to notice Logan Porter driving a different quad bike down the road, still without a number plate. The Grange staff applauded but there wasn't much enthusiasm from anyone else. Emma guessed half the riders were under 18 and the younger ones had ponies which belonged in a gymkhana. She passed her tray of glasses to another of the Grange staff and headed back to the farm shop.

The field left the road and crossed more parkland until they passed through a gate into a curving valley filled with trees. Out of sight of the Grange and the police, the masters pulled aside to let the pack of hounds run on.

Chloe and Jack looked on from their vantage point. The hounds had been quiet but suddenly their barks became frantic.

"That was quick," shouted Chloe and she joined Jack running down the slope towards the trees where a couple of other sabs were waiting. A fox burst out of the treeline and ran across the open ground in front of them. The sabs ran towards the route the fox had taken. One of the sabs sprayed citronella on the ground and Jack started rating the hounds even before they broke from the trees.

"Back to 'im!" he shouted repeatedly, interspersed with, "Leave it!"

He unfolded a homemade whip constructed of a light wood handle, some climbing rope and a bootlace which delivered the cracking sound.

One of the others, standing to the side pulled a hunting horn out of her rucksack and blew long mournful notes. As the hounds appeared, they hesitated and then stopped completely, the dogs looked around, confused by the differing instructions they were hearing. The terrain in the wood was not very rideable and the field had to take a longer route following the vehicle track. The first to appear was Logan Porter on his quad bike.

Chloe watched him swing around in a circle behind the sabs before stopping. Porter wore a green face covering revealing black, bulging eyes and long, dark eyebrows pasted to his forehead.

"Fuck off, you're trespassing!" he shouted.

Chloe couldn't stop herself laughing as she imagined the inside of his face-covering wet with spittle. Jack was busy sending another group message showing their location on a map and telling everyone the fox had headed west. The first riders appeared and they waited for the red jackets of the magistrate Jeremy Cockerill and the Duke. But it was the Lady Master who addressed them, "The police are here and I'll be reporting you for harassment and aggravated trespass." If it was meant to be a warning, it didn't work.

"Course you are, love," came the reply.

As they waited for the stragglers, it was clear the field would be less than half the number who left the Grange. The younger riders on their ponies and several parents separated from the rest.

After what seemed like an age, the *Hunt* continued with the hounds trying to follow the scent of the fox. Chloe heard short bursts of excited barking but then a hound would swing in a circle, scent lost. The sabs walked and sometimes ran to keep pace.

Chapter 32

Raven had been riding his mountain bike as well, not all the way from home, as he did drive a short distance. Chloe had briefed him and suggested the top of Catchbrow Hill would be a useful vantage point. She included him in the messaging so he had a running commentary. He wheeled the bike towards the top of the hill, counting the entrances to an extended badger sett. Many were sporting fresh piles of earth and stone from recent excavations. The terrain was a mix of shrubs, trees and rough grass. He decided to leave the bike in a holly thicket close to the top. There were already several people up there and he didn't know if they were friendly or not. He tried to keep an open mind but the group of six men thirty metres along the ridge exuded *hunt support*. They were dressed in well-worn greens with padded gilets or waxed jackets and a couple of flat caps thrown in. They all turned to scan him as he arrived. Then a couple of minutes later Raven sensed someone else approaching through the trees. It was Sergeant Carson, dressed in plain clothes. Raven nodded a greeting and Carson returned the same. There was an awkward silence as Raven reminded himself he hadn't wanted to speak to any police if he could help it.

"Lots of messages coming through," said Carson.

Raven's phone was pinging continuously.

"Don't worry, I'm not going to be looking over your shoulder," Paul continued then he leant in, "I'm here for interest and to action some of the information you sent us."

They spent a few minutes watching as the hunt approached a boggy hollow with low willow trees, some of them more like bushes. Raven sent a message: *Hunt at Wet Sitch*

Then he used his binoculars to take a closer look at the quad bike behind the riders.

"That's Logan Porter, on a different quad this time."

He offered the binoculars to Carson.

"I can see that, Raven."

Carson stepped back into the trees to make a call. His Constable Xan Philips answered.

"Sir?"

"Right, Xan you can go and check out Middle Beck Farm. Porter's involved with the hunt as expected, on a red quad bike this time. See if you can find the one that's been stolen."

Carson walked back to monitor the hunt.

"Our friends here have clocked you talking to me. If you've come in that unmarked Peugeot down there you might find it on bricks when you get back," observed Raven.

Carson turned to look at the group but suddenly they'd all turned the other way.

"They wouldn't dare," he said.

"Not if you were in uniform," replied Raven.

*

Xan was expecting the call and he'd parked a short distance from the farm. He turned off the surfaced road and made his way down a wide track to a collection of barns, some constructed from stone. Those had warped roofs and looked hundreds of years old, as did the farmhouse. There were also taller steel-framed buildings some with open sides. At first sight, he couldn't see the quad bike.

Xan knocked on the door of the farmhouse, but there was no reply. He kept trying for a couple of minutes and was about to give up when the door was opened by a stooped weather-beaten man who looked to be in his seventies.

"George Carter? I'm making some enquiries about a quad bike that was reported as stolen."

"Sorry, I was just having a sleep," said George. "Can you tell me what you're looking for?"

Xan explained they had evidence the quad bike was parked in one of the barns.

"Bastard never told me it was stolen," muttered George.

"Someone told you to hide the quad?" The constable asked.

The reply was clear, "Logan Porter. I hope you're not blaming me for any theft."

Xan didn't offer any reassurance.

"Can we take a look?"

George took them to the rear of the buildings and pointed to the vehicle in the open-sided shed just as Chloe had filmed. George explained that Logan had told him he'd leave the quad in the barn and didn't explain why.

"Sounds a bit odd, Mister Carter, why didn't you just say no?"

George screwed his face up until his eyes were slits.

"You don't say no to a man like Logan Porter." He spat on the ground. "He's all lah-di-dah the Duke this, the Duke that, but menacing like. I own this farm, but the Duke owns everything else around here. They'd just make my life a misery. Take the thing away I don't want it here."

"Right, I'll need a statement from you just so we're all clear about everything that's happened."

"I'll get the kettle on," said George.

Xan took some photos of the quad bike and the surroundings then went back to the car for his laptop and some crime scene tape. He wound strips of tape around the quad so it was clearly of police interest to anyone who looked.

George had made some tea which was remarkably drinkable.

"You here on your own?" Xan asked.

"I am. My wife died a few years back and the lad's got a better-paid job, can't blame him. I get some help in, but it's just me."

Then they started the long process of producing a written statement in the language the police required.

*

From the top of Catchbrow Hill, Raven could see several black-clad sabs close to the shrubs in Wet Sitch and others were jogging across the open fields to join them. The hounds were crisscrossing the area, picking up a scent but quickly losing it. Then all of a sudden, a fox leapt out of one of the shrubs. Immediately the huntsmen were sending rapid sharp notes from the hunting horn and Raven could hear shouts of "On, on, on!" and all that noise was mixed with the sabs shouting their own instructions by voice and using their own hunting horn to gather the hounds. The dogs were confused as was Raven. But it gave the fox a head start until the Hunt, hounds and sabs all followed. Raven needed to move position in order to keep watching and he noticed the hunt support had left the top of Catchbrow. Carson was busy on his phone. Raven moved over the brow of the hill to look down on the road and there were the four men approaching Carson's vehicle.

Raven pulled the video camera from his pocket and started filming. Their approach to the Peugeot was casual, hands in pockets. Then one of the groups looked down the road to the left and another looked to the right. There must have been some kind of signal because the remaining two bent down and took a wheel each, using the whole of their bodies to jab something into the tyres before yanking the implement sideways. Both men tucked their weapons away but one looked back up the slope before leaving. It was only a short distance to their pick-up and Raven concentrated on filming the registration plate. When he zoomed in even more, it took all his effort to stop the camera from shaking. The men drove away and only then did Raven notice Carson descending the top of the slope. Raven sent a message:

I was right about the hunt support and your tyres. I'll send a video later

Then he thought Carson might want to take some action immediately, so he watched the clip on the small camera screen and sent a description of the pick-up and the registration before heading back to his bike.

Carson could see the flat tyres from a distance, but before he could get to the vehicle he heard shouting, barking and the thump of a road traffic collision over to his left. He could see the hunt on the road and a few of the riders congregating around a saloon car that had stopped. Other riders and dogs followed by some of the sabs were continuing across the pasture on the far side of the road. He pulled out his phone to report everything to the control room and saw Raven Harley's messages which meant he could put out an alert for the pick-up. No one could tell him if the liaison officers and squad car that had been deployed earlier had just been on ceremonial duties or if they were still in the area. Carson buried his anger at the thugs who'd damaged his car and the lack of colleagues. He started jogging down the road towards the RTC.

A few minutes later, he was squeezing by horses and elbowing past a crowd of people who had congregated on the road. There were actually two cars with front-offside wings locked together. One of the drivers was motionless behind the wheel where an airbag had obviously inflated. In front of that vehicle were four hounds. Three were dead and the fourth was being cradled by one of the sabs.

Carson waved his ID and shouted, "Police, move back!" The crowd responded slowly. The nearest driver had climbed out of his vehicle and was leaning against the driver's door.

"Are you going to be ok for half an hour?" Paul asked.

The reply took some effort: "Yes, you need to take a look at the old lady there," he said pointing at the other car. Paul traversed the wreckage and tried the driver's door which was buckled. It wouldn't open. It was a three-door hatchback and he tried the passenger door, but that was clearly locked and he assumed the boot would be as well. He phoned his control room with an update and requested an ambulance and fire crew with cutting equipment, urgently.

One of the sabs had come over, face covering pulled down.

"I'm Jed," he said. "Can I help?"

Paul's head was spinning with everything that had happened and he told himself to focus.

"This lady is the priority. We have to get inside," he said out loud. At least he had something of a plan now.

Jed wrenched a large rock from the dry-stone wall at the side of the road.

"Shall I?" He asked.

Paul nodded and with one swing of the boulder Jed smashed the passenger window then pulled down his sleeve and tried to sweep the glass from the seat. They managed to open the door and Paul clambered in.

*

Xan was working his way through the statement in George Carter's kitchen when they saw the flash of ginger-red streak across the field behind.

"Aye, she'll be heading for the setts in the covert there," said George.

Xan felt like he needed a translator. A few moments later, everything was clear as the hounds appeared followed by three riders all moving in the direction of the fox.

"My cows are in that field!" shouted George as he scraped back his chair. Xan followed him outside to see half a dozen sabs running towards the covert.

Some of the dogs had peeled off and were chasing the cows sending them into panic and George was hobbling across the field trying to calm his animals.

Xan took a more measured pace as his radio requested his location and his phone beeped with messages. The thick walls of the farmhouse must have cut off all signals. He had to sort out this situation before he could help Carson.

The hounds were barking frantically at the large well-worn entrance to a badger sett. Guarding the tunnel were six masked sabs, Jack and Chloe among them. The riders were waiting and turned when they heard a quad bike enter the field. It was Logan Porter arriving with his terriers and spades to dig out the fox. But when Porter saw the uniformed officer he paused, unsure what to do.

Xan had received very little training in the Hunting Act and the implication had been clear: don't get involved. And if you do get involved your job is to protect rural communities going about their lawful activities. But Xan couldn't see much in the way of lawful activity. That gave him a chance to speak.

"You're in breach of section one of the Hunting Act. Go home. Now!"

They didn't move. Xan pointed towards the road.

"I've got to attend a road traffic collision over there with a possible fatality and I'm not wasting any more time here. You," he said pointing at Jeremy Cockerill in his red jacket, "get down off your horse; I'm arresting you for obstruction."

That did the trick and Cockerill pulled his horse around and started to leave. Seth gathered the hounds and followed. Porter on his quad had disappeared as well. Xan left the sabs at the badger sett without speaking a word to them then he made his way back to the farmhouse to collect his laptop. George was still trying to calm his animals.

Xan made his way towards the collision, parked as close as possible and left the blue lights flashing. Paul was still in the front of the crashed vehicle, trying to monitor the driver. He leant back in the passenger seat when Xan arrived.

"She's breathing and I can feel a pulse but she's not conscious," said Paul. "I don't know if that's because of the collision or if the crash brought on a medical problem. She might have damaged her neck so I don't want to move her. Any other ideas?"

"I think you've got it covered, sir. I'll ask around for a blanket and start taking some details from the witnesses," replied Xan.

Raven was still near the top of the slope. He'd witnessed and filmed the hunt spilling out onto the road without a care for any vehicles that might be around. The collision seemed inevitable. He messaged Chloe:

Hope. you are ok. Total carnage on the road, crashed cars, dogs killed and looks like one driver seriously injured. Hunt has disappeared now.

He didn't have to wait long for a reply:

Yes, ok, we missed all that. Managed to save a fox. Police did their job for once x

Then a follow up:

Fox hiding in a badger sett. We're just waiting to see if scumbags return

Raven replied:

Pretty sure they're keeping out of the way. They'll be back at the kennels by now. Police taking statements here. Ambulance arrived.

Raven watched the scene a little longer. Traffic was backing up from both sides and drivers were struggling to turn around. A fire engine was having difficulty passing all the cars. It was a scene of chaos. The huntsmen seemed to think they could act out their roles in a sealed bubble, keeping their idea of the countryside alive by chasing and killing vermin. But that bubble had burst spilling rancid pus into the lives of the people who happened to be on that road at the wrong time. The Hunt had poisoned everything in their path.

Over to his left, he saw a couple of riders moving away from the road. The Duke in his red jacket was very obvious and he was accompanied by his partner. They were leaving others to take the blame.

Raven decided to head back as well glad he could ride off-road. He'd send the video files to Sergeant Carson later.

Chapter 33

Word of the crash had filtered through to the farm shop. People spread the word on the pretext of making sure their friends avoided the road that was blocked. But they all knew the Hunt was responsible. Emma didn't hear any criticism, that wasn't done in these parts but she had a sense that people wanted to say more.

She expected Logan to be delayed and he'd miss his session in the pub. Catching a fox was the reason to celebrate all afternoon. And not catching one wasn't much different. She wasn't sure if buying a drink from the shop was a good idea but felt as if she needed to make some kind of gesture towards him. So, she left work at 4.00 p.m. with a carrier bag of beer and whisky. The house was empty and she set about making some food, a pie that would keep in the oven.

Seth had managed to round up *a dozen couple* of hounds. He'd been told four had been killed on the road. That left four unaccounted. He was changing out of his hunting clothes when Logan turned up driving Seth's quad bike.

"Duke wants to see us at six," said Logan.

"Not surprised," replied Seth. "I've got two couple missing. Need to get out and have a look before they wander into the path of any more cars."

"Get your togs on and hop on the back of here," said Logan.

Seth stuffed a hunting horn into his jacket and they set off. They were two men on a one-person quad, no number plate and no helmets driving on a public road. But nobody was going to stop them, not around here. They made their way towards Middle Beck Farm, pausing frequently to blow the hunting horn and shouting as loud as they could to gather the dogs.

The hounds eventually responded to the calls and ran behind the quad as Logan drove back towards the kennels. Soon a car was coming towards them and Logan swerved into the middle of the road, forcing it to stop. He didn't bother telling the driver the road was blocked further on. At the kennels, Seth put the hounds with the rest of the pack then they swapped to the pick-up and headed to the lodge, making their way to a small office at the side.

The Duke brought a cloud of whisky fumes with him before slumping into a chair. Seth and Logan remained standing.

"Well?"

It was Seth who replied. "The hounds lost the scent around Copper Fold but a few had strayed further and a different fox shot out of Farriers Hollow. That's what split up the hounds. I was at the front with Mr Cockerill. The fox was straight across the road and we followed. I'd no idea about the crash."

The Duke looked at Logan. "And you?"

"I was taking a slightly different route to get the quad through some gates. But I could tell they were all heading for Middle Beck so that's where I went as well."

The colour rose in the Duke's cheeks and he spat his words.

"I pay you to keep those hounds under control. I still don't know if one of the drivers is dead or not. But for certain there's an injunction heading our way to keep us off the public highway. It's a total fuck up and I'll have to spend I don't know how much picking up the pieces."

Now he was gasping for breath.

"All when I made it very clear today had to be a complete success. Get out the pair of you."

"Yes, Your Grace," they said in unison.

Eddie spent a couple of minutes calming down then he heard his phone ping, a WhatsApp message from Jonas the accountant.

50k transferred to your account

"It'll take a lot more than that to sort out this shambles of a hunt," muttered Eddie to the empty room.

*

Logan and Seth maintained their chastened look until they were out on the road away from the lodge. It was Seth who spoke first, "I've had the express instructions to make sure the hounds keep up with the fox, no matter what, so we get the kill. And when I do that I get a bollocking for not holding the hands of the stragglers. For fuck's sake, it's a hunt!"

"He needs to dip in his pockets does the Duke," said Logan. "We can't do everything he needs more paid staff, not bloody amateurs."

The dressing down was painful and humiliating, whatever they did was wrong and it was always Logan and his colleagues who shouldered the blame.

"Fuck it," said Logan. "Are you going to the pub?"

"I've got to feed them," said Seth. "And at the moment, I like those hounds better than them fuckers in the Grange. Some lads are going to collect the dogs that were killed on the road when the police have finished. That's one less job for me. Then those hounds will be going straight in the grinder."

Dead hounds used to feed the hunt pack didn't even register as worthy of comment. Logan dropped Seth at the kennels and then headed back to his house. As he went in Emma muted the TV.

"Food's ready when you are and there's some beer and whisky on the side," she said.

He splashed his face and hands in the kitchen sink, drying himself on a tea towel. Then he sat down at the table and started on the drink.

*

It was shaping up to be a long day for Sergeant Carson. A specialist team had arrived to record the position of the vehicles involved in the collision and collect as much data as they could. The ambulance crew had managed to revive the female driver working on the theory the impact, seatbelt and airbag had triggered a cardiac event resulting in her losing consciousness. The last Paul heard was the lady speaking very loudly about that *bloody horse* in the road.

They recovered a dashcam from the other vehicle and the second driver confirmed a horse and rider appeared from nowhere, in the middle of the road and the lady had swerved into him to avoid the horse. And there were dogs everywhere. Paul had asked his colleagues at the station to search for complaints of the hunt on public roads. And the sab who helped him confirmed they'd logged several incidents with the police. The Hunt was a limited company supposedly going about the lawful business of trail hunting. There were lots of laws to stop protesters from interfering but not many options to stop a repeat of this fiasco. Requesting a court for an injunction against the Hunt looked like the best course of action.

The owner of the pick-up Raven had reported to him had a conviction for driving without insurance. That looked like a good place to start. Given a police vehicle had been damaged, he'd have no problem devoting some resources to get those thugs prosecuted.

Chapter 34

Raven took some tea and a plate of toast back to bed. Sunday stretched out in front of him. He yawned and tried to shake off the exhaustion. When he'd returned home after the hunt, he made himself send the video files to the sergeant hoping the police could get a prosecution for the damage. He'd have a word with Chloe later but the videos weren't for social media just yet.

He'd slept for ten hours and only now realised how frantic the last couple of weeks had been. He still felt on edge all the time, expecting the next thing to happen and fear was constantly churning in his mind. It drained him, especially as he'd tried to carry on as if nothing had happened.

His relationship with Becky was over. He didn't even want to be friends but she was going to be in his life, an arm's length business deal, mutually beneficial. She knew how to tap into his need, finding his weakness. He was coming to realise it wasn't about putting up defences and barriers but accepting who he was and hanging onto the most important thing in his life. That was Chloe if she'd have him.

Today there'd be Becky and Madison from Kerbstone, a pub lunch and smiles all around until he signed up. He tried not to be cynical, maybe they really wanted to help.

Meanwhile, he had a couple of hours and the house could be cleaner. Chloe could come around any time. The laundry basket was full and it was a good drying day. But maybe doing the sheets was a bit too hopeful.

At lunchtime, he drove to the Dragon and found Becky and Madison at a corner table, a couple of menus open in front of them. They all opted for soft drinks and ordered a selection of sandwiches and bowls of chips.

Madison started to explain how Kerbstone worked with activists. She was in her twenties, blonde hair pulled back, had kind eyes and her smile seemed genuine. Becky was trying to look cool but Raven sensed she was hanging on Madison's every word. This was Becky's world.

"I'd expect you to be wary of us," Madison said. "Most activists spend their lives battling against the whole culture of big companies with lots of money. Let me show you what we've done with other people, it's not much more than putting our logo at the end of one of your videos."

Raven looked at some examples which seemed ok.

"Then we'd want something more personal about you. Our customers would be bored with an in-depth interview. But if you decide to go for it, we could go out somewhere this afternoon and record a few one-liners," she continued.

The food arrived and Raven tucked in. Soon his companions were offering their leftovers which went down just as well.

"That's filled a hole," he said then he started to spell out what he wanted. "I've had a lot of trouble over the last few weeks and I don't know where I am with it all. I need somebody to back me up, who I can trust."

Raven pulled a tablet from his rucksack and showed them the video of the masked intruder breaking down his door.

"Oh my God, what happened?" Madison asked.

Raven explained about standing at the top of the stairs with the chainsaw and how the intruder had fallen backwards.

"In the middle of the night? Wow, that's some image," she said completely captivated.

Then Becky leant over to Madison and spoke in a stage whisper, "He sleeps in the buff you know…"

Both women shrieked with laughter and after a moment Raven joined in as well. He had been clothed that night but he didn't want to spoil the image. After the horrors of the last fortnight, it was good to lose himself and if everyone was flirting, why not?

The laughter subsided and Madison put on her work face again.

"Sorry," she started. "That's where we can help, that story is absolute dynamite."

"There is more," he said, "and it explains where I am at the moment."

Raven showed them a second video of his arrest a few days before.

"It was the same officers who came round to my house. I've got a solicitor on it but they explained it will take years and they'll probably end up having to sue the police for assault rather than the police taking action themselves. I don't know how much that's going to end up costing?"

"Right," said Madison serious now. "That would be part of the deal we'd cover your legal expenses, within reason. And our legal department could help move things along sometimes solicitors can be very slow. So money…"

Madison explained they could have an arrangement where Raven was paid every month and either party could terminate at any time but Kerbstone would keep and use any material they'd already received. The amount they were offering was what Raven earned in a good month so there was a chance to double his income. And that was something he could offer Chloe if she didn't go back to social work. There were more options for them, if there was going to be *them* and that had to be a good thing.

They had enough leads to connect the devices and Raven transferred the files.

"I trust you to do the right thing with those," he said, realising he'd agreed to work with them.

Madison wanted to film somewhere a short walk from the road with some rocks and moorland as a background. They set off in a two-vehicle convoy to High Ridge. In a lay-by on the edge of the moors, Raven was offered a range of t-shirts, jackets and trousers and he left most in the back of the van. He just swapped his fleece and they walked up to some rocks.

Becky set up the tripod and camera while Raven made himself comfortable on a rock.

"I'll probably ask the same question a few times, Raven, just say what comes into your head."

They did a sound check where they heard Raven had toast for breakfast. Then Madison came over and started fussing with his thick blue-black hair. It was cut short, almost shaved at the sides and longer on top and she couldn't decide whether that should be flattened or wayward. She settled on the latter.

"Your left profile is your best, just twist around slightly to the right. Look at me, not the camera."

Raven did his best to oblige but felt uncomfortable with this sort of attention.

"Why do you do it?"

"*For the animals.*"

"They put the frighteners on you by beating down your door."

"*That's not going to stop me.*"

"Who's going to win?"

"*Nature.*"

"Why do you keep going?"

"*To get justice.*"

After twenty minutes, Raven wasn't sure if he sounded genuine or pretentious. But Madison seemed happy.

"Thanks, Raven," she said eventually. "I've done a few of these with people from very different backgrounds and you're all driven by the same values. It's hard to describe in a few words, but we're messing up the planet big time, most people don't even know that but you guys *do know* and you put yourselves on the line to stop it."

That sounded genuine and it did make Raven think about why he did all this stuff. They agreed to sort the paperwork over the coming week.

By now, Raven had a much clearer idea of what was involved but did Kerbstone know?

"They'll be organising petitions against you and they'll have an army of trolls dig up all sorts of lies about me, to try and discredit the whole thing," Raven said. "And at the same time, they'll have a few people take a more subtle approach, pretending to agree then spreading doubts, saying there's more pressing problems in the world than stopping the shooting industry. I don't even know who *they* are, but someone's paying PR experts a lot of money."

"I've seen your video about the pheasant shoot. That bunch of so-and-so's aren't going to buy anything from us, ever. Our customers live on social media and they know all about trolls. That's why the videos you've given me are so important. They show what happens to people who won't be silenced. Our supporters want to be you, as brave as you. I can see it's making you cringe but you'll get used to it."

"Right," said Raven. "I need a walk."

And he headed out onto the moors. He still wasn't sure if he was doing the right thing with Kerbstone. But the conversation had made him think about what and who he was up against. After a while, he realised it wasn't helping to be in that world, that'd consumed him over the past few weeks. So, he sat down in the heather, planting himself on the ground. He closed his eyes and felt what was around, the smell of damp earth, springy stems of the dwarf shrubs, the wind on his face and the burbling calls of grouse in the distance. His mind would fill with the same problems and he'd pull himself back to everything around him, now.

He wasn't clock watching but eventually it was time to move on and that movement had its own rhythm and pleasure. It was a brief sojourn into a world of *could-be* and it was a bird of prey that brought him back to *what-is*. A female hen harrier was scouring the moor, flying about five metres above the heather, dropping down at the sight of a vole then continuing its search. It was a beautiful bird but if it was around for any time the gamekeepers would know about it soon enough. Through binoculars, Raven could see this female didn't have a satellite transmitter which made it even more vulnerable. The harrier wouldn't take on a fully grown grouse at this time of year, but that didn't make any difference to the gamekeepers. The killing of predators leading up to next year's breeding season had already started and the gamekeepers would exterminate every bird of prey if they could get away with it.

Raven had to move around to keep track of the harrier and as the light was fading another harrier appeared as a silhouette so it was difficult to determine the sex. Male harriers were much lighter and Raven fancied that's what he was watching. Eventually, both birds headed towards a small wooded valley. It took Raven a moment to remember the name: Fletchers Sitch.

Finn Sutherland kept himself still in the heather. Dressed in full camouflage, including hat and face covering he was invisible to the world around. Certainly, the two harriers hadn't seen him and neither had the man wandering all over his moor. He was sure it was Raven Harley. If Finn had been back on his home patch in Scotland, he'd have dispatched those harriers by now. But down here, the moors were full of people. He'd had his instructions from Parbolde: carry on, do your job, get me lots of grouse, we've got lawyers to deal with the police. Doing his job meant not getting caught. Tomorrow he'd rely on those lawyers to do their work but today was his domain. He'd spotted solitary harriers on this part of the estate, their presence had attracted others and that made his job easier. These birds gathered together in the autumn and winter in communal roosts, Fletchers Sitch was a new one.

Finn's WhatsApp group had been ranting about Raven Harley and how to get rid of him. Plenty had been done over the last few weeks but he just kept on coming, wrecking lives. The Duke, Parbolde and Tranchard didn't participate in the group, but it was obvious what they wanted. A plan started to form in Finn's mind, but he needed to act now. He stood up and pretended not to notice Raven in the distance. Instead, Finn made a show of pointing his binoculars down towards the lip of the valley where the harriers were settling down to roost in a patch of long heather and rushes. Then he turned and walked back to his all-terrain vehicle that was parked in a stream gully. The trap had been set.

Raven was shocked to see the gamekeeper appear and it looked like he'd stood to gain a better view of the harriers. The birds were roosting together, Raven had heard about this, but no one would ever share the locations. And the gamekeeper had seen it as well. It was obvious what was going to happen, maybe they'd wait until more harriers were attracted to the same roost. But there was only ever going to be one outcome around here: those birds would be killed and it would happen at night. Raven had all the night vision gear as well and he'd make sure those birds were safe.

Chapter 35

Sergeant Paul Carson knocked on the glass door of Superintendent Farlow's office. After a moment, Farlow waved him in and offered a seat.

"I've read the reports from the weekend," Farlow started. "Quite some disruption from the RTC and of course, it made a lot of news, not just the usual social media but a slot on the TV bulletin as well. It was a severe disruption to the public when it's our job to keep things running smoothly. And I see amongst all that one of our vehicles was damaged."

"Not just damaged, sir, it was intentional, two tyres slashed on the unmarked car I've been using for my other work," replied Carson.

"Where are we with all that?"

"The RTC: dashcam footage shows it was caused by a huntsman on horseback going straight into the road along with several hounds, causing the vehicles to swerve into each other. One driver lost consciousness but is ok now."

"Can we identify the huntsman?"

"It's Jeremy Cockerill, the magistrate and I've informed the chief magistrate's office, especially as we'll be interviewing him soon regarding breaches of the Hunting Act. I've had a word with Traffic and they put me on their contact in the Highways Agency. Looks like everyone has agreed this warrants an injunction against the Hunt using the public highway. So, I'll liaise with the appropriate people and we'll get something before the High Court as a matter of urgency."

"And the vehicle damage?"

"Four white male suspects drove away in a pick-up registered to Archie Cartwright who's a temporary gamekeeper at Fairview Mill pheasant shoot. We'll interview him in a day or two. The catalogue of rural crime continued with criminal damage to the Torsen family van."

"Forensics has taken a look at the tyres of the camper," Paul added. "Looks identical to the damage to our vehicle and there were several fingerprints and a clear palm print above the wheel arches of the van. You'd expect that but Cartwright did lean against our police vehicle before doing the tyres, so we need the results from the van to place him there."

"Is there more?" Farlow asked.

"I know the badger cull has grabbed a lot of our resources but one of the protesters has come forward, with some reluctance to provide dashcam footage of Cartwright climbing into his pick-up a few hundred yards from the camper. The timing fits in with Torsen's statement: 2:03 a.m."

"Why the reluctance?" Farlow asked.

"The witness also recorded what she described as police brutality at the badger cull that evening, an incident involving PC Colne."

Farlow tried his hardest to keep an expressionless face. But Carson and others would know Tom Colne was one of Farlow's close circles. Farlow had risen through the ranks smoothly but there was a rough edge to Colne that had been useful, now he'd overstepped the line in words and actions too many times. The chief made it clear Farlow's job and influence were teetering, any sign of favouritism and he'd be out.

"Get a full statement from the protester, all the incidents and pass the complaints onto Professional Standards, tell them that's come from me. Anything else?"

"DNA from the break-in at Raven Harley's house has been identified as from Ryan Walker, another gamekeeper at the pheasant shoot," said Carson who kept a steady gaze at the superintendent. Farlow's association with the shoot was looking more and more damaging. Farlow was shaking his head from side to side, he couldn't brazen this out.

"Good work, Sergeant," said the superintendent. "Obviously, you know I attended the shoot so it's appropriate that you deal directly with the chief on this. Follow the evidence and if you have enough to bring charges then do that. Keep me informed of any outcomes and I'll make sure everything runs as smoothly as possible."

Paul left the office thinking it was the only thing Farlow could have said. Paul would make sure their conversation was reported to the chief and it was clear any interference would be bad news for Farlow.

Paul went back to the main office and made his way to Xan's desk.

"Has Sutherland arrived?" He asked his constable.

"He has indeed along with his solicitor. We're honoured to have the young Mister Hargreaves, Julian."

Proctor and Hargreaves were the go-to solicitors for landowners and the monied and they prided themselves on successive generations continuing the family firm.

"The videos and photographs are all on here," Xan continued, showing his sergeant a tablet.

The officers made their way to the interview room and as they entered solicitor and suspect stopped their whispered conversation.

"Sorry, did you need more time?" Paul asked.

"No we'd like to clear this up as soon as possible," said the solicitor.

Paul and Xan sat down and started the recording device. Everyone introduced themselves and Paul explained the interview was being conducted under caution. Finn Sutherland was lounging in his chair, looking smugly confident, he'd dressed in a gamekeeper's shoot day uniform of jacket, trousers and waistcoat in shades of green and brown but he'd undone the top button of his shirt and loosened his tie. *I can dress smartly but I don't need to for you lot.*

Julian Hargreaves looked familiar and Paul realised they'd probably seen him on the video of the shoot, wearing his tweeds.

"Mister Sutherland, can you confirm you are the head gamekeeper at Fairview Mill pheasant shoot?" Paul asked.

"No comment," replied Sutherland.

"That's not a problem for us we can get your wife to confirm your employment details." The comment was aimed to antagonise.

"You leave her out of it, you bastard," said Finn Sutherland, not so cool now, leaning over the desk, weight on his forearms. Hargreaves placed a hand on Sutherland's arm. *Calm down.*

"We can confirm your employment from any number of sources if you don't want to cooperate," pressed Carson. "And who knows what we might uncover when we start interviewing people?"

Hargreaves intervened. "I appreciate you have a job to do officer but as far as I'm aware we're talking about allegations of minor offences that aren't even recordable. If you have evidence I think we should all see it."

Carson knew the solicitor was trying to sow doubt, that this interview was a waste of everyone's time. But just like Sutherland, he had to keep cool. He nodded to Xan.

"Constable Philips, can you play the first section of the video?"

Xan did as asked. Their technicians had slowed down the footage and highlighted the sparrowhawk flying around the pheasant pens.

"We have an expert who confirms the species as sparrowhawk, a protected bird of prey," said Paul.

Xan continued the video showing the commotion as the bird tried to free itself from the trap.

"It goes on a long time doesn't it," said Paul. "There are enough frames of this video showing the sparrowhawk through the foliage to confirm the bird has both legs crushed in the trap and it tries to free itself for four and a half minutes before collapsing when the bird is left dangling by its broken legs."

Paul was careful not to express his disgust.

The next section of the video was again enhanced and showed Finn Sutherland, clearly identified by his face, removing the bird and trap.

Sutherland looked towards his solicitor who remained impassive.

"Why did you use a trap that's been illegal for over fifty years, Mister Sutherland?" Paul asked.

"No comment," was the reply.

"Next, we're going to look at this Larsen trap," said Paul. "A certified veterinary surgeon gave her expert opinion, following an examination of the crow that was found in the trap. The bird was suffering unnecessarily due to neglect. The crow had to be euthanised and a post-mortem examination confirmed the vet's observations."

"Very interesting officer, but how is that related to my client?" Hargreaves asked.

Paul knew that was crucial to obtaining a conviction. Sutherland had to be linked to the trap. Xan continued with the video that showed a gamekeeper approaching the trap. Two birds could be seen inside with the footage slowed and highlighted. The gamekeeper reached down to pull one bird from the trap, leaving the other in place, to draw yet more crows into captivity. The captured bird was then beaten against the vehicle. Again Sutherland's face and the vehicle registration were highlighted.

Paul realised everyone was waiting for him to speak. He'd been thinking about the poem he'd heard at the school fundraiser and the plight of the birds. Willow's message had been innocent and genuine. And who could argue with that? Except for part of a community telling Carson *we're fighting for our way of life, they're taking it away from us.* But Raven Harley and his friends were only showing the reality of what happened in this *way of life.* All the video footage had come from the activists. Wasn't it the job of Paul and his colleagues to gather evidence? He found himself shaking his head. Then he said quietly:

"If we decide to charge you, Mister Sutherland, we'll photograph you and have an expert make a comparison between you and the person shown in these videos. Is there anything you want to say?"

Finn Sutherland remained quiet so it was his solicitor who spoke:

"We can provide our own expert, officer. And I think you'll find you're wasting valuable resources on a trivial case you can never hope to win."

The interview was voluntary so Paul thanked them for attending and asked Xan to show them out. Unless the politics had changed overnight the chief would agree to charge Sutherland.

*

Julian Hargreaves and Finn Sutherland didn't speak until they were sitting in Hargreaves Volvo making the short journey back towards the solicitor's office.

Hargreaves noticed his client's Scottish accent grew stronger as he became more stressed. Finn muttered a few barely comprehensible words.

Do you think they'll charge me? Hargreaves assumed.

"Farlow seems to think this is all coming from the chief constable, if that's the case then the usual concerns from the Crown Prosecution Service will be overruled. So, I'm afraid, yes, it does look likely. We'll take a look at their evidence, but on both counts it looks like there are clear images of your face which doesn't help. We can argue the crow was fine the day before and you've been trained in using those traps. We'll need an expert to look at the sparrowhawk footage to see if we can cast some doubt on the species and what's actually happened. I take it the police didn't find the traps you used?"

"Buried. Nobody will find them," replied Sutherland.

"Good because they DNA test them these days. How the hell did someone get a camera in there, I thought you had CCTV?"

"Fucked if I know. There was nothing on my cameras."

Sutherland shifted in his seat. They were in the uncomfortable confines of a multi-storey car park. Hargreaves had driven up to level 2 and they were looking at Sutherland's pick-up with a ticket on the windscreen.

"Ah," said the solicitor, "it's because you've parked across two bays. Don't think our company discount will cover that."

Hargreaves left his client tearing the wrapping from the parking notice and the solicitor made sure he parked neatly between two white lines.

When Finn Sutherland finally made it home, he remained in the pick-up, staring across the moor but not seeing it. If he was convicted, he wouldn't be able to use the General Licences for killing crows and all the other vermin and he'd probably lose his gun licence as well. He'd lose his job, his house and his vehicle. There was one person to blame for all that and he needed to be taken out of the picture permanently. Finn ran through the scenarios until he had one that was foolproof.

Lily's car pulled in behind his. He lowered the window as she walked up.

"You're back, love," she said. "Are you all set for tomorrow? I'll sort you some food then I have to dash down to the hotel to meet Mister Tranchard."

"The beaters will be there, they want their money. I just have to be there nice and early to send them off to the right place."

Lily blew her cheeks out. "I hope so it's been a nightmare with all the cancellations then trying to get new bookings."

Lily walked over to the house and Finn realised she hadn't asked how it had gone with the police. They both assumed it would all go away like it usually did. He phoned Jayden, one of the temporary keepers, and arranged to meet at Fairview to go through everything for the shoot tomorrow. Finn's team of four was now two with Ryan sent up north and Archie being questioned for criminal damage.

*

At 7.00 p.m., Gerald Tranchard sat in the lounge of the Midham Stables Country House Hotel. Since he'd been dragged into the cesspit of Parbolde's estate management, he might as well have some compensation. The glass of malt whisky in his hand was a start. He'd received a message from Lily Sutherland saying there was another last-minute cancellation for the shoot. They were scrambling to fill places after a block booking from an investment firm had been withdrawn. All because of the publicity in the last week. Tranchard needed order in his life. That had nothing to do with the comfort of a routine and all about those around him knowing their place. If they didn't see that, they had to be shown. The only people he respected were those who had the wealth and knew how to use it. Ancestry helped. He'd given his instructions and they'd been carried out for no result other than creating more problems. Now he felt stabs of panic as everything was spiralling out of control. The pheasant shoot, the hunt and even the badger cull were all a demonstration of how his elite controlled England. There was no purpose other than to show they *could* and they *did* and they wanted everyone to see. But what was on show right now was chaos.

It was Parbolde's shoot but Tranchard was feeling used. The estate had needed new gamekeepers *and* an agent to do all the running around. Instead, Parbolde brought in his trusted, experienced keeper from Scotland who was turning out to be a liability. Tranchard was lured by the prospect of easy money for a little paperwork and recruitment of staff. He expected his cut for minimal effort and if that led to a paper loss for the business it was filled with Parbolde's dirty money. It wasn't just the money that was soiled, Tranchard felt as if he was up to his knees in a midden. Instead of punters begging to be let in, he had to dream up inducements for their patronage.

So, here he was offering dinner bed and breakfast in the hotel as part of a reduced-price package and he had to play the gracious host. It was humiliating. He hoped the clients knew one end of a gun from the other but maybe that was too much to ask. The hotel was owned by the Duke and Tranchard had a free room, it was the least Eddie could do after all the favours he'd received. Tranchard would get the Sutherlands to do all the work and he'd messaged Lily to ask if she could fill the vacant seat at the table. It would help to have someone else to share the hosting duties. Lily had just walked in, she was wearing a long dress low cut at the front and Tranchard never realised she was so attractive. He waved her over, forgetting his disgust at the situation.

"You're a life saver, Lily," he said turning on the charm. "Come and have a drink."

She perched on the edge of a seat, looking nervous.

"I'm so sorry about the bookings Mr Tranchard, this latest one wouldn't transfer the money and I had to phone him to confirm he wasn't coming."

Tranchard summoned a waiter. "A glass of champagne for my colleague," he requested then he turned his eyes back to Lily noticing a red flush had appeared on her chest. Her soft Scottish accent, deference and embarrassment brought him a sigh of pleasure. For a moment order had been restored and he wondered when he should mention his room.

It didn't occur to Tranchard that Lily was eyeing an overweight, balding man in his fifties who couldn't take his eyes off her breasts. He was her boss and it was obvious what he was thinking. His creepiness was embarrassing and she hoped she'd be able to nudge him away without making things worse for Finn. Tranchard would be paying the lawyer's fees, but there was a limit to what she would do. She had a good life with Finn, better than most but she had some self-respect as well. She was here to charm the guests and smooth the way for a successful shoot and that was all.

A flute was placed delicately on the table between them. Lily took a sip and Tranchard raised his glass.

"Don't worry about that. It gives me the pleasure of your company, Lily. And do call me Gerald, cheers."

Lily hoped her smile looked genuine. She leant back in her chair for a minute before the guests arrived.

A couple of hours later, Tranchard surveyed their private dining room, hands resting on his belly after partridge followed by venison. Lily was in full swing recounting stories from the estate in Scotland. It was a good job she was here because if he'd spent another minute talking to these people his contempt would have spilled over. As expected, some of them didn't even own their own guns and his gamekeepers would have to make full use of the weapons in the gun room at the lodge. There were still ten thousand pheasants to shoot and that wouldn't require any skill even for these novices. The clients were a source of cash but these people would never *belong*. He was bored and angry. All this had become necessary after the fuck-ups caused by one person who'd had plenty of warnings, but wouldn't listen. Finn Sutherland had some ideas which needed to be fleshed out. Sutherland's anger matched his own and that was necessary for the gamekeeper to do what was required.

Through the meal, Tranchard had been sent alerts and messages about a promotion from a clothing company featuring Raven Harley. There'd been some response already on social media, but amongst all that Tranchard now needed to push a narrative that would prepare and justify what needed to happen.

Chapter 36

When Raven had finished work, he went home to unload his tools and grab a bite to eat. He kept on checking his phone but the messages from Chloe hadn't changed.

I'm heading to Fletcher's Sitch. Hen Harriers roosting and gamekeepers around. Come along if you're free.

Love to, but arranged to go out to badger cull—there's no sign of an end. I've been called into the office tomorrow. Wish me luck!

Raven knew he was obsessing. Chloe wouldn't change her mind and he had to go on his own. He took a close look at the map which showed Fletcher's Sitch as a small wooded valley just off one of the roads that traversed the uplands. He decided to park at the far side of the road and approach from the opposite direction to Sunday's hike.

The cameras and a flask went into a small rucksack then he noticed the clothes from Kerbstone piled up on a chair. Already the wrappers were gathering dust and his mind wandered to keeping the house clean in case Chloe visited. He was back to obsessing and dithering so he shook his head, grabbed the rucksack and left. He had an hour to get in place before twilight.

His plan turned out to be a good one with a parking spot off the road where the van wouldn't be seen. He crossed the road a couple of hundred metres from Fletcher's Sitch and worked his way up a parallel stream bed where he was hidden from view. As that gully dried out on the moortop, he had a view down across to the deep heather that had attracted the harriers. He settled with his body hidden by the gully and his arms and head above scanning the area in the last of the light.

It wasn't long before the harriers showed up and a third bird appeared to join the two he'd seen on Sunday. It was difficult to tell in the fading light but there seemed to be one pale grey adult male and two brown females, though they could both be juveniles at this time of year. He managed to capture the birds in flight on his camera.

Raven switched to the night vision scope which also recorded video and that camera showed the faint outlines of the three harriers roosting on the ground above some scattered Scots pines. There was no sign of any gamekeepers which was good but it also meant Raven had to decide how long to wait.

Soon his phone was vibrating with notifications. He resisted the temptation to look before he'd spent more time searching the area for white shapes which indicated the warm bodies of people or animals.

Eventually, he checked his phone. Kerbstone hadn't wasted any time in putting out a video, but Raven couldn't watch it yet because there weren't enough signals. There were plenty of comments on social media from supporters and trolls. So, he spent the next two hours alternating his checks of the area with the growing stream of vitriol.

@Alllifeisprecious (2148 posts 752 followers) Oh my God hope u r ok

@Janet06982355 (0 posts 0 followers) Should have put petrol through the door

@Stopruralpov (1109 posts 3998 followers) @KerbstnStrWear *You have a great selection of clothes, but are you sure you know what you're doing? @RvnHarley has spent most of last 2 wks under arrest and in a #police cell*

@Tony3334598 (0 posts 0 followers) *Terrorists like @RvnHarley should be put on the plane to Rwanda*

It was properly dark now and there was still no sign of people or vehicles. The harriers hadn't shifted from their roost. Raven had seen lots of similar posts on social media. Usually, they were drowned out by positive comments but this time it felt like an organised campaign.

And as he expected here was the petition:

@RrlJustice (598 posts 16443 followers) Sign here to stop @KerbstnStrWear paying extremist @RvnHarley fat £££s to terrorise hardworking rural people… 749 of target 1000 signatures

The gamekeepers could turn up at any time but Raven wasn't going to stay here all night. The temperature was dropping and his arms and legs felt stiff. He stretched and filled his lungs with cold air scented with damp peat and vegetation shutting down for autumn. That along with the silence of the moor was comforting. His eyes had adjusted and he started down without a torch. Three cars had passed in two hours and now a fourth was approaching. He crouched in the gully to see if it pulled in but without a pause, the lights continued towards town and he would soon join them.

*

It had been another ten-hour day in the fields and Anton joined the queue for the shower. The only other native Russian speakers were the minders. All the rest of his work colleagues spoke their home languages from a range of Eastern European countries and communication between the workers was a few words of English. Anton wasn't alone in dreaming farmwork would just be a stepping stone to a better-paid job and permanent residency. They were living in purpose-built portable units but six were squeezed in a room instead of four.

The door to the shower opened with a cloud of steam and Anton shuffled up the queue. Kirill, one of the minders appeared, on his way to the eating area.

"When are we getting our money?" Anton asked in his native tongue.

Kirill stopped and then took a couple of steps closer until his chest was almost pressing against Anton.

"When you've paid your debts," the blunt reply.

Anton could smell alcohol and cigarettes on Kirill's breath. Then he was shoved back against the wall before Kirill grabbed his cheek, squeezing the flesh.

Nearly a year before Anton had signed every piece of paper they put in front of him. Rodian Shenkov had toured the villages just outside Yekaterinburg, driving a Mercedes and telling everyone who'd listen he'd made a fortune working abroad, to come home a *big man*.

All the men in Anton's extended family had worked in the mines, underground or open cast and they all had health problems. It was a family trait to cough incessantly and hobble on legs that had been crushed or broken in accidents. It was no future and Anton needed to grasp any way out.

The paperwork had been in English and he'd signed for a Seasonal Worker Visa, supposedly to pick fruit and vegetables. Somehow that had switched to poultry for the Christmas rush and then he was back in the fields. They were all given £50 a week spending money and that disappeared on alcohol and top-ups for his phone. He was promised £500 per week in his hand but immediately he had to pay for the long overland trip to the UK as well as the £1270 in a bank account so UK Immigration was happy he could sustain himself. That should have all been cleared in a month but instead, they were stuck on pocket money for ten-hour days, six days a week. Anton had picked up as many snippets of information as he could. His sponsoring company was Greenway Resources and one of the men behind it was Sergei Yvprestov who still had interests in the Sverdlovsk Oblast mines near Anton's home as well as more lucrative oil and gas exploration further north. Back home Yvprestov was one of the elite and untouchable by the law. It seemed like he had the same status here.

As well as the debts Anton had of course handed over his passport for *safekeeping*. He was stuck. And now this thug was squeezing his cheek like a playground bully. Anton imagined shoving his knee into Kirill's groin, but he held back his anger.

"Looks like I'll have to send Rodian around to fuck your sister Galina again," spat Kirill.

His family had received visits from Rodian, just to let them know Anton had to behave, but nothing had happened so far. It was the lack of a passport that stopped Anton from leaving. He'd searched the minder room and found nothing. And every week they were told if they were picked up without a passport, Immigration would dump them in a camp. Even that was sounding more attractive now.

Eventually, Kirill let go and Anton tried to scrub himself clean in the shower.

Chapter 37

Just a few hours later and well before sunrise, Sergeant Paul Carson addressed a small team of his colleagues and introduced Chief Inspector Samantha Charter from the National Crime Agency and Steven Hove, a Home Office Immigration Enforcement Officer. Two squad cars and two minibuses were paying a visit to the Duke of Midham's extensive agricultural holdings to check all the temporary workers. More officers would be called if necessary. The small convoy made its way out of town, over the moorland and down into the farmland beyond. Intelligence had told them the workers were housed in portacabins close to where Paul Carson and Dew Foster had seen them. The police vehicles stopped outside the compound and officers did their best to surround the buildings. The chief inspector and immigration officer banged on the door of the largest building and soon a couple of lights were switched on inside. Then there was a lot of shouting as officers at the rear of the buildings tried to stop two men from escaping.

Paul ran towards the commotion. In the half-light of dawn, he could see a couple of his officers rolling on the ground trying to restrain two thickset men who were punching and kicking. He dived into the fracas, kneeling on the suspect and then using both hands to drag a flailing arm away from his officer. Between them, they managed to apply the handcuffs.

Paul looked over and was relieved to see Xan had got the better of his opponent and soon they were able to take the two men to the police vans where they were secured inside. Everything seemed calm in the buildings and when Paul looked in he saw bleary-eyed workers sitting quietly on the edge of their bunks, looking as if they couldn't take in what was happening.

Soon the officials had organised two spaces to interview the workers. Paul assisted the National Crime Agency officer and their first interviewee was Anton.

"We're here to check your visas are in order," asked Samantha Charter. It didn't take any prompting to start Anton giving the full details of his story. For

Charter, it was a familiar tale: lots of broken promises and coercion with just enough spending money and the bare minimum of accommodation to keep the workforce from running away.

"Thank you, Anton, your English is very good. You've no idea where we can find your passport and visa?" Charter asked.

"No," came Anton's reply. "This is their office," pointing to the room around them. "I've searched everywhere."

"And you've been in the UK for a year?" Paul asked.

Anton nodded.

"And the other workers have been here just as long?"

"Some longer than me. Some not so long," said Anton.

Paul turned to his colleague. "Beyond six months then, so most if not all of the workers are illegal?"

"Looks like it," said Charter. Then she thanked Anton.

"I just want to go home and I want to be paid," he said. "They told us if we were caught you'd put us in a concentration camp. Is that true?"

"You'll be given decent accommodation and we'll put you on a plane to Russia as soon as we can. But we need to find out what's been going on here first."

Anton wasn't entirely convinced. He was used to a world where police were in the pockets of the *pakhan* or organised crime as they'd say in this part of the world.

When Anton had been escorted back to the bunkrooms, Samantha Charter checked in with her office. Paul got the drift of the conversation: "*Greenway Resources...owned by Greenway Global which is registered offshore, their UK office doesn't actually exist and there's just an email address. How the fuck did the Home Office approve that one? And the link to Sergei Yvprestov? Suspected but not proven.*"

"Did you get that?" She asked Paul.

He nodded. "This is the Duke's land around here. He must know what's going on?"

"Our Duke will be up to his neck in it," Samantha replied. "But as far as appearances go, I think we'll find he'll tell us he's outsourced his labour using a Home Office approved agency. All perfectly legitimate as far as he's concerned."

"I hate to say it but a deluge of publicity might help. Having this on the six o'clock news would soon galvanise public opinion."

"Not just yet," said Samantha. "We need to do more digging on the money laundering but somebody will have noticed what's happened this morning for sure. The press will be taking an interest soon enough."

"Those two thugs need to be in police custody, not an immigration centre."

"We'll square it with the judge. We'll need statements from Anton and others but there'll be plenty enough to charge them under the Modern Slavery Act and hold them in custody. As always, getting their bosses is the problem."

Paul spent another couple of hours interviewing the workers then they took the minders back to the station. They wouldn't speak at all so it was going to take some time to find interpreters. They'd see if fingerprints, DNA and facial recognition came up with anything, nationally and Europe-wide. Paul made a little bet with himself that Procter & Hargreaves would magically appear to represent them.

*

Chloe walked into her office at 10.00 a.m. as requested. It had only been two weeks but the open plan space seemed alien and her eyes took in the shabbiness of it for the first time. Then her colleagues started to look up from their screens and she saw warmth and friendship. There was no hint of criticism. Her desk was empty and she walked straight past and into manager Dave's office. He gestured for her to push the glass door closed. His smile was genuine as well.

"You look great, Chloe," he said. "Amazing what a fortnight away from this place can do for you."

Chloe felt embarrassed at the greeting so she shrugged her shoulders and smiled.

"Today then," Dave said, "they're waiting for you in the conference room. As you might expect they've set up a Child Practice Review. The lead is a recently retired Director of Social Services and just to warn you, her questioning can be a bit harsh."

"Thanks, I'll try to keep cool. Are they going to let me see a copy of the notes?"

"Probably not," said Dave.

"Oh dear," replied Chloe. "I'm not sure I can remember every last detail over the last 18 months."

"Just do your best. If I'm still in a job after this, you have my complete backing," he said as he stood to escort her to the conference room. Dave introduced her to the inquiry team and then left. Chloe stood awkwardly, unsure if she should take the empty seat at the end of the long rectangular table.

The grey-haired lady sitting at the far end of the table pushed her glasses up her nose and started proceedings.

"I'm Elizabeth Freeman, head of the Review. Please take a seat, Ms Turner."

The review panel comprised representatives of the agencies involved in the care of Leo Corbet, including a consultant paediatrician and a police inspector.

Without the assistance of her notes, Chloe was asked to describe Leo, his parents and their situation. The initial referral had come about from a concerned neighbour and Chloe had visited roughly every two weeks. Eventually, the questioning concentrated on one detail.

"The only bruising you ever noticed was on Leo's knees and shins?"

"That's right," replied Chloe. "I had seen the rest of his body numerous times especially when he was younger and just wearing a nappy. As soon as he was walking, he was very active, not manic just full of energy and running all around their flat. At least twice when I was there I saw him bump into furniture. And then on other occasions when I arrived, I noticed bruising on his lower limbs, talked it through with Mum and the explanations seemed to fit with what I was seeing."

"Did you make a note of these injuries?"

"As far as I recall I did. I'm not being awkward here, but you have my notes perhaps you can tell me?"

There was a stony silence until Elizabeth Freeman continued, "Did you ask the paediatricians for their opinion?"

Chloe had long chats with her mum when she was training trying to find out what a normal childhood looked like and what signs indicated problems. The message from her mum was Chloe had been on the go all the time and only got fractious when she'd been unable to burn off her energy. She couldn't remember being two years old but recalled plenty of bumps and bruises.

"Honestly, I can't remember. The main concerns were around Dad and when he showed up we had continued reports from concerned neighbours. And then concerns about Leo's failure to thrive which I did discuss with the medics."

"I see," said Freeman. "The post-mortem determined lower leg bruising was not accidental and if that had been picked up earlier, Leo could have been saved."

The words hit Chloe like a sledgehammer. It was her fault.

"Moving on, it was a very junior registrar who gave an opinion on Leo's failure to thrive with a *let's wait and see* recommendation. Were you happy with that assessment?"

That sounded like a consultant shifting the blame onto a junior colleague. If *only you'd told me...*

"It's not my place to be *happy* as you put it, with that type of assessment. I was dealing with a team of qualified medical professionals supervised by a consultant."

"I see," said Freeman making a note on her pad.

The grilling continued and Chloe found herself repeating her replies and getting flustered. After an hour, she was told she could leave and it was made clear she shouldn't speak to any of her colleagues. Chloe's mind filled with one thought: it was the walk of shame through her office. The inquisition had been humiliating, her face was flushed and everyone was staring. They were actually concerned, friendly faces but it didn't feel like that. So, she stared at the carpet tiles and walked past as quickly as possible. Outside the air was sweet but couldn't clear the acrid taste in her mouth. Freeman may as well have told her she had an incurable disease, Chloe was helpless in the face of *something else* and that left her with the crushing weight of injustice squeezing her chest. Then that seemed selfish. A child had died and Chloe carried the guilt. Somehow she thought of Raven, he always seemed to ground himself in nature, a tree or a mountainside but that wouldn't help until her mind had cleared.

*

Lily greeted the clients in the car park at Fairview Mill.

"Morning, sir," they liked that, pushing their chests out because they were important people. There were no women this time. It had been a difficult conversation with Sue Thornton at the school:

"It's a crisis at Finn's work, I really need a day off," she'd explained.

"We have a class full of children Lily, you can't just abandon them," came the reply.

Then Lily tried to explain if she didn't help him now they may well be packing up and leaving and that wouldn't help Sue and St Mary's at all.

"Yes, I did hear he'd been arrested."

Those words stabbed her ear and she imagined blood trickling down her neck.

"It's those antis planting evidence and ruining the lives of honest, hardworking folk." Her accusation, made in thick Glasgow dialect was bitter and hollow, even Lily could see that now. The silent seconds stretched out until Sue Thornton cut the conversation:

"Let me know when you're back."

The night before Finn had been in bed when the taxi drew up in the yard. He guessed it was past midnight. Lily came in trying to be quiet and after a while, he told her to turn on the light.

"Sorry," she said joining him.

They lay side by side unable to sleep until Lily said, "Tranchard was being an old lech tonight. Really creepy."

It wasn't a surprise to Finn.

"Oh yes?"

And Lily described the wandering eyes and the references to his hotel room.

"I'll fucking kill him if he lays a finger on you," replied Finn.

Lily slept but he couldn't. His threat was empty; Tranchard, Parbolde and the rest of them knew it. Finn had to lay there and suck up the humiliation. Their house, his job, his vehicle and the lawyers' fees, *they* said yes or no. And given half the chance Tranchard would fuck his wife just because he could. It always felt just out of reach, the good life. There was always another bird to kill, another *polis* to sweet-talk and another *anti* to intimidate. Well, that's how it had been. Now, it was more life and death. Finn wanted to choose a side but there was only one on offer. He was a gamekeeper unless Tranchard said otherwise and then he was nothing.

So, as Lily greeted the clients Finn scoured the woods for any sign of Raven Harley and his chums. There'd be no videos today. Eventually, he joined everyone outside the mill. And there was one of the punters with his hand on Lily's elbow, enjoying a drink or two before the shoot, everyone laughing. Finn walked past and phoned his underkeeper Jayden.

"Beaters all in place?" He asked. "Ok start the drive." Then turning to the guns he shouted, "We're ready to begin."

There were thousands of pheasants and the punters couldn't fail to shoot a van load.

Raven was back to doing a full day's work that absorbed him, leaving no space to think about everything that had happened. The message from Chloe surprised him:

If you're out checking the harriers tonight, ok if I join you? I'll make some food at half five if you like.

Of course, that was alright and it led to some banter with his workmates.

"Are you singing, Raven? You look like a happy man," asked Mark. And Raven knew he was smiling. After work, he grabbed the cameras and drove around to Siobhan's house. Mark took him to one side of the kitchen.

"They're talking about work."

Raven nodded and tucked into a sandwich. Fifteen minutes later Chloe emerged from the lounge and gave Raven a hug. The smell of her body, he missed it so much.

"Ready?" He asked. She grabbed her bag and they went out to the van. He watched the road and even without speaking it was comforting to share the car with her.

After a few minutes, she pointed to the view. "The simple stuff, Ray, it's just lovely."

Then a minute later, "It was awful today. Dave warned me in his way but they just made me feel it was my fault, completely. I know you'll say it's not, but I can't help but feel responsible. The whole thing, the job I don't know if I can do it anymore no matter how the review turns out."

"Did it help to talk to Shiv?"

"Yeah, everyone in the office feels awful. They all support me and they're terrified it will happen to them. But just now that doesn't make it feel any better."

"What would?" Raven asked.

"That's the problem. If I resigned, I'd just be running away. But I can't face going back at all."

Raven explained the deal with Kerbstone. He slowed the van and pulled onto the verge.

"I'm not sure I've done the right thing. But putting that to one side gives more options. I don't know how long it will work but right now money's a lot easier. I want to say for us because I really do want to get back together."

Chloe reached over and put her hand over his.

"I've been thinking about that as well. But I don't just want to dive in and carry on as if nothing happened."

"If you're not desperate for cash, maybe you can think about the job more realistically. And, I don't know maybe we could go on a date?"

Chloe laughed. "Meet you at the bus stop then. Snogging before the number seven turns up…"

Raven laughed as well then Chloe suggested they get a move on to check the harriers. Raven guided them up the same route as before and they caught sight of the raptors dropping into the vegetation to roost. They were lost from view until the night vision camera revealed the location.

Raven's phone was going mad. It was on silent but vibrating all the time. Eventually, he had a look and saw the notifications about a new video Kerbstone had produced. It loaded this time and Chloe leant over to watch.

There was a scene from the pheasant shoot with fat, bald men in ridiculous baggy checked tweeds, all brandishing guns.

This bunch has a petition to boycott our clothes
Just because we support those who Stop Cruelty and Save the Environment

There was Raven wearing a Kerbstone jacket and showing his best side.

Kerbstone Style with a Conscience

"Oh God," groaned Raven.

"You'll get used to it," said Chloe. "I better get the shackles on you. You'll have a few more fans before the days out."

Chloe scanned the valley once more as Raven checked more social media. A thread from @RrlJustice was getting a lot of attention:

Our conservation work is vital for wildlife and biodiversity
Countrymen understand the balance of nature and humane management—it takes a lifetime to learn
Temporary restraints and no harm capture treat wildlife with compassion
Only when absolutely necessary will they use lethal force
Extremists and saboteurs damage and disrupt vital work night and day
Unless they learn to keep out of the way it's an accident waiting to happen

The rebranding of snares as temporary restraints didn't fool Raven. They were vicious traps that caused huge suffering. And the rest was a thinly veiled warning: if we see you nosing around we'll shoot you.

Their rabid followers were slavering at the prospect:

@Bethany2844571: *Accidently Shoot the F**kers!*

It was a different tactic and no surprise. Raven's urban life was gun-free. Out here in the countryside, the opposite was true but there was absolutely no reason for all these people to have weapons. The gamekeepers still hadn't turned up so they walked carefully down to the road and Raven drove them back into town. When they reached Chloe's place, they sat for a moment before she leant over and kissed his cheek.

"I'll give it the rest of the week up there," he said. "Maybe we could have that date on Friday?"

Chapter 38

Paul Carson hoped the chief would approve his overtime. It was stacking up. The National Crime Agency and Immigration had done much of the work, but there was still Kirill and Dmitry to process. The workers had no hesitation in naming them but of course, couldn't supply any other details. So, it was a matter of taking photographs, fingerprints and DNA to be circulated around the UK and Europe. Today it was fox hunting once more and Raven Harley had provided a telephone statement to back up the video he'd sent. And there was a further statement from Chloe Turner. Procter & Hargreaves solicitors had taken over the waiting area.

First up was magistrate Jeremy Cockerill accompanied by Sebastian Procter, one of the senior partners. They sat down around a table in the interview room where Xan explained the interview would be recorded.

Jeremy Cockerill couldn't very well go for a *No Comment* routine. He was a magistrate after all and not prepared to give that up. He admitted attending the hunt eleven days before at Upper Denling Wood but insisted they were legally following a trail.

Xan explained the police had edited the video for the purposes of the interview and he placed the laptop at the head of the table so everyone could see. "There's the captive fox being released and what looks like you, Mr Cockerill, in the same frame, approaching, blowing a hunting horn and shouting *On, On, On* with the hounds running past you chasing the fox. We've checked and can't see any valid exemptions in force."

Sebastian Procter attempted to earn his fee: "My client was legally following a trail and had no idea that fox would appear."

Paul enjoyed standing back and seeing the efforts of these lawyers. Procter wasn't landing Logan Porter in it 100% but it wasn't far off. It was time to interject:

"We have identified the person who released the fox and we'll be interviewing them shortly. They are a paid employee of the Midham Hunt and you, Mr Cockerill, are the master of that hunt. We are sure of these facts and unless you can provide an explanation we will charge you," said Paul.

Procter and Cockerill looked at one another, but there wasn't even a whispered conversation.

"My client has an exemplary character and I think you'll find a court will believe his version of events," Procter tried.

"Thank you, Mr Procter," said Paul. "We've been in touch with the chief magistrate's office and they indicated should this be brought to trial the case would be referred to the Crown Court where Mr Cockerill will receive a fair hearing."

Paul nodded and Constable Xan Philips charged Jeremy Cockerill under Section 1 of the Hunting Act 2004. Procter's swagger evaporated and the colour rose in Cockerill's face.

"Now to other matters," said Paul.

Xan showed Raven's footage of the melee when the Hunt came onto the road below Catchbrow Hill. There was a huntsman wearing a red jacket astride a black horse charging onto the highway. Hounds were everywhere. The soundtrack consisted of gusts of wind, traffic noise, dogs barking and a lot of shouting, the same *On, On, On*. And then high-pitched shrieks from animals followed by a dull thump. Xan paused the laptop.

"Catchbrow Hill last Saturday," said Paul. "We now have some dashcam footage."

Xan continued and they watched as rider and horse loomed onto the road, the car jerked down as brakes were applied and only then did the rider glance to the right towards the vehicle. Xan paused the video. Below the black hunter hat were the unmistakable pink cheeks of Jeremy Cockerill.

"Continue," said Paul.

In a moment, a vehicle appeared from the other direction and the horse had moved onto that side of the carriageway. The second driver swerved to avoid the horse but that resulted in a collision with several hounds. The impact on the dogs sent them flying into the air and the trajectory of the second car brought it crashing into the first vehicle. Paul described the action being taken as a result:

"Two insurance companies have asked for our help in identifying the horse rider with a view to civil proceedings due to the injuries to drivers and damage to vehicles. And we are assisting Highways to request an injunction from the High Court to prevent any similar incidents from recurring."

"We'll ask for the original footage before any of that happens," replied Procter, trying to sound in control. "It looks manipulated to me and I'll be interested to see what our own experts make of it."

The RTC at Catchbrow was verging on a major incident with three emergency services involved all because the great and good of *Midhamshire* were illegally chasing a fox. He ignored the lawyer. Paul knew claims of manipulation were feeble and he couldn't resist emphasising procedure.

"As I'm sure you're aware, Mr Cockerill, now you've been arrested and charged, you'll be photographed and we'll take your fingerprints and a sample of your DNA. That will help us in multiple aspects of our investigations particularly confirmation of the people involved."

Then he asked Xan to get the custody team to record Cockerill's identifying features and make sure both men would be escorted from the building so they couldn't converse with the others in the waiting area.

Paul used the time to get his notes in order for the interview with Logan Porter. A few minutes later, Xan came back and sat down.

"Well, I'm impressed, sir, you were totally cool there and he's a fucking magistrate with the best lawyer money can buy."

Paul smiled and patted his colleague on the shoulder. "The chief said to follow the evidence and here we are. Now let's see what Porter has to say."

The first thing Paul noticed was the presence of Michael Hargreaves, another senior partner in the law firm. It looked as if the Duke was taking a keen interest in the welfare of his terrier man and that in itself showed how important the archaic ritual of hunting was to this section of the aristocracy. Paul introduced himself and Xan and once again explained the interview would be recorded.

They started with the date, time and location of the Denling Wood hunt and Xan paused the video at the point where Logan Porter released the bagged fox. Paul looked across the table and saw a solid square man in his forties. There were dark smudges under the slits that were Porter's eyes and his best country attire of jacket, shirt and tie in matching greens were straining over his belly. Some different clothes and slightly more Slavic features and Porter could have been one of the *modern slavery* minders. Violence oozed from his pores.

"What's that in your possession, Mr Porter?"

Logan looked at his lawyer and then said, "No comment."

"As is your right, Mr Porter, so let me explain. We have witness statements from that location on that day and our technical staff confirmed the video has not been manipulated. You are releasing a fox in your possession and within five seconds hunting hounds are chasing that fox and within a few minutes, the fox has been killed. Our vet confirmed the pad on the foreleg of the fox had been sliced with a knife or similar implement. Can you provide any explanation?"

"No comment."

"My constable will charge you under Section 4 of the Animal Welfare Act 2006 Allowing Unnecessary Suffering due to releasing a fox in your care to be killed by hounds."

Once Xan made the formal charge, Paul continued, "Now in the early hours, two nights later you phoned our control room directly."

Xan played the audio of Logan's call and they listened to him reporting his quad bike stolen after a break-in.

"Do you still maintain your quad bike was stolen?" Paul asked.

This time there was a whispered conversation between lawyer and client before Logan spoke.

"No comment."

Paul went through the video Chloe had taken and described Xan's discovery of the quad bike the day of the Catchbrow Hill hunt.

"We arrested a suspect on the basis of your initial call to us and that was your intention, wasn't it? But in fact, the quad bike hadn't been stolen at all and you continued to use it. Do you have anything to say, Mr Porter?"

"It's all a misunderstanding, Sergeant," interjected Michael Hargreaves. "George Carter borrowed the quad bike. Farmers and countrymen are always helping out each other."

"We have a statement from George Carter who supplied a different version of events," replied Paul.

"My client faces constant harassment from violent extremists when all he seeks to do is support his family and his local community. These extremists filmed their break-in of my client's property, why don't you arrest them instead of heaping further harassment on my client? There's clear bias, Sergeant, and I'll be complaining to the police and crime commissioner and your chief constable."

Paul was expecting the tirade but he had the evidence and he hoped he had the backing of his chief. But the Duke and his lawyers wielded huge influence. The saving grace here was any detailed look into these events would reveal Superintendent Farlow as dodgy if not corrupt. The chief was smoothing that over and dealing with Farlow in her own way. Putting Paul in charge of these investigations was a clear sign of that rationale.

"I'll supply you with the contact details, Mr Hargreaves, once we've finished our business here. Now do you have anything further to add?"

Logan Porter was well-practised in the hard stare but Michael Hargreaves had a lot to learn in that department. Paul had seen it all before and it made him more determined to do his job.

Paul nodded to his colleague and Xan charged the terrier man with perverting the course of justice contrary to common law.

Archie Cartwright and his lawyer could wait. Paul and Xan went back to their office for a cup of tea.

"Are the CPS going to follow through on all this?" Xan asked.

Paul swirled the tea in his cup to cool it a little before taking a sip. "I did run it past them and remind them of their purpose, you know, prosecute if it's likely to be successful *and* in the public interest. It seems our chief had got in first with the public interest side of things. She'd stressed our need to increase public confidence that we tackle rural crime."

"It has felt quite a lot of the time that I've had to look the other way," said Xan. "And after a while morale just goes through the floor."

"You've been here long enough to know we have umpteen initiatives but mainly they're just for show. We'll just have to wait and see if this is a real change or not," replied Paul. He didn't add that his morale had been through the floor and it was only now he felt he was actually doing his job properly. "Any news on the DNA sample we took from Raven Harley's house?"

"The one at the bottom of his stairs?" Xan asked.

"Yes."

"Came back this morning, that's pretty quick for our lab. It's a match for Ryan Walker who as you know is one of the gamekeepers at High Ridge and Fairview. And that tied in with the index Harley gave us which belonged to one of the High Ridge pick-ups, seen near his house earlier that day."

"Still no sign of Ryan Walker?"

"He's disappeared," said Xan.

"Parbolde has an estate in Scotland. He'll be up there or more likely at one of their neighbours. Let's get an arrest warrant issued and see what our colleagues up north make of it."

Xan would suggest his colleague PC Tom Colne sort out the paperwork on that one given he'd attended the scene. Colne had some making up to do as Professional Standards were now investigating his conduct at the arrest of Raven Harley and a further complaint from Willow's family after the school fete. Complaints were part of daily life for a front-line police officer but Xan had his suspicions about Tom Colne. He was one of Superintendent Farlow's drinking buddies and liked to go sport shooting, but there was no way he could afford that on his wages. Xan couldn't believe their control room would supply false information about Raven Harley's *antisocial* driving history unless they'd been primed by someone as senior as Farlow. There were plenty of Xan's colleagues who thought Raven Harley and his mates were a pain in the neck, or worse, troublemakers that needed to be stamped on hard. In this case that meant crossing a line which had become blatantly obvious to Harley and his lawyer. The complaint would be spun out for a couple of years or more and there was no way someone as senior as Farlow would be criticised for anything. And if Tom Colne was as *in* as he appeared then the only blame would be apportioned to overworked civilian admin staff. On top of that, what made Xan really angry was having to drive an over-the-limit Farlow after his lunch with the Duke; it was enough to send any honest police officer running for the door.

They finished their tea and returned to the interview room where Xan checked the video clips were in order.

"So, we start with our vehicle then we'll move onto the campervan?" Xan asked.

Paul nodded and Xan collected gamekeeper Archie Cartwright and his solicitor Julian Hargreaves.

After the usual no-comment routine and the solicitor questioning the relevance of the video, Paul looked at the suspect who tried to stare back, but soon dropped his eyes to the desk and shifted in his seat.

"I saw you, Mr Cartwright. I was there ten metres away from you. We've enhanced the video. You looked back up the hill after slashing the tyre," said Paul.

They watched the footage with a clear image of Cartwright's face. Cartwright had a whispered conversation with Hargreaves who decided to switch tactics.

"My client saw you with a known extremist who'd been arrested for criminal damage, theft, antisocial behaviour and intimidation. Quite simply, in such a remote location he was in fear for his life. The only intention was to delay any pursuit and avoid further intimidation."

It was laughable of course and Hargreaves should have known the police would take every action possible when their own property had been damaged. Some of that information might have been gleaned from the videos that appeared but not that level of detail. It was obvious one or more officers were leaking information.

"I see," said Paul. "You can discuss that with the judge. What we are dealing with is £400 for new tyres, the cost of vehicle recovery and following that damage, which made the vehicle un-driveable, an officer was hampered in carrying out their duties during a serious incident. As further evidence, we also have an ANPR image of Mr Cartwright driving his vehicle shortly afterwards which places him in the area."

Paul and Xan gathered their paperwork before Paul continued, "The night of St Mary's School fete, the tyres of Mal Torsen's campervan were damaged when he was parked on Moor Lane. We have witness and dashcam footage that places you a couple of hundred metres away shortly after the damage occurred. What were you doing in the area, Mister Cartwright?"

"No comment."

The response was expected and Paul continued. "We also have clear fingerprints and palm prints from around the wheel arch on Mister Torsen's vehicle. Have you made physical contact with the vehicle Mister Cartwright? If you have can you explain why?"

But of course, the response was the same and Paul explained Archie Cartwright would be charged with criminal damage for the first incident and his fingerprints would be taken. If there was a match for the prints on the camper, he would be charged for that damage as well.

For once, Paul didn't mind if their day's work was leaked and news spread around the community.

Chapter 39

Edward Fraine hated being in the same room as his wife Sophie but she'd insisted on this meeting. They were in one of the formal rooms at the Grange and the Duke and Duchess were sitting on opposite sides of a long polished table. The Agricultural Manager William Cassell sat next to the Duchess. The Duke ensured his management team all had strictly defined areas of responsibility so none of them had an overview of the extent of the scams in place. Cassell dealt with livestock and crops but wasn't involved in timber or moorland management so wouldn't know about the false invoicing there.

There wasn't any small talk.

"You wanted to meet?" The Duke asked.

"People are saying the raid on our crop pickers is scandalous. And we're the butt of everyone's jokes," said the Duchess.

They hated each other but still shared the arrogance and haughtiness of their *position*. It was beneath them to have personal involvement in such matters as hiring and managing farm workers.

"No one's ever laughed at our family for long," replied the Duke. The Duchess turned to Cassell who thought it prudent not to mention the agency that provided the workers had been recommended by the Duke. Instead, he said, "The agency was government approved and it's their responsibility to make sure all the necessary permits were in place. But the problem I have is even though it's autumn there are a lot of crops in the ground that need to be harvested. Then we have an increasing amount of work at Midham Turkeys in the run-up to Christmas."

"So, go to another agency," said the Duke.

"I've made enquiries, Your Grace, but since Brexit, it's much harder to source cheap labour, especially at short notice. We're talking about doubling the cost which would turn it into a loss-making venture."

Beneath his facade of brusqueness, the Duke's mind was racing ahead. Loss-making meant the £50k he'd earmarked for the hunt would be needed to prop up the *Home Farm*. The glossy brochures and professional website for the Grange showed the Duke with rolled-up shirtsleeves cradling a newborn lamb in a spotless barn. But he had absolutely no interest in farming. It was something his hirelings did to provide a lot of money. It was their place while the Duke's place was wearing a red jacket and leading his hunt.

"Then hire fewer people and work them hard."

"If I do that, Your Grace, they'll just leave."

It was left unsaid that the previous workers couldn't leave.

"Bump up the prices in the farm shop," the Duke tried.

The manager couldn't avoid sighing. The Duke had absolutely no idea what it took to run an agricultural business or where the produce actually ended up.

"The prices in the shop are already premium. People will pay that but there is a limit. The real problem is the shop only takes around 5% of what we produce. The rest goes to the wholesale market. We've looked at creating our own branded range of products but we don't produce enough to supply a UK-wide supermarket chain. We're too big for one shop and not big enough to go national. These things take years to set up."

It was too much for Edward Fraine who hadn't followed any of that.

"For God's sake, just do what you have to do," he said to Cassell.

They were all silent for a moment before the Duke continued "What are people saying? Do I need to sort it out?"

"We're a hashtag, darling," replied his wife. "#Midham Grange Modern Slavery followed by *#KeepingUpOldTraditions.* And then there's the joke about the Hunt…"

The colour rose in the Duke's face and his frown knotted his eyebrows.

How many members of the Midham Hunt does it take to cross the road?
One to cross and ten to pick up the pieces.

The agricultural manager plucked up the courage to speak his mind. "If I may, Your Graces, I just provide the produce but we're coming up to our busiest season. Social media takes off like wildfire and unless we grab the narrative this is all we'll be remembered for. People will stop coming. It can be fixed, but you need to hire a public relations consultant. Get another message out there."

"William's right," said the Duchess. "The lawyers will recommend someone, I'm sure."

The Duke was already paying Sebastian Procter a fortune. He was expecting an update from Jeremy Cockerill and the solicitors about the police interviews. The silence didn't feel like good news. He hated to say it, but Sophie was right.

"I'll give Procter a call," he said.

The Duchess and Cassell stood up and left, he made the call and was put straight through. The lawyer explained about the charges for Cockerill and Porter, the insurance claim and the effort being put into an injunction to ban the hunt from the public highway.

"A PR firm, Your Grace? Yes, I'd definitely recommend that. I'll make a call now," said Sebastian Procter.

Eddie stabbed the off symbol on his phone and pulled himself out of his chair to look out across the manicured parkland. He wasn't beaten. He needed to take charge, that's all.

Chapter 40

Following the arrests and charges, there was endless paperwork for Paul Carson. On top of that, he was trying to pull everything together so they could charge Finn Sutherland with wildlife crimes. Then his phone buzzed: Dew Foster.

"The raid didn't stay quiet for long," she said. "We need to move quickly at our end before everyone has covered their tracks. Everything we have implicates the Duke and that's a result. But we've still got nothing on Nathan Parbolde and Sergei Yvprestov. So, the thinking at the moment is we'll raid the offices at Midham Grange on Friday along with the accountant Jonas Farland and hope the Duke can be shamed into naming others. We'll contact your chief constable directly, I'm afraid your office is leaking like a sieve."

Paul moved into a small glass-box office and closed the door. "Ok, I'll wait for instructions from the chief at my end. Superintendent Farlow is an obvious candidate for any leaks."

"Yes, we know about him. But we had a bit of luck with someone else as well. Have you seen the social media posts by @WhackaCrim? They show a great deal of knowledge about arrests you've made, something that could only come from an officer. The same name crops up in a police officer's WhatsApp group with vile suggestions about what to do with asylum seekers, misogynistic comments and the rest. And we traced that mobile number back to your colleague PC Tom Colne."

Paul tried to compute all the incidents where PC Colne had been involved. "Professional Standards are looking into him. Whether they do anything is another matter. In the meantime, he's on completely normal duties. He was at the raid the other day."

"He might have been the leak for that one but we'll have to investigate further. Given everything else he's said I'd expect him to be a fan of modern slavery."

Paul shook his head in disbelief.

"The only way we can keep him out of things is to suspend him which is above my pay grade."

"Ok, Paul, I'll be in touch."

*

Raven took comfort in his routine of driving out to Fletchers Sitch. From the parking spot, he made his way carefully onto the moor opposite the hen harrier roost and concentrated on trying to get some video clips of the birds wheeling above the heather. The sun had set and he was aiming for a silhouette against a patch of dark blue sky that had appeared behind a gap in the clouds. Tonight another harrier had appeared, pale-coloured it looked like a male but the light wasn't good enough to be sure. That made four birds at the roost. A little later, the night vision camera confirmed they were all in the same place. Any normal person with that information would avoid the area so there was no chance of disturbance. But Raven knew hen harriers were still Britain's rarest bird of prey. They'd been persecuted close to extinction and four at one roost could be killed by a single shotgun blast. The main diet for hen harriers was voles. They didn't kill many grouse and the persecution on these moors had no reason. Harriers were a bird of prey and gamekeepers thought they took grouse chicks and prevented grouse from flying towards the guns on a shoot day. That was enough to kill them year-round.

With no sign of gamekeepers, Raven checked his phone. The raid on Midham Estate farm workers was massive news with links showing how slave trade profits had doubled the size of the stately home and purchased thousands of acres of prime farmland. And of course, when slavery was abolished, the Dukes of Midham received the equivalent of millions of pounds in government compensation. As Raven was reading, he kept on turning to his night vision camera but there was no sign of any people. Chloe was helping to stop badgers being killed in the cull zone a few miles away. Maybe he should have joined her.

*

Finn Sutherland was well away from Fletchers Sitch on the far side of the road. His brief had been to watch and not be seen. He noted where Raven Harley

197

parked his van and the route he took onto the moor. There'd been just enough light to pinpoint the location where he laid up. His approach up the gully left him hidden most of the time with just a few seconds in the open. And when he reached his vantage point, his body was hidden in the stream bed with just his head poking above when he checked his camera. They'd need to draw him out somehow. He phoned his boss using WhatsApp and passed on the details.

Nathan Parbolde took the call and relayed the information to the others in the room. He wasn't sure of the best course of action but sensed desperation for a plan. Sutherland had described how the latest shoot at Fairview had fallen to quite pathetic depths. The corporate clients had cancelled, fees for the day had to halve with a sweetener of a dinner bed and breakfast at The Stables thrown in and still they couldn't fill all the places. Half the clients had never shot before and were unlikely to return. Parbolde's instruction had been to create the finest and most exclusive pheasant shoot in England. But within two weeks those dreams had been trodden into the autumnal mire.

Parbolde had needed new gamekeepers and thought Sutherland would be experienced enough to manage the estate day to day with minimal involvement from Gerald Tranchard. But Finn Sutherland had been sloppy and was at the root of all the negative publicity. Tranchard had sent Porter and Ryan Walker to put the frighteners on Raven Harley and Farlow was supposed to ensure Raven was prosecuted. But whatever was done Raven Harley kept coming. Parbolde was starting to feel random stabs of panic. He bought people to do all the dirty work even if that involved violence and killing. If they failed him, they were discarded with no comeback. He realised his panic stemmed from feeling humiliated and helpless. His self-assured swagger had melted away and he was left stuttering. This wasn't a corrupt businessman in a sanctioned country who wouldn't be missed. Raven Harley had a *following*. They had to be watertight or they would be found out. Parbolde found himself listening to Tranchard add yet more layers of doubt:

"We've all heard of the girl who read the poem: *Willow*. Our community out there should be spitting in her face but instead, farmers are offering her family somewhere to live and everyone is talking about the thugs and bullies who tried to drive them out. It needs to be clear: without us, the *countryside* dies. Instead of hugging those crusties people need to fear for their jobs, their lives if they turn against us. We need to show everyone who's in charge."

They were sitting in the lounge at Midham Lodge and Tranchard's call left everyone in silence. Parbolde was taken back to his boarding school world where he was desperate to establish himself on the top step of a hierarchy of peers. He did that by breaking the rules and the law where no one else would dare. He stole, bullied and used enough violence to make everyone else fall in line. It had served him well in his life, but he'd also learnt the value of caution. He wouldn't be the first to volunteer but he did offer his thoughts.

"Going after a ten-year-old girl was a mistake. But Gerald is right. We need to show we're in charge. Raven Harley is a legitimate target."

The Duke was in his own world. His right leg was twitching and jerking nervously and he kept trying to still it by crossing his legs but he couldn't calm himself.

"My Duchy is a fucking hashtag. People are laughing at me," he said.

Without even speaking Sergei held the room with an air of calm and self-assurance, sitting relaxed, but upright in one of the Duke's armchairs. He noticed Parbolde's demeanour still looked a little forced. Nathan had a way to go before he could be a true *pakhan*. Sergei addressed the Duke's concerns first:

"They're just *krestyanin* Eddie, peasants. Who cares if they have papers or not? They're worth nothing. They'll be put in a hotel somewhere without any money while the government decides what to do with them. Then we'll threaten them and tempt them and before you know it they'll be begging to be on a farm again. Business goes on," said Sergei. And then he clicked his fingers. The sound was clear and metallic, a slab of ice-cold steel breaking in two. The nervous fidgeting stopped. "You have your *Dacha* and your *Shire* and if you hide in the comfort of that you'll always have to play to the tune of the *chinovniki*. Little men Eddie, bureaucrats. You have all this," he said opening his arms, "because your ancestors crossed the seas. Tobacco, sugar, cotton, they owned people and forced them to work. That's how they made a profit." And then he looked straight at the Duke, who dropped his eyes to the carpet. "It's not the time to wobble."

There was silence in the room broken only by the wind gusting outside. Then Sergei addressed Tranchard, "The girl and her poem? Fuck that. If we want the *countryside* behind us, we'll build them a new school, that'll show who has the money. It's simple those who support us do well, those against suffer. Back home her whole family would have disappeared."

Tranchard forgot his failures and started to feel a sense of excitement. Sergei was taking charge. "We did have the police sewn up and they should have calmed everything down, arrested a few extremists, discredited the rest and put out the message: there's nothing to see here. But the problem stems from the new Chief Constable Madelaine Chatton and I don't have anything on her, no leverage at all. And if we did anything she'd want to investigate. That's why I've put out a clear message: guns are used in the countryside night and day and anyone poking around in the wrong place might have an unfortunate accident."

The Duke recovered his composure and tried to offer something useful:

"We owned Fletchers Sitch at one time. There are a few quarry workings and a couple of old mineshafts amongst the trees with old tracks leading up there. Very easy for someone to *disappear* if that's the message we want to put out?"

"My keeper said we'd have to draw him out, otherwise he's too well hidden," chipped in Parbolde. "Finn Sutherland is desperate to do something."

"I can say the same for Logan Porter," said the Duke.

"Can we rely on them?" Sergei asked.

Everyone knew what this meant coming from the Russians and the penalty for failure. Sergei didn't hear any disagreement so he continued, "What about disposal?"

"No point burying him," said Parbolde. "Peat preserves bodies for centuries."

"He needs to be disappeared," said Sergei.

"I may have the solution," said the Duke. "We have an abattoir for fallen stock. There's a small incinerator but that would generate some smoke. Otherwise, there's a superfine pulveriser. I've just spent a fortune on a new one. It grinds everything into a paste, including bones and it can all be fed to the dogs."

Again no one spoke. Nathan Parbolde looked around the room. Sergei was smiling but the Duke was plagued by anxiety once more. *This was real.* There was the skeleton of a plan, but who would pull the trigger? Parbolde had never killed anyone himself but had been in plenty of meetings like this before. There'd always been a professional to carry out the orders. Finn Sutherland and Logan Porter were thugs but they weren't trained killers. There were plenty of stories of Porter using his bulk and his fists at hunts but an assassination was in another league. If they panicked, they'd end up confessing to the police and implicating everyone else. His own men Callum and Sean would kill for a price he was sure but Nathan used them for close contact muscle. If they did a job like this, he'd end up paying them to disappear and it'd be a pain in the neck to replace them. For Nathan, this was all about saving face and cementing the hierarchy. He and Sergei were the players here and he was entwined in Sergei's world. The Duke was a bumbling aristocrat and Tranchard was just a fixer, an agent, someone hired to make things happen. Parbolde hoped Sergei wouldn't pressurise him into a hands-on role but the Russian was unpredictable. It had probably been a rite of passage for the oligarch to kill someone with his bare hands.

Sergei slapped his palms down on his knees and grinned.

"I have Vasily Zaytsev's M1891 Mosin Nagant, the exact weapon that disposed of hundreds of Nazis at Stalingrad. This is the perfect opportunity to try it out. Akim is ex-military, he can be my spotter."

The tension lifted. They were all used to giving orders but this plot had brought them uncomfortably close to acting as foot soldiers.

"I have to make a call," said Sergei getting up to walk into the kitchen where Akim and Pyotr were waiting. Sergei phoned the staff at his mansion outside Yekaterinburg and gave instructions for a night scope to be fitted to the M1891 and for the rifle to be tested and zeroed then flown to the UK by private jet. Once he'd had his fun he'd leave straight away for some heli-skiing in the Alps, there'd been early snow in the mountains. The shooting would bind Parbolde, the Duke and Tranchard to him. They were involved just as much as he was. *Conspiracy to murder*. Having control over them would be useful in other businesses. Pulling the trigger was a simple step along the way. There'd be plenty of times ahead where he'd need them to do something illegal for him and this was the way to force them to do it.

The others took the opportunity to plan their alibis. Tranchard would speak to Sutherland and Porter later. Then in the evening, he'd join the Duke and Parbolde for a public meal at The Stables. The body would be taken to the abattoir for immediate disposal and Harley's van would be driven away and torched. Callum and Sean would deal with that.

Sergei appeared in the doorway and beckoned Nathan. They went outside.

"There'll be a helicopter waiting at 8.30 p.m. in the usual place," said Sergei. Nathan knew this was a clearing sometimes used for pheasant shooting on the Duke's land.

"There's a space for you if you want to vacate the area?" Sergei asked.

"Sounds good. Amelia's forgotten what I look like."

"Turn up unannounced," said Sergei, "I'll be going on to see Lara and the boys."

It was all familiar to Parbolde. The helicopter would take Sergei to an airfield near London for his private jet and Switzerland. Nathan would carry on to his own mansion in the home counties. And they'd all be far away from whatever happened.

Chapter 41

At last, Chloe had time to check her messages.

Another harrier appeared. All safe tonight x

She smiled. Her anger at Raven was receding like the waves of an ebb tide slipping down a shingle beach. Thoughts of him were soothing. She found herself questioning why she'd been so angry at all. Then it came back to her: Becky Vickers. Raven's offer of financial stability sounded so grown up, parental even, at the best possible time. Chloe couldn't face going back to social work, not at the moment. But it had meant so much to her. If they sacked her at least that would solve her dilemma. When a child had died, people who'd never met her looked for scapegoats.

Raven and his sponsorship meant Becky Vickers would be a feature of their lives. Becky was looking out for herself and no one else so Raven was a ticket to greater things. Becky wouldn't be disappearing any time soon.

And when Chloe thought of it like that, how could she trust Raven was being honest? She'd always had her independence and she'd looked after him when he'd needed her. But the other way round?

She groaned then told herself trust had to start somewhere. Raven had never shown any sign of manipulating or controlling. If it didn't work out, Chloe would be gone, for good. Trying to work out exactly what had led to him going with Becky would drive her mad. He did seem to know he'd messed up and what he'd lost.

Her next breath out was an involuntary sigh and she shook her head to try and clear the negativity. A flask provided a welcome mouthful of tea before her phone buzzed again. More scumbags in untaxed SUVs were spotted and the badger cull continued into the night.

She followed the map that had been sent with the message and she started to notice what was not there. There was no Logan Porter and no police, just thugs in 4×4s lurking around fields where badger setts had been mapped. Shining a bright light at them for twenty minutes was sending them on their way, usually to another sett but Chloe had the feeling protesters were winning. There was no justification for the slaughter but it tapped into the countryside tradition of *exterminating vermin* and it seemed everyone with a gun licence had signed up to be a cull operative. Chloe imagined the rural life of fighting an endless invasion of creatures must be exhausting. Countless badgers had died yet Bovine TB was still there in cattle herds. But on this patch, there'd been insufficient mortality. The cull continued because targets hadn't been met. Chloe was determined they never would.

*

Emma couldn't get used to Logan being around in the evening. The television was on and she kept glancing across at him in his armchair. He was muttering to himself, then his phone rang and he signalled for her to mute the programme. It sounded like a WhatsApp call with gaps in the dialogue as the Wi-Fi caught up.

"Yes, Mr Tranchard, tomorrow…I'll follow Finn. Just hang on a second."

He looked at Emma and mouthed *get out.*

She pulled herself up from the sofa and stepped out of the lounge. The door was warped and dragged on the carpet so didn't shut properly. She ducked around the doorframe into the corridor and listened.

"Yes, I can open it up any time…absolutely no problem with that…I can use the incinerator as well, but best leave that until the morning, you know, the usual time we have it on."

Then Logan listened for a while before ending with, "You can rely on me. I won't let you down."

Emma walked into the kitchen and switched on the kettle. She leant back on the worktop and wondered what he was up to but before she could piece it together she felt a stab of pain in her stomach that made her gasp. It wasn't indigestion and for a second she felt really frightened. Then it was over and she could breathe again. Her forehead was covered in cold sweat and she shivered. She didn't want him to think she'd been listening so quickly made two mugs of tea and struggled to open the door to the lounge. He had a glass of whisky in his hand so she placed his tea on a table at the side.

"Actually, I don't feel well, Logan, I'm going to take this up to bed."

There wasn't a flicker of sympathy in his voice, "I'll join you."

"No, we agreed. I'm in the spare room."

"You agreed," he shouted, "if you lock the door, I'll kick it in."

"If you come in there, Logan, I'll tell the police you raped me and they can add that to…"

She didn't say the words *perverting the course of justice* but he heard them all the same. He stood up face purple with rage, grabbed the tea cup and threw it into the fireplace then shouldered past her. A moment later she heard the engine of his pick-up. He'd be in the pub in a few minutes.

Emma tried to calm herself then went back to the kitchen for a mop and bucket and did her best to clean up the mess.

A couple of hours later, she heard a key being fumbled in the front door and realised she'd left the door unlocked. Eventually, he tried the handle and pushed the door open before tumbling inside with a curse. He must have left the pick-up at the pub. It took another half an hour for him to stagger up to bed and a few minutes later she heard him snoring.

Sleep didn't come easily to Emma she felt something was wrong in her body. She was woken by the alarm in the morning but struggled out of bed. She didn't seem to have any energy and was finding it hard to concentrate. But the thought of calling in sick and spending the day at home with Logan was unbearable. So, she made some breakfast as quietly as she could and hoped that would revive her. Then a five-minute drive took her to the farm shop and she opened up as usual.

The shop was usually quiet first thing. The locals rarely came in and most of their customers were visitors. Some of these had done a tour of the Grange and others had spent a couple of hours walking around the parkland.

At about 9.30 a.m., Emma recognised her first customer but couldn't immediately think of her name so settled for 'Good morning'. It was a woman who lived nearby and was in her forties. She wore a green waxed jacket over a padded body warmer. "Still a bit chilly today," said Emma, the usual fallback. Then she remembered, it was Laura who was prodding some carrots in a plastic tray and tutting.

"Morning," Laura replied, "I needed some vegetables, but everything is twice the price it is in town."

Emma could do without this. Laura had no intention of buying anything.

"Well, it is the finest produce hand-picked on the Duke's estate," tried Emma.

Laura replaced the carrot in the tray and walked over to the counter and leant in towards Emma. "And who picked them? Slave labour is what they're saying."

Emma tried to make a joke of it. "You haven't seen the wages here," she offered.

Laura placed both hands on the counter and leant closer still. "Your husband's been arrested as well, hasn't he?"

It wasn't really a question, but a probe for gossip as Laura's face contorted into a sneer. Emma felt the cold sweat on her forehead again. She wanted to lean on the counter as well but that would have brought her even closer to Laura. Instead, Emma sat back in the chair next to the till. She looked up at Laura and said, "Sorry, I'm not feeling well."

Laura pushed herself upright and looked Emma in the face, "I don't know how you can live with the shame? It's disgusting," she said before walking out of the shop.

Emma stared at the floor. She hadn't done anything wrong but was still an object of abuse *by association.* She was sure the Duke and Duchess would smooth everything over soon enough but the hidden rot would remain. Logan wouldn't change and she felt she was drowning, trying to carry on a decent life as the weight of corruption was pulling her down.

She was saved, for a moment by her colleague Jessica who breezed through the door saying, "Poor you, you've had Laura Fenton in, tongue like barbed wire that one, bet she said how rubbish all our stuff was?" And then Jessica paused when she saw Emma's grey clammy face. "Oh, are you alright?"

Emma shook her head and then asked "Have got any pads in your bag? I think my period has started."

Jessica started swinging her shoulder bag around to her front and searched through the contents. When she looked again, Emma was doubled up in pain clutching her stomach. "Come on, let's get you into the back."

They had a small staff room just behind the till and Jessica helped Emma into a chair before offering her a pad. "They're never usually this bad, are they?" She asked.

Emma shook her head. "That's better the spasm's going. No, it's not like any period I've ever had. I don't know what's going on?"

"Let's get you to the doctor then," said Jessica as she brought up the number for the GP surgery. She pushed the key for the speaker so they could both hear the recorded message:

The surgery is fully booked today. Please call at 8.00 a.m. tomorrow for an on-the-day appointment. Our local pharmacist can offer advice and off-the-counter medication.

"Bugger that," said Jessica, "I'll take you down there."

"You can't, you'll have to close up and we'll both be sacked," protested Emma.

"The Duke can manage without us for an hour," said Jessica taking charge.

It took fifteen minutes to drive to the surgery and Jessica helped Emma out of the car. The front door was locked and it took a couple of minutes banging before one of the receptionists opened up and they helped Emma into one of the nurse's rooms. Emma lay down on the examination couch and Jessica leant against the wall. It was half an hour before the doctor came in and Emma could describe her symptoms.

"I'll need to examine you," he said, "probably best if we have a chaperone, are you ok with the receptionist, we don't have any nurses on today?"

Emma nodded and the doctor looked at Jessica. "Do you mind waiting in the corridor?" He asked.

The doctor pushed two fingers around her abdomen and found one place on her right side that was extremely painful.

"Do you think you could be pregnant?" He asked.

"I shouldn't be, you fitted a coil about five years ago," replied Emma.

"When was your last period?"

Emma tried to think, but her mind seemed blank. "I think about seven or eight weeks ago but they have been getting a bit irregular. I thought it was an age thing. Peri-menopause, is it? My mum had it quite young."

"Ok," he replied, "the right-sided pain might be appendicitis or it could be an ectopic pregnancy. Could you manage to do a pregnancy test for me?"

The doctor looked really worried and that scared Emma. The receptionist helped her to the toilet for a urine sample. The doctor was on the phone when they returned and they waited a few minutes for the result. She was pregnant.

"Ok, I'm almost certain you have an ectopic pregnancy. I'll explain what that means. The foetus normally develops in the uterus but in this case, it's lodged in the fallopian tube and that's causing the pain. You need a small procedure immediately to remove the foetus otherwise the tube can rupture and that would be serious. Do you have any questions?"

Emma shook her head but then asked, "Can you do that here?"

"No, we have to get you to the hospital. And that's the problem, I've been onto ambulance control and they're telling me they can't get anyone here for four hours."

"Jessica will take me, I'm sure," said Emma.

"You're my patient. I have a duty towards you and I need to take you."

Emma thought about the full waiting room and all the people there who might have an urgent problem. "If there was this rupture or whatever, could you sort it out in the back of your car?"

"Probably not," he replied honestly.

"Right you just phone ahead, Jessica will take me and I'll take responsibility if anything goes wrong, ok?"

They helped Emma back to the car and she told Jessica to drive steadily. Half an hour later as they drove through the hospital grounds, they passed a line of about thirty ambulances waiting to unload their patients into A&E. Jessica drove right up to the doors and ran out for a wheelchair. Then she pushed Emma inside and told the receptionist, hidden behind plates of security glass that it was urgent and Emma was expected.

Jessica went back to the car and drove away looking for a parking place. Ten minutes later, she was back and Emma was still sitting outside the receptionist's cubicle. Jessica banged on the glass.

"For fuck's sake, she could die if she's not seen!"

The receptionist pointed soundlessly to the nurse striding up the corridor. Again Jessica pushed the wheelchair as the nurse tried to take a history. They went straight to a booth for an ultrasound scan and within a minute a doctor arrived who soon confirmed the GP's diagnosis. Emma was told she'd need a general anaesthetic and it was left to the nurse to go through the consent form. Emma couldn't take in what she had to agree and just heard: *fallopian tube removed...could affect your chances of getting pregnant*. She did her best to sign and was taken off to be prepped.

Jessica made her way back to reception and made sure they had her details and that she'd be waiting. Next, she stepped outside to phone the Grange, but everything seemed so chaotic she didn't think they'd notice the shop wasn't open. "Make sure you tell her husband, Logan," she said before going back inside to look for a coffee.

Emma had no idea of the time. She was in a bed, one of six in a bay and on a ward. The blinds were pulled down and it could have been the middle of the night. She wanted to sleep but had a raging thirst. There was a glass of water next to her and she drank. A nurse came into the bay with a female doctor.

"You're awake," said the doctor.

"Just about," Emma managed.

"The procedure went well, it's kind of a keyhole thing; there are two small holes in your abdomen, one near your belly button and another on your right side. Two stitches in each. We removed the fallopian tube and we've monitored you this afternoon. Everything looks fine and you should be able to go home tomorrow."

"So, the baby, er, foetus has gone?" Emma asked.

"Yes, there was no other option. It was lodged in the tube which looked close to rupturing so it was a good job you got here when you did. You must have been in a lot of pain. We had to remove the IUD as well so you'll need to use some other contraception."

Emma couldn't take it in. The doctor left and the nurse came over.

"Can I get you a sandwich and a cup of tea, love?"

Emma nodded.

"Oh and your colleague from work is outside, do you want to see her? She's been worried sick."

Emma burst into tears when she saw Jessica.

"You poor dear," said Jessica placing her hand on Emma's arm. "No sign of Logan then?"

The tea and sandwich arrived along with Emma's appetite and Jessica was soon dispatched down the ward for a refill.

Chapter 42

Sergei Yvprestov regarded his manor house as a convenient stopover when he was in the north of the UK. It was an investment and one of many properties around Europe. His name wasn't directly linked with the dwelling because the house and grounds were owned by a company registered offshore. The house had a carefully upgraded interior and a remote-controlled gate had been added to the perimeter wall. There were security cameras and razor wire inside the wall which were not visible from outside and the house was screened by trees. There was no ostentatious show of wealth just a few signs of someone seeking privacy.

There was also enough room to land a helicopter giving Sergei the option of using this site or woodland clearing nearby that wasn't linked to him. Today's cargo was a vintage sniper rifle and two briefcases full of cash and to avoid any prying eyes the helicopter landed in the grounds. Akim and Pyotr unloaded the cargo and sent the helicopter to be refuelled for the return trip to London that night.

Sergei was waiting in his study and Akim carefully placed the rifle case on the desk. Sergei clicked open the fastenings and cradled the rifle in his arms, running his fingers over the polished wood of the butt. Then he put the rifle to his shoulder and looked through the sight.

Akim leant over to turn on the scope before saying, "The main function is a night scope. It's digital and works in daylight as well," pointing to a small switch. "But it's probably not as good in natural light as a top-quality optical scope which is how the rifle would have been used originally."

"Thank you, boys, that'll be just fine," said Sergei sighing with anticipation. "Pyotr, do you have time to take the cash along to Jonas?"

"Yes, sir, they're expecting it." He was known as Peter at the Grange and spoke perfect English. He knew how to charm and the female staff in accounts always looked forward to seeing him. He couldn't resist flirting and it would be a pleasurable errand.

Sergei was keen to set up a target on the grounds so he could check the sight and take a little practice. But the noise of gunshots travelled and he wanted nothing to connect him to the anticipated shooting. So, he went back to his spreadsheets until it was time to prepare.

*

Logan was sitting at the kitchen table and couldn't keep still. He scraped back the chair, stood up and threw the remains of his tea down the sink. He looked at the clock on the dresser and saw he still had an hour before he needed to leave so he filled the kettle once more and switched it on.

He needed to get the job done and show everyone he could be trusted. And once he had that status the charges against him would be dropped. They had that kind of influence. Right now everything had to appear routine, but it was Emma as always who ruined it all. People were flapping around after her. He stabbed the keys on his phone to read the text once more: *I've left a couple of messages for you, Logan. Emma has been taken to hospital in town for an emergency. Don't have any more details so please phone the hospital for more information. William Cassell.*

Logan thought Cassell was the farm manager, what did anything have to do with him?

*

Raven was driving home and thinking about his date with Chloe. He was feeling nervous and told himself to calm down. What was the best thing he could do? Listen to her. Her life was upside down and she couldn't even talk about social work as a career any more. He imagined she didn't know how she felt about him, her work and what she wanted to do with her life, just about everything then. He'd tell her again how much she meant to him but what could he say about getting off with Becky? He thought he was unhappy and Becky was an instant fix. Only it turned out she wasn't. What would he do next time? Talk more and listen more. At that time, Chloe hadn't been speaking much, but she was communicating in other ways. Raven realised he'd been too wrapped up in himself to see that. Everything was clear in his mind now but he knew he'd be a tongue-tied schoolboy trying to get the words out when he saw her. He parked outside the house. It felt like one last night on the moors before a new start in his life. He ran through a checklist in his mind of everything he'd need then unloaded his tools from the van before a bite to eat.

*

Sergei and Akim sat in the rear of the blacked-out Range Rover while Pyotr drove them towards Fletcher's Sitch.

"You changed the plates?" Sergei asked.

"Yes, boss," replied Pyotr politely even though he'd already confirmed it to his *pakhan*.

Akim had recced the route earlier that day. "Stop here," he said.

Pyotr pulled two wheels onto the verge. "Clear, boss," he said after checking the mirrors.

Sergei opened the door and dashed up the hill for twenty metres before sitting back in the heather. There was no one else around and he watched Akim casually open the boot and lift out a small rucksack and a black canvas gun bag. A few seconds later, he was leading Sergei up the slope; both men crouched over and walked quickly for fifty metres or so before stopping to look around. They still had half an hour before Raven was expected, more than enough time to reach their hide.

Akim had chosen a flat patch of long heather on the rim of the valley opposite Raven. Akim had cut some of the heather but left a stand of tall plants at the front to conceal their position. He gestured to his boss and Sergei lay down before Akim passed him the rifle. The barrel was hidden in the plants yet Sergei still had a clear view right across the slope opposite. Sergei had insisted he would shoot without a tripod because he was convinced that's what Zaytsev would have done. Akim wasn't sure but didn't argue and he checked his own view of the slope. Akim was the spotter and would follow Raven's progress then direct Sergei when to shoot. He'd been hunting with his boss before and knew Sergei could lay still for an hour or more when needed. They expected Raven to have some night vision gear but he shouldn't be looking up to their hide unless he was exceptionally thorough. Harley was here for one purpose: to keep an eye on the roosting birds who would be a hundred metres along from their hide. The light was fading. It wouldn't be long.

Raven drove out of town and parked in the regular place. Autumn was advancing and even though it hadn't rained recently he could smell the damp earth and see his breath condensing in wisps of vapour. The sounds were of birds settling down to roost in secret and that reminded him he needed to get up the hill to catch sight of the harriers. He remained hidden behind a tangle of hazel and checked the road in both directions: nothing. He crossed and made his way up into the streambed, crouching low where the banks were shallow. It was a routine way of moving around the moors. If someone was intent on following him, he'd be seen. Otherwise, he wasn't that obvious and he'd be the one doing the watching.

But this time, there was someone checking his progress. Sergei concentrated on keeping still just as they agreed and it was Akim who was smoothly adjusting his shoulders to keep track of Raven through optical binoculars. Their quarry was moving in the way Finn had described, keeping to the gully and only revealing brief glimpses of his profile.

"Target moving up the gully as planned," said Akim quietly. Their plan was to take a shot when it was dark so they could escape immediately with minimal chance of being seen. But if an opportunity presented itself before then they would take it. Akim felt the anticipation and excitement grow and knew his boss would be feeling the same. They weren't shooting cardboard ducks at a fairground. Harley moved like a *Spetznaz*. This was a contest.

Raven continued his crouched progress up the gully, the exercise felt healthy and natural and he took a smooth, deep lungful of air. On his last visit, he'd taken a slightly different position where he'd found a small nick in the edge of the gully. He just had to push aside a few stalks of heather and he was able to watch the roost site without lifting his head above the lip of the ground. He settled down in this position and watched for the harriers.

Opposite Akim was trying to get a clear view but Raven's position meant he was partially obscured. Akim described the location in a whisper and Sergei slowly twisted around and settled his eye on the gun sight which was still in the daylight setting even though the light had almost gone. All he could see was the rusty-coloured fading flowers of heather plants. He flicked the scope to its night setting and let his eyes adjust. He knew the scope would be the best money could buy, but even so all it revealed was a faint light smudge on the hillside. He wanted one clear shot and the key to that was patience and not revealing his position.

"We need to wait for Finn to create the diversion," he whispered back to Akim.

Chloe was sitting in her car waiting for Logan Porter to leave his house so she could follow him into the cull zone. Eventually, as the light had nearly gone she saw the headlights of his pick-up and expected him to turn right into the kill area. Instead, he turned left. She thought he was being devious so she spun her car around and followed but within a couple of minutes, he was on a lane that led up to the moors. Everyone was sure badgers in those areas would be targeted as well, but it was outside the official area. She tried to convince herself it was a good sign and Logan Porter with all the charges hanging over him had given up on killing badgers, at least for now. So, she checked her messages and drove towards some of the setts where her colleagues had last seen cull operatives.

Logan Porter drove to Keepers Cottage and found Finn Sutherland waiting in the yard. There were two vehicles: a pick-up truck and a six-wheel all-terrain vehicle with an open compartment at the rear, large enough to take a body. Porter swung round behind the ATV and lowered his window for instructions.

"I'll take the ATV down the road, Logan. Give me five minutes, it only does about thirty, then follow on."

Logan was impatient to get started but knew he had to follow instructions exactly. So, he checked his watch and timed his wait. When he drove down the road, he found Finn dragging open the five-bar metal gate at the mouth of Fletcher's Sitch. It wasn't used much and needed maintenance. The track in the valley only ran for a couple of hundred metres to a turning circle before the dale filled with vegetation. At the track end, Finn parked his ATV at the side and Logan positioned his pick-up at right angles so someone in the passenger seat would have a clear shot up the valley. Finn grabbed a stained canvas sack from the rear of the ATV and walked about thirty metres ahead before dumping the contents on a patch of grass. The partridges from last week's shoot were rotting nicely and would attract a fox, but they were after different prey tonight. Logan could barely make out what Finn had done because the sun had set half an hour before and twilight was fading into dark. When Finn was in the passenger seat, Logan checked the roof spotlight illuminated the bait. It was all for show: if they'd really been after a fox they'd use night scopes on their rifles.

The two men sat in darkness for a few minutes, gamekeepers about their legitimate business. They'd made no attempt to keep quiet so Raven Harley would be well and truly alerted by now.

Raven had heard the clatter of diesel engines and he twisted his head around to take in the view down the valley. With the headlights and later the spotlight, he saw two vehicles and two men. Fifteen minutes earlier he'd seen the harriers arrive at their roost and managed to get a few seconds of video. The gamekeepers below had gone through the sham of putting out bait for a mammal but Raven was sure it was the raptors they were after. Raven had put the night vision camera on a short tripod and he soon found the white glow of the pick-up with the profile of a man inside. He took a short video clip and then waited.

Ten minutes later, the doors of the pick-up opened and two men started to make their way up the valley. As they approached the section underneath Raven's position, they were suddenly lost from view as the steep sides of the valley hid them. Raven pulled himself forward on his elbows and re-sited the tripod.

Across the valley, the white glow of Raven's head filled Akim's night sight binoculars.

"Now," he said.

Raven still wasn't picking up the men and he pulled his head away from the camera to try to re-orientate his view. The camera exploded at his side falling back into the gully. Then he heard the sound of the shot. Without thinking, he lay flat on the ground and shuffled back urgently. He slumped into the gully with his heart thumping. He found the camera, mangled, but still attached to the tripod. It had definitely been a shot, but it can't have been from the gamekeepers below. There was someone else with a rifle and they were trying to kill him. They had night vision and he was a glowing target. He made himself think. The shooter must be on the opposite side of the valley with a lot of rough ground separating them so they wouldn't be near, not at the moment. It was the same for the gamekeepers but they had an ATV which could get to him in a couple of minutes. Calmer now, he felt around the camera and released the memory card which he put into his pocket. The camera went into his rucksack. He tapped a message to Chloe:

At Fletcher's Sitch, they're shooting at me

Should he call the police? It didn't seem worth it, they'd take hours to get here if they came at all. The message hadn't gone so he raised his arm level with the lip of the gully. Seconds later, there was another shot, but the message was sent. How far did this gully extend? He couldn't remember but they all petered out higher up the moor where he'd be a target once more.

He needed a solution before they came for him. They had night vision that picked up the faintest heat of a body. A bright light would dazzle them. But it would need to be something much more than a torch beam.

Chloe checked her phone and couldn't believe the message. Then a sudden realisation: Logan Porter wasn't killing badgers tonight; he was on the moors trying to kill Raven. She drove.

Raven's father had joked about always taking a survival kit on the hills. Somehow that had stuck in Raven's mind. His first survival kit filled half the rucksack with warm clothes, food and shelter. Over the years, it had shrunk to a small plastic bag with a folding knife and spoon. And a lighter. Raven's eyes were getting accustomed to the gloom and he could make out a few shapes. He felt in the bottom of his bag and tore open the plastic then reached up and felt the vegetation on the gully lip. On the side furthest away from the shooter, there was dried grass and heather. On every walk, he'd passed signs telling him the moors were tinder dry. He hoped they were true and flicked on the lighter. The grass caught and the air whistled with another shot. He tried another patch of grass and there was no shot this time. Maybe the shooter had to reload. Soon the smouldering grass was fanned by the wind which sent the flames over the moor away from Raven.

Across the valley, Sergei blinked into the night scope which was filled with a dazzling white ball of light.

"Switch back to daylight," Akim said. Sergei did as suggested then waited for one last shot.

Tall heather plants on the edge of the gully were alight across six or seven metres as Raven crouched down. One last deep breath and he sprang over the edge of his refuge, curled into a ball and rolled through the flames along with another bullet. As a teenager, he'd leapt over a bonfire for a dare and never thought he'd need those skills again. He kept the fire directly behind him and crawled through the heather on his elbows almost flat to the ground putting more distance between him and the shooter with every second.

"Time to go boss," said Akim.

"Fuck," said Sergei staring at the flames. He'd been denied the delicious feeling of a kill. But more than that was the bald acceptance he'd been out-smarted. He handed Akim the rifle, spare ammunition and used bullet casings.

"Call Pyotr," he said glancing at his watch, "we'll make the collection as planned."

A few minutes later, Chloe sped around a bend and slammed on her brakes as the road was partially blocked by an SUV. She managed to stop just in front of the vehicle and stared at the number plate to memorise the registration. Then she crawled past and accelerated again, Fletcher's Sitch must be close. She flew past the track then slammed on her brakes once more and reversed. She still had one of her work notepads in the car and jotted the registration of the SUV before driving slowly through the open gate and up the track. Main beam headlights soon illuminated the ATV and pick-up. Chloe had to leave the engine running so the headlights didn't dim and she climbed out to take a look. The vehicles were empty and the short valley was lit by flames leaping into the night sky. What the hell was going on?

She sent Raven a message: *At Fletcher's Sitch. Are you ok?*

But there was no reply. It was just like the cull: there were men with guns and the way to make them go away was to shine a bright light. There was no hiding from her car headlights. She worked out the fire was just about where she'd sat with Raven and that can't have been a coincidence.

She dialled 999 and asked for the Fire Service, explaining she'd been driving back to town and had seen the fire on the hill.

"It's normally the gamekeepers who deal with moorland fires. I can't find any record of their mobiles, would you happen to have them?" The operator asked.

"You must be joking," replied Chloe.

"Ah, well in that case, would you be able to keep an eye on it and get back to us if it's spreading? I'll see if I can find someone to contact at our end."

As instructed, Finn and Logan were waiting about 400 metres up the valley in some dense undergrowth. They were looking at the flames above them and knew someone else was around because of the glow of car headlights.

"Who the fuck is that down at the parking?" Finn spat. "I knew Raven Harley was a terrorist and now he's set fire to my moor."

For once, Logan was trying to be calm. "We had our instructions, but I've no idea if they got him or not. The fire gives us an excuse to get up there even if it's attracted attention. We'll do a thorough search, just like they told us. Now, is that fire going to spread? Do we need to phone around the other estates and get the keepers out here?"

"Shouldn't be a problem," said Finn. "There's a recently burnt patch just in from there so it should die out in about twenty minutes. But I do need to check. And yes let's see if we managed to get him."

The last words were spoken without conviction and Finn had the feeling Raven Harley was away over the moor. They made their way back towards the vehicles and saw a blonde-haired woman wearing a dark jacket pointing a video camera at them.

Finn couldn't control himself, "Fucking antis," he snarled. "Are you the arsonist who set fire to my moor? I'm calling the police."

Chloe ran her eyes over the two men facing her: Logan Porter and Finn Sutherland, both carrying rifles and ready to kill. "They can join the Fire Service then," she said simply.

Finn stepped forward a pace and Logan grabbed his arm, pulling him towards the ATV. Both men squeezed into the front and Chloe watched as Sutherland picked a line up the hillside towards the fire. But now the flames were dying down leaving the valley to hold the acid stench of burnt peat.

Chloe felt her phone vibrate with a message: *Meet you at the road junction about a mile towards town.*

She spun the car around and drove back to the road.

Sergei and Akim sat in the back of the Range Rover as Pyotr drove carefully towards the woodland clearing. "Do you want me to torch the car?" He asked his passengers.

"Just swap the plates," said Sergei. "Do it now. Then tidy up here and make your way out to Switzerland tomorrow."

"Will do boss. And the rifle?"

"Make sure that gets home," replied Sergei.

Pyotr knew that meant a return journey to Yekaterinburg the same way it arrived: by private jet. Nathan Parbolde was waiting in his vehicle at the clearing and stepped out to greet Sergei.

"Nice dinner?" Sergei asked.

"Of course, and you?"

"Good sport, to be continued," said Sergei cryptically.

They heard the helicopter and the landing lights were turned on.

*

Chloe stopped at the junction and leant over to unlock the passenger door. Raven soon appeared out of the darkness and as soon as he'd closed the door Chloe set off towards town.

"Sorry I'm heading back," she said. 'Do you want to pick up the van?'

Raven couldn't reply immediately. "Tomorrow," he said eventually.

Chloe drove as far as the street lights of the suburbs before glancing across at him.

"Ok?" She asked.

"Hope so," he said. "I'll tell you everything over a cup of tea."

Ten minutes later, Chloe was leaning on the doorframe in the kitchen, watching Raven, arms wrapped around his chest fighting spasms of shaking.

"I'd put some sugar in if I could find any," she said. She took the drinks and joined Raven at the table. He sipped the hot tea and explained the action. And she went through what happened after she arrived.

"So, Sutherland and Porter were acting as a decoy to get you out into the open?" She asked.

"As soon as I moved, that's when the sniper fired. Some bit of kit they must have had to see me so well, it was pitch black and I was wearing dark clothes. They had it all planned."

"Who was the shooter then?" Chloe asked, but every *countryman* had a night scope for shooting badgers. "I took a registration number," she continued, "it was a blacked-out Range Rover, quite posh looking, new. And parked on the road just underneath where they were firing."

She wasn't sure he'd heard or taken in what she said.

"Bastards will be calling me an arsonist forever and a day."

"The fire was just about out when I left and those two thugs were going up to check anyway. But I don't think they're going to publicise any of this. For God's sake, Raven they tried to kill you!"

Raven stared down at the table and wrapped both hands around the mug.

After a few moments, Chloe put her hand on his wrist. "If you give me the memory card, I'll make some copies and see what you recorded. Why don't you take a shower?" She suggested, putting her other arm around his shoulders, tenderly. "You smell like a kipper factory."

He looked at her and tried a smile. They'd had a weekend on the northeast coast, staying in a cottage just down the street from a smokehouse. It seemed like a different, simple life and so long ago. He stood up, unsteadily and caught his shoulder on the door as he made his way upstairs to the bathroom.

She remembered the night vision camera had been really expensive and now it was wrecked. But it had managed to capture something of the impact of the bullet and Raven's expletive as he survived. Along with the registration, there was enough to take to the police. Chloe really wanted to check the harriers were all right, but that would have to wait. She gathered together the computer equipment, checked the door was locked and made her way upstairs.

Raven was in bed dressed in a hoodie, sweat pants and thick socks. She joined him, cradling his back and hugging him tight as his spasms of shaking continued, until he was still and breathing deeply.

Chapter 43

Logan waited in his pick-up as Finn drove up the road towards Keeper's Cottage. The fire had only spread for twenty metres just as Finn predicted. There was no sign of a body in the gully or the moor beyond. All day he had to keep his emotions in check but the image of taking Raven Harley to the abattoir kept filling his mind. To be turned into dog meat was all that scum deserved. But the anticipation was gone and he could feel the rage building. They hadn't been told who was doing the shooting and he had the feeling if he found out it would be followed by a bullet in his head. And then there was the message about Emma. Maybe a hospital visit would strengthen his alibi if the police started asking questions. He was desperate for a strong drink, but that would have to wait. He started the engine and turned right towards town.

Despite everything that had happened, it was still only 9.00 p.m. when he pushed open the main doors of the hospital. The receptionist gave him a ward number and as soon as he left the area near accident and emergency, the windowless corridors of polished flooring and painted walls were quiet and empty. He eventually found the ward with a series of six bedded side rooms down one side and storage and office space on the other. He asked for his wife at the nurse's station.

"Oh, you're in luck, Mr Cameron should be able to update you."

Logan looked puzzled.

"The consultant gynaecologist," she explained before taking Logan to one of the side rooms. The consultant was perched on the end of a bed chatting with a middle-aged woman. Logan could see Emma asleep on the opposite side of the room. The nurse left and Logan hovered in the corridor.

After a minute or so, Mr Cameron stood up and saw a thickset, square, solid man, green waxed jacket undone, over layers of grubby clothes that looked like they'd been painted on weeks before. As he approached, he could smell wood smoke and what was it? He realised it was the smell from a dissecting table before a cadaver had been preserved in formaldehyde: dead flesh and cold blood.

Logan saw the hesitancy and thought he needed to explain, "Logan Porter here to see my wife Emma. Sorry about the clothes, I've come straight from work, been flat out today. We work at Midham Grange for the Duke."

"Ah yes," said the consultant softening, "lovely house." Then he took Logan into one of the offices. "Right, Emma Porter, we operated this morning and removed an ectopic pregnancy."

Logan just heard the last word. The son he'd always wanted. And then Cameron continued confusingly.

"It was an emergency and we had to remove the fallopian tube as well, that's standard."

"So, the baby's gone?" Logan asked, not at all sure of what he was hearing.

"Yes, I'm afraid so," said the consultant, sounding very matter-of-fact. Logan didn't respond so Cameron elucidated, "Pregnancies are never viable outside the uterus." Logan was still quiet so Cameron ploughed on, "And of course, ectopic pregnancies are more likely where an old-style IUD has been fitted."

Logan looked at him blankly. What the hell was an IUD? And before he knew it the consultant had ushered him out into the corridor and Logan was left trying to catch what he said, "We'll be discharging your wife tomorrow. Stop by around midday and you can collect her."

"Thank you," said Logan to the consultant's back as the medic disappeared down the corridor. Logan made his way back to the pick-up and tried a few searches on his phone. At first, he was looking at a list of articles about Improvised Explosive Devices in Afghanistan. Then he tried again and found an 'Intrauterine device'. Emma had been using contraception all this time and she hadn't told him. He felt the rage rise from the pit of his stomach up into his chest urging him to scream. Then more slowly, coldly he worked out how he needed this to end. For now, he'd play the loving husband and collect her tomorrow. But first, that drink.

*

Chloe woke to the clatter of teacups as Raven brought a tray into the bedroom. The alarm clock said it was 6.30 a.m. He looked bright but the dark smudges under his eyes were back and the skin on his face looked thin and grey.

"You're a bit cheery," she said yawning. "What time do you call this?"

"Nice morning," he said drawing the curtains. "Mark's coming to pick me up in an hour. Mind you they'll be gossiping."

She didn't imagine spending their first night back together would be quite like this.

"Don't count your chickens, mate, you've got to woo me on a date first," she said.

He placed the tray on the bedside table and passed her a mug of tea, then some toast.

"We're still on for tonight then."

"Yeah," said Chloe. "Just don't get into any more scrapes before that."

After breakfast, Chloe took the van keys and borrowed Raven's bike for the ride out to Fletcher's Sitch. She had a job convincing him it was safe.

"I think they're after you, Ray, not me. They had it all planned and they failed. We can talk it through later. This morning I'm sure I'll find your van exactly as you left it."

*

Sergeant Paul Carson received the call at 5.00 a.m. Officers from the National Crime Agency were raiding Midham Grange. Paul was to attend with half a dozen officers from the early shift. He was at the station at 6.30 a.m. preparing to brief his team when they arrived at seven. His mobile rang it was Dew Foster.

"Sorry about the lack of warning, Paul but it is best if we don't have any leaks. My team will be taking the Grange, well the offices mainly especially the accountants. Can you take two officers to the farm shop and the rest of you go to the Duke's shooting lodge? No need to break down any doors at the shop it's more about talking to the staff about the way they deal with cash, securing the till and card machine if they have one. The lodge is a different matter. Ram the gates if they don't let you in, so you'd better go in a pick-up. Secure all laptops, devices and documents. Take lots of evidence bags and boxes. And find out where the safe is located, there will be one."

"The search warrants?" Paul asked.

"Just emailed so print them off."

"Ok, I'll keep you informed. Basically, we're looking for bags of cash and all the documents we can find."

"That's right," said Dew. "I'll give it thirty minutes before it makes the national news."

Paul was glad he wasn't making the decisions. It would be a huge embarrassment for the National Crime Agency if they didn't find anything.

*

The raids were coordinated for 8.00 a.m. Xan Philips drove one of the covered pick-ups they used for rural crime work. Since being ordered to chauffeur an over-the-limit Superintendent Farlow after his Sunday lunch with the Duke, Xan was looking forward to seeing the discomfort on the Duke's face when his house was searched. It was time the same laws applied to everyone.

This time his passenger was Paul Carson, armed with a search warrant. Xan stopped outside the solid wood gates and spoke into the intercom:

"Police we have a warrant to search the premises. Can you let us in, please?"

Nothing happened.

"They'll be panicking now, probably waking up the Duke and asking what to do. I hope they open the gates soon, if we ram them it'll make a right mess of the bumper on this one, not like the old Land Rovers which were like tanks," said Paul. "Let's give them five minutes."

Eventually, the gates did open and they drove along a smooth track to the lodge. A saloon car with four officers followed. The front door looked almost as solid as the gate and they waited once more. When they were admitted, they were shown into the dining room where the Duke was self-consciously trying to pull a cashmere cardigan closed as he spoke on the phone. The aristocrat hadn't had time to comb his hair or dress properly. For a moment, the police listened in on the conversation:

"Yes, my dear they're here as well. Get Procter and Hargreaves on it…they're taking your mobile, what?"

Paul Carson held the search warrant in one hand and beckoned for the phone with the other. "Here's the warrant, sir, we'll need all your devices."

The Duke straightened his back, just as he'd been schooled to do but his cardigan slipped open to reveal a crumpled checked shirt with buttons fastened into the wrong holes. But he wasn't giving up.

"Address me as Your Grace, officer, just as your chief constable does," he ordered.

"Certainly, sir," replied Paul struggling to suppress a smirk. "It was the chief who sent me this morning, now, your phone, please. You are of course free to use your landline."

The Duke handed over his phone.

"To save time, could you direct us to your office, any laptops or computers and your safe or strongbox?"

"The housekeeper will show you. Now leave me alone," said the Duke, slumping into a chair. He stared out of the window and muttered to himself. Parbolde and the Russian, they'd got him into this but of course, they'd jetted off last night and were nowhere to be seen. Sophie had told him the National Crime Agency was searching the Grange on suspicion of money laundering and all their bank accounts would be frozen. That would mean the Grange would have to close. His only hope was that Parbolde had been as clever as he made out, and they'd find nothing. He held onto one thought: he'd be cleared, heads would roll in the police and he'd receive more compensation than his ancestors were paid for the slaves they had to give up. It was a slim hope.

Dew Foster and her team were searching the offices at the Grange when the accountant Jonas Farland walked in. He'd seen the police cars and dark vans parked on the gravel directly in front of the grand portico entrance where the stone flags had been worn smooth by prime ministers and Royalty. Now they were being raided, how had they found out? He thought about running, but he was, in reality, a lowly salaryman. The bonuses were fantastic when everything went well but this was a disaster. He tried to ensure every thread of finance ended in an offshore company with opaque ownership, but if they spent enough time they would find plenty. He would be pleasant but offer minimal cooperation. He'd seen the minders who accompanied Parbolde and the Russian and had no doubt of the consequences for himself and his family if he pointed the finger. Officially he was the Duke's accountant but it was the other two who pulled the invisible strings. He placed his briefcase on the floor next to his desk.

"I'm Jonas Farland, chief accountant, how can I help, officers?"

Dew Foster introduced herself and asked for the keys to the strong room.

Farland reached into his pocket. "This is one set, the Duke has the other and you'll probably find those in his safe," he said.

The strong room was situated adjacent to the main office area and was a windowless space encased in concrete. The door was solid steel, similar to a bank vault.

"If you could do the honours?" Dew Foster asked.

Farland used two long keys to open the door, pushed it inwards then followed Foster inside.

"We'll start with these then," said Foster pointing to the suitcases that Pyotr had delivered the previous evening. Farland lifted the first case onto a small table in the centre of the room and flipped it open. Wads of used £50 and £20 notes filled the space.

"How much is there?" Foster asked.

Farland knew the exact amount but he had to start acting his role, something that was new to him.

"Um, we have to do a series of reconciliations before I can give you an accurate answer," he said.

"Ball Park?" Foster asked.

"Around a hundred thousand," he replied. "You'll find the Grange is a cash-rich business with a complex financial structure."

"And the other case?"

"Similar," said Farland.

Dew Foster called in a colleague and asked them to make arrangements for a security company to transport the contents of the strong room once her team had done a basic inventory. She asked Farland to wait at his desk while she tried to grasp everything they'd found so far. It would need painstaking bookwork to prove these two suitcases of cash hadn't been generated legitimately by the business. Of course, it was blatant money laundering but proving that was another matter. Paul Carson phoned with an update:

"We've seized the Duke's devices and his housekeeper kindly opened the safe for us, which is wardrobe size with a lot of documents and also a big bag of cash. Tens of thousands I would say. The key was hidden in a copy of *Hard Times* on his bookshelf would you believe?"

"Ok, we've got a security van to collect all the cash. I'll send it up when it's finished here. It's going to take months to go through everything and we'll have to find a way to let them continue with the business otherwise we could end up paying millions in compensation."

"Glad you're sorting that one," said Paul.

It was going to be a long day of gathering evidence.

Chapter 44

Chloe found some trails and tracks to follow on her bike ride to Fletcher's Sitch. It was uphill all the way from town but that gave her time to take in the change of habitat from improved pasture to rough grazing and finally moorland. Sunshine gave the trees a golden glow of autumn altogether a pleasant rural scene that gave no hint of the rancid efforts of a few people who thought breeding and money made them *better*. Raven ignored their threats and continued to expose the corruption. He kept on pushing and was paying the price.

The van was intact and Chloe lifted the bike into the back and locked the doors. She looked across to where the drama had taken place and the only difference was a smudge of black on the edge of the steep valley side. Instead of following the route she'd taken before Chloe climbed through the heather and saplings on the opposite side, looking for signs of the shooter. She kept glancing over at the burnt patch and looked for a vantage point that gave a clear view. Eventually, it didn't take any skill to identify an area where long stems of heather had been cut right at ground level, large enough for two men. She took some photographs and eventually spotted the dull metal of a bullet casing that looked as if it had been pushed into the ground. After taking another photo, she took a small plastic bag from her rucksack, put her hand inside and used that as a glove to pick up the bullet before putting a knot in the bag. It was another piece of evidence to pass on to the police.

For completeness, Chloe wanted to take a few photos of the location where Raven had nearly been killed. There, she said to herself it had been life or death. And yet she wasn't acknowledging the enormity of that. Would she be next? Maybe, they could try to talk about that later?

Crossing the valley looked impossible with scrub, boulders and trees. But walking around the top looked easy enough, with lots of recently burnt patches providing a simple path. All this area was engineered for grouse shooting with only small, difficult-to-access areas like Fletcher's Sitch remaining untouched. No wonder the hen harriers had chosen it for a roost.

Fifteen minutes later, Chloe took some photos of the gully and burnt area where Raven had escaped. The ATV that Sutherland and Porter had used had left obvious tracks across the vegetation but there was nothing else to see. Chloe made her way down and drove to the park where Raven was working. They were sawing up an ash tree with die-back.

Her arrival was an excuse for a tea break. The fresh air and exercise had given Raven some colour in his cheeks. It didn't take much to get him back to normal. She left him with the van keys and cycled back to *theirs*. It took a while to put together the file of evidence and it was up to Raven if he wanted to pass it on to the police. There might be fingerprints or DNA on the bullet casing but that wouldn't prove it had been used last night. Then it was time to go back to Siobhan's and get ready for her date.

*

At 4.00 p.m., Logan Porter was pacing up and down the corridor outside Emma's ward. The consultant had said midday, but he'd been told to wait, something to do with a ward round and discharge, he didn't understand a word of it.

Eventually, a nurse backed through the double doors, pulling a wheelchair. She swung it around and Emma gave Logan a weak smile.

"We'll just have to wait for someone to take you down to the car park," said the nurse. "Emma could really do with another day on the ward, but you know, we've been told to discharge as soon as we can. She's got some pain relief and a prescription for more."

Logan looked down at his wife clutching a bottle of medication and a sheet of paper. "Porter's my name so I think we'll manage without any help," he said brightly.

The nurse laughed, but Emma didn't have the energy to say anything. Going back with Logan was the last thing she wanted. He sounded charming but she never saw that side of him at home. Logan wheeled her out to the pick-up which he'd left parked on a grass verge and helped her into the passenger seat, then let the wheelchair career down the slope until it bumped into a kerb and toppled over. *Not so caring now*. On the journey home, she could tell he was brooding, he cursed at every traffic light and queue; there was no point trying to talk to him when he was like this.

In the house, he was no different and Emma sat down at the kitchen table. "Sorry, Logan, I'm exhausted, I just need to go to bed."

He grabbed her chin between his forefinger and thumb and twisted her head around. *Familiar pain and helplessness.*

"You need to explain what the doctor told me," he said.

Emma tried to shake her head. "Later," was all she could manage.

"Fuck's sake," he spat, releasing her. Then he walked out to the yard.

Emma pushed herself up and made her way slowly upstairs to the spare room and climbed into bed fully clothed.

During the cull dead badgers had been sealed in thick polythene sacks and stored before being collected for incineration. Logan's outhouse was one of the stores. The cull was ending tonight and he had a clipboard in his hand, trying to reconcile the bagged carcasses with the claims from operatives. They'd submitted paperwork for around twice as many as they'd actually killed. It didn't bother Logan but he wasn't sure how much checking took place later on. Then he heard a vehicle pull into the yard. His first thought was the police coming to accuse and harass him even more. But it was a smart new SUV, one of the smaller Range Rovers and he recognised the woman who stepped out. It was Jasmine wearing some oven gloves and carrying a baking tray wrapped in foil. He made his way over.

"We heard Emma had been let out of the hospital. I've baked a lasagne for you. I don't suppose you'll be up to doing any cooking?"

Logan flipped back to charming. "That's lovely, come in a minute," he said.

"It's hot now if you want some or I can show you how to reheat it in the oven?"

"Let's have some now," said Logan pleasantly. He took a couple of plates from the cupboard. "Emma's gone up to bed but I'm sure she'd like some."

Jasmine searched for the kettle and some clean cups. Then Logan came closer and lowered his voice.

"I'm glad you came. I'm really worried about, Emma, she hasn't been herself for ages and seemed really down and talking about leaving. I don't know what to do?"

He'd learnt that much from the attempt on Raven Harley. Plan ahead, spread misinformation and confusion. Then act. Jasmine nodded keen to hear more.

"Why don't you go up and have a chat?" Logan offered.

Jasmine busied herself serving the lasagne and making tea, then took a tray upstairs. Beyond the kitchen the house smelt damp and wallpaper was peeling above the skirting boards. She'd seen worse in the village, but this was one of the Duke's properties. How could he rent it in such a state?

"Here you are, love, I've brought you some food," said Jasmine pushing open the door to Emma's room. Emma looked groggy and pale. "Oh you poor dear," Jasmine continued, "can you manage something?"

Emma pushed herself up in bed. "This is a surprise, maybe I can," she said.

Jasmine perched on the end of the bed. After a few minutes when Emma had managed some food she asked, "Is everything alright? You know…"

Emma shrugged her shoulders. "I don't know?"

Jasmine didn't press her anymore and when she went downstairs, Logan had cleared his plate and had gone out.

*

Raven and Chloe met at the bus stop even though they were just going to the pub around the corner. He gave her a hug and took her hand as they walked. The Heron was quiet and they ordered some food and drinks at the bar before finding a table. Raven turned off his phone and tucked it away in his pocket.

"Financial irregularities at Midham Grange who'd have thought it?" He said.

"Money laundering more like," replied Chloe. "That's all over social media. And no surprise to me." She took a sip of her drink. "Did you find the folder I left?"

"Yes, I saw that. Good that you found that bullet casing, I don't feel like going back there in a hurry," replied Raven.

"Are you going to report it to the police? If you're worried about the fire, I checked that as well and it only went as far as the next burnt patch."

"Maybe I should give it to my *legal team*. That sounds pretentious, doesn't it?"

"If your *sponsors*," and she emphasised the word, "are paying for that why not?"

They laughed. Sponsorship and legal teams seemed a long way from saving animals.

"I feel nervous, Chloe. I had a speech all prepared and I knew I'd forget it as soon as I saw you."

She didn't help him. And Chloe felt just as tongue-tied. The thought of having a child had lodged in her mind. She didn't know if that's what she wanted and she'd never really spoken to Raven about it either. Then of course anything they'd discussed before needed to be scrubbed clean if they were starting again. Right now he needed to do this alone and say what he really thought.

Raven took a deep breath. "I'm really sorry for what I did. I don't need sponsors or likes on social media, what I need is you. And I want another chance to show you. I could ditch everything else tomorrow."

Chloe couldn't look him in the eye so she stared at the table in front. "You needed to say that, Ray, and yes I want to start again. And I know we need to put it behind us, talking is good but I can't keep blaming you forever."

Raven reached over and took her hand. "I need to talk more and listen more, Chloe." He paused. "Right, can we get drunk now?" He asked, raising his glass.

"Good idea," she said. "You can overthink these things."

The food and more drinks slipped down easily. But after an hour or so, Chloe was ready to go.

"I want to get out to Nether Beck tomorrow and see if they're going to load up all those dead badgers, nobody's managed to get any video yet."

"Can I come with you for that?" Raven asked. "It's just with everything that's happened, it'd be better if there were two of us."

"It's a deal," said Chloe. "I'll pick you up at six. And maybe I could move back in when we're finished out there?"

She leant over and kissed him on the lips and then made her way out. *See how it goes* she told herself.

Chapter 45

Raven waited outside the house with a rucksack filled with cameras, flasks and sandwiches. They may as well be comfortable as they waited for any action at the farm. After Chloe left, he had another drink then at home he was dusting, vacuuming and changing sheets for a couple of hours before bed. This morning one load of washing was already hanging on the line and another was churning around in the machine. He saw the lights on Chloe's car and lifted his bag.

"I wasn't sure you'd be up for this, I thought you might need a break?" She said as they drove.

"Expect I might collapse in a heap at some point, but I'm better doing something at the moment," he replied.

They parked a few minutes from the farm and made their way to the same location they'd used before, at the top of a slope looking down into the yard where Logan Porter's pick-up was parked. Once they were in place, Raven made a start on his breakfast as a weak sun tried to find a way through the cloud.

*

Logan Porter woke as it was getting light and for a moment felt disorientated. His mouth was dry and then he remembered: Emma was back in the *spare room* and he'd been to the pub. He pulled on some clothes and made his way down to the kitchen for some tea. Then he noticed her phone on the worktop. She must have left it there yesterday.

He tried the buttons at the side and the screen lit up. *Enter pin number*. He replaced the phone on the worktop and sat at the table with his mug. What else hadn't she told him? Then he tried the phone again. He needed four digits and tried *1234*. But he was no good with these devices. What about her birthday, the third of February, he tried *0302* and that didn't work either.

One more try, day, month, year *3283* and he was in.

Most of the symbols on the screen had little coloured blobs next to them. He tapped on one for emails which showed about twenty unread messages. Tranchard was always going on WhatsApp to send secret stuff, but that seemed to be filled with messages from every woman in the village: *Hope you are ok. Let me know if I can help? x*

Then he tried Twitter and tapped on Emma's photo: *Choose account* appeared. He saw @EmmaPorter24 but also @Countryview987 which looked like one of Tranchard's secret accounts. He needed to find out more. One of the buttons at the bottom of the screen looked like an envelope: Direct Messages and when he explored further there was a list of every *anti* in the area including @RvnHarley. He couldn't believe what he was seeing. Raven Harley had ruined his life and spread lies everywhere. Everyone wanted him dead and here was Emma, his own wife passing on every secret she could find.

Logan looked through the messages.

Check out Fairview Mill pheasant shoot. Looks well dodgy.

That had sent Harley out with his cameras and resulted in Finn Sutherland being arrested and the Duke being made to look like an idiot. Logan was convinced Harley was behind everything but Emma hadn't really given him that much.

He tried @MidhamSabs and there was a list of every hunt meet with dates and locations. That's why the sabs were there every time. That's why he'd been arrested for releasing the bagged fox they'd been in the exact location waiting to film him.

His blood was boiling and he could have crushed the phone in his hand. Then there was the message: *Padlocks – try Logan Porter's birthday 230582*

There it was, she was telling them how to break in. He was still convinced Harley was one of the sabs but anyway, that's what had resulted in Logan being charged with perverting the course of justice. He was looking at prison time because his wife was a traitor.

He looked up to see Emma standing in the doorway. She spoke before he had a chance to do anything, "Logan, I'm sorry I didn't tell you about the coil I had fitted. I didn't think I could talk to you about it."

Emma looked at him and felt a fear she'd never known. He looked as if he was going to explode. He spoke quietly but each word carried menace.

"I wanted a son and you made that impossible. You've lied to me for years with your IUD, that's what that stuck-up doctor told me."

The words hung between them and Emma saw the phone in his hand, her phone. He held the screen up towards her, an accusation and she realised he knew everything.

"Don't do anything stupid, Logan, I'll leave right now, you'll never see me again."

But it was too late. In a second, he was out of his chair. He grabbed her and threw her onto the floor with a force that filled her body with pain and took the breath from her lungs. Then he was back with a gun in his hand.

"Get up," he shouted.

She staggered to her feet and he grabbed her arm, pulling her into the hall and then out into the yard.

*

"We're on," said Chloe. "Fucking hell, what's he doing?"

Raven dropped his coffee cup onto the grass and looked down into the yard. There was Porter, rifle in one hand, dragging his wife towards the pick-up. He opened the hatchback and seemed to lift her inside with one arm. Then he locked the door. In a few seconds, he was driving out of the yard.

Raven and Chloe grabbed their bags and ran down to the car.

"He went left," said Raven.

Chloe started to follow. "They're going to the kennels," she shouted. But in seconds their path was blocked by a large van. "Fuck, they've come to collect the badgers."

That didn't matter now. "You can get on the verge," said Raven and they squeezed past the van. A minute later, Chloe swung the car through the stone arch that opened into a courtyard. They could hear dogs barking behind some of the doors but Porter had backed his pick-up into the wide entrance of the abattoir. They jumped out and squeezed past the vehicle.

Raven gagged on the stench of blood and disinfectant. The high ceiling space was filled with stainless steel machinery for cutting and grinding bone and flesh. Porter was standing next to a huge butcher's block, a solid table used for carving up large animals. But this time he had one hand gripping the arm of his wife and in the other a cleaver with a polished blade that looked like it could remove her head in one swipe.

When he saw Raven and Chloe, he let go of Emma and reached for his rifle, holding it awkwardly in one hand. The barrel was pointing at Raven who had a camera in his hand. Porter felt triumphant. The people who had betrayed him and ruined his life were all gathered in one place. And any evidence they'd been here would vanish in a few minutes.

"Raven fucking Harley you've come to the right place," shouted Porter and he took a step away from Emma and flicked on the grinder which crunched some bone remaining in the funnel. He knew this would distract them and he put the cleaver onto the bench keeping his eyes on Raven and Chloe before taking the rifle in both hands.

Emma shuffled her feet as well and glanced over her shoulder at the bench behind. Logan didn't notice because he was looking straight forward, his jaw clenched, and his finger on the trigger.

As Logan took aim Raven and Chloe both dived onto the floor and Emma twisted around to grab a boning knife which she plunged into the right side of Logan's stomach. His shot hit the roof and he dropped the rifle onto the floor, trying to work out what had happened.

Emma staggered back leaving the knife in him. Logan yanked it out on an impulse and stood facing her, a dark, wet patch spreading through his clothes, liquid dripping onto the concrete under his feet. He held the knife in a hand wet with his own blood and tried to lunge at her.

She screamed and stepped back as he staggered and collapsed on the floor, unmoving now with the knife still clenched in his fist.

Chloe and Raven pushed themselves up and rushed over to Emma. Chloe took her by the shoulder and walked her away from Logan.

Raven switched off the grinder then dialled 999 and asked for police and ambulance. "We're at Midham Kennels. A man's been stabbed, we're not sure if he's dead. Nobody's in danger anymore."

"Stay on the line caller. Services are on their way."

A paramedic on a motorbike was first to arrive. He parked in the yard and stood nervously at the entrance to the abattoir. Chloe was still comforting Emma.

"It's safe," shouted Raven.

Logan hadn't moved and was lying in a pool of blood, knife still in hand. The paramedic quickly pulled on some gloves and checked for breathing and a pulse, then spoke into his radio: "Victim no sign of life."

Then they all stepped back as the police arrived.

Chapter 46

Raven, Chloe and Emma were driven back to the police station in separate cars. Raven felt as if he'd worn a groove down the hall but this time he had the luxury of waiting in one of the interview rooms. He gave his statement and was offered some tea. He didn't think he was being accused of Porter's murder but the officers wouldn't clarify if he was being interviewed as a witness or a suspect. The video on his and Chloe's cameras told the story better than they could. But his two previous visits had left a bitter scar. He was half expecting a couple of burly officers to come in and slap him in handcuffs.

So, it was a surprise when a female detective came in accompanied by Chloe.

"Your stories check out so we're letting you go. We'll need you as witnesses and we're not sure what charges Emma Porter will face."

The officer paused and Raven wanted to ask, *Why don't you let her go as well? She's the victim here.*

But the detective did continue, "If she faces any charges at all. The custody sergeant will sort out some transport for you."

In the reception area, the sergeant was another familiar face.

"Right, Raven, we've had a whip round and we're sending you on holiday. Crime statistics are through the roof and each one is related to you somehow."

"Thanks, pal," managed Raven, "maybe I should get a season ticket for that interview room."

It was gallows humour but somehow seemed appropriate. A young constable drove them home. Raven had no idea of the time, but it was dark and Chloe had leant into his shoulder. He wouldn't be letting her go.

They went into the house. "Are you hungry?" He asked.

"No," said Chloe, "I just feel dirty. I need a shower, but don't have any clean clothes."

"You left some in a cupboard in the spare room. I'll sort it for you."

Hot water wasn't enough. By the time Raven joined her in bed and wrapped his body around her back, all she could smell was the stench of the slaughterhouse, it dripped from her skin. And when she closed her eyes there was Logan Porter in a pool of his own blood and in the background the sound of bone being ground in some awful machine. She tried to concentrate on the smell of freshly laundered sheets which helped her to drift off for a few minutes, but then she was back with those images assaulting her senses.

The house was quiet with no sound from outside. The dead of night. She couldn't hear a breath from Raven either.

"Are you awake?" She asked.

He was and she rolled over towards him. They had sex and then they slept.

*

It was 10.00 a.m. when they woke. Raven had left a neat pile of folded clothes on a chair by her side of the bed, but instead of dressing in those she took his t-shirt.

"Where are you going?" He asked.

"Just making some tea, I'll be back in a minute."

The kettle had just boiled when she saw a figure approaching the kitchen door. It was Becky. Chloe opened the door before she could knock. Becky took a step back, surprised and Chloe felt she was being scanned from head to toe as Becky's eyes lingered at the bottom hem of Raven's t-shirt.

Becky was wearing a jacket over a short top which revealed a shiny navel piercing.

"Nice," said Chloe, tilting her head towards Becky's stomach.

Becky was suddenly embarrassed and wrapped her arm to cover herself.

"Um, I just wanted to ask Raven about a video," Becky said.

Chloe was relieved to see Becky discomfited. She'd imagined a self-assured seductress that Raven was powerless to resist but instead, Becky looked young and unsure.

"Just send him a text and I'm sure he'll meet up," said Chloe ending with a smile.

"Um, I'll do that. Sorry to bother you."

And Becky turned and walked away. Chloe took the tea upstairs.

"Was that someone at the door?" Raven asked.

"Just Becky in her sexiest outfit," replied Chloe.

"Oh shit, I'm really sorry," said Raven.

It was good timing actually. She got the message.

Raven was quiet for a few moments. "Did you open the door dressed in my t-shirt and nothing else?"

"I did," said Chloe. "That's what I was telling her."

Raven laughed and pulled her towards him.

Postscript

Emma was left in limbo for several weeks. She was a suspect in the murder of Logan Porter but wasn't charged. A national campaign evolved with calls for her to be cleared, but the police didn't act until an image was leaked of Logan Porter grasping her arm and holding a cleaver in his other hand, amongst a background of evil-looking machinery in the slaughterhouse. Finally cleared, Emma moved in with her sister.

Finn Sutherland was charged and convicted of killing a sparrowhawk and causing unnecessary suffering to a crow. He was fined £500 on each count, paid for by his employer Nathan Parbolde. Sutherland's lawyers argued successfully their client's human rights would be compromised if he lost his livelihood and Sutherland continued to work as a gamekeeper at High Ridge and Fairview. Archie Cartwright was fined £500 and ordered to pay £1000 compensation for damage to a police car. Cartwright's fingerprints were found on the campervan and he was convicted of the damage to that vehicle with an identical fine and compensation. Nathan Parbolde paid all costs and gave Cartwright a full-time job as a gamekeeper. Despite an arrest warrant, Ryan Walker has not been located.

Raven and Jack receive an increasing number of tip-offs and other information from the local community.

The Duke of Midham insisted he was unaware of being used by unscrupulous businessmen and knew nothing about human trafficking or money laundering. The Crown Prosecution Service decided it was not in the public interest to prosecute. The Duke was allowed access to his £2 million profits from Russian oil exploration but had to pay £1.75 million in a tax settlement with HMRC. The Duke's public relations consultants portrayed him as an absent-minded benefactor and photographed him riding around his *park* on an e-bike emphasising the farmland was going organic but not mentioning this would take several years.

Accountant Jonas Farland was sentenced to five years in prison for financial irregularities and money laundering. The judge said the sentence would have been reduced had Farland named the individuals behind the schemes. Despite extensive searches, the names Nathan Parbolde and Sergei Yvprestov were not linked to any of the shell companies involved. The two Russian gang masters were convicted under the Modern Slavery Act and sentenced to three years in prison, to be deported at completion of their sentences. No link was found to Sergei Yvprestov.

Jeremy Cockerill was convicted of hunting with dogs and fined £738, the courts had obscure procedures for calculating fines to the last penny and more humiliating for Cockerill was the loss of his position in the judiciary. The Midham hunt was served with an injunction barring the use of the public highway. Lawyers are still arguing if Jeremy Cockerill was liable for the road traffic collision. After 500 years, the Midham Hunt folded, but a few members joined neighbouring hunts and hunting continued on some of the Midham *country*.

Cory Fuller and colleagues at Fuller & Wainwright are pursuing their complaints about police actions relating to Raven Harley. It will be years before a resolution. Fuller submitted the evidence regarding the attempted shooting of Raven Harley and a fingerprint was retrieved from the bullet casing but no match was found on the police database.

Chloe Turner and her social work department were not found liable for the death of Leo Corbet but Chloe was required to attend a three-month refresher training course. Chloe and Raven decided they both wanted children, just not yet.

Printed in Great Britain
by Amazon

47005826R00137